THE BEECHWOOD FLUTE

Pendred Noyce

Minneapolis

Minneapolis

SECOND EDITION DECEMBER 2022
THE BEECHWOOD FLUTE Copyright © 2016 by Pendred Noyce.
All rights reserved.

This is a work of fiction. Names, characters, places and incidents either are the product of the author's imagination or are used fictitiously. Any resemblance to actual persons living or dead, events, or locales are entirely coincidental.

No part of this book may be used or reproduced in any manner whatsoever without written permission except in the case of brief quotations used in critical articles and reviews. For information, write to Calumet Editions, 6800 France Avenue South, Suite 370, Edina, MN 55435.

10 9 8 7 6 5 4 3 2

Cover design: Barnas Monteith
Book interior: Gary Lindberg

ISBN: 978-1-960250-38-4

To Warren Wilde, my high school English teacher, who inspired and uplifted a generation of young people.

Also by Pendred Noyce

Lost in Lexicon (Scarletta/Mighty Media)

The Ice Castle (Scarletta/Mighty Media)

New Frontiers in Formative Assessment (co-editor with Daniel T. Hickey, Harvard Education Press)

The Desperate Case of the Diamond Chip (Tumblehome Learning)

The Vicious Case of the Viral Vaccine (Tumblehome Learning)

The Baffling Case of the Battered Brain (Tumblehome Learning)

The Perilous Case of the Zombie Potion (Tumblehome Learning)

The Cryptic Case of the Coded Fair (with Bob and Barbara Tinker) (Tumblehome Learning)

The Contaminated Case of the Cooking Contest (with Peter Wong) (Tumblehome Learning)

Magnificent Minds: Sixteen Pioneering Women in Science and Medicine (Tumblehome Learning)

Remarkable Minds: Seventeen More Pioneering Women in Science and Medicine (Tumblehome Learning)

Mosquitoes Don't Bite Me (coming 2017) (Tumblehome Learning)

THE BEECHWOOD FLUTE

Pendred Noyce

Part One:
The Birchwood Flute

Chapter 1

When he reached the bluff overlooking the village, Kiran leaned his flute against the trunk of a fir tree and drew his wooden sword. Ryan stood waiting for him, boots planted in the dirt, sword slicing the air.

"Took your time, snake spit," Ryan said.

Ryan's shoulders bulged in his tunic and despite the morning cold, sweat already trickled down his neck.

Kiran took a step forward. "I'm ready," he said, hoping his voice didn't betray him. He wasn't ready. He'd been crazy to ask Ryan to meet him for an extra practice session. They were both sixteen, but Ryan was a head taller than Kiran and heavily muscled. Ryan didn't need more practice.

Ryan let his sword tip touch the ground. His black hair lay matted on his forehead and his lip curled. "Are you sure, flute boy? Bulo's not here to call a halt this time."

Kiran nodded and raised his sword, edging closer.

Ryan sprang toward him and slashed his sword downward. Kiran parried, sidling backward and turning his sword as Bulo, their trainer, had taught them. He was quick, but the bones of his forearms felt as if they would shatter each time his sword caught one of Ryan's two-handed strikes. Sweat started on his forehead and his breath grated.

The larger boy drove him away from the forest edge, then paused for an instant and swung wide, sword whipping in from Kiran's left.

Kiran leaped sideways. His right foot landed on a rock, his ankle rolled, and he fell hard, dropping his weapon. At once he tried to wriggle after it, but Ryan shoved a booted foot against his chest and pinned him.

Ryan shook the sweat out of his face and grinned. "Saved you, music boy. You'd have gone off the cliff."

Kiran turned his head. It was true. A few feet away, the land plummeted down the brushy slope toward the village. He would have retreated right off the edge if Ryan hadn't turned him. He ground his teeth.

Ryan placed the point of his sword on Kiran's throat. "Poor little flute boy, whipped again. What will that prune-face priest do to you when you turn up dirty? And how will you explain to your famous father?" He lifted Kiran's chin with the sword point. "Oops, I'm sorry, I mean what *would* you say, if your daddy hadn't run off in a panic and let Savages rip him to pieces?"

With a cry of fury, Kiran arched his body upward, kicking out with both feet at Ryan's knees. In the same motion, he swiped Ryan's sword away from his throat with his right wrist. As Ryan lurched back, Kiran leaped to his feet. The pain in his ankle made him stagger.

Then Ryan jumped him, snarling, sword thrown aside, his fists pummeling Kiran's face and head while Kiran's own fists pattered uselessly on Ryan's arms. Kiran crashed back to the ground with Ryan on top of him. Ryan grabbed his ears, yanked his head upward, and smashed it against the ground.

"Give up!" Ryan shouted. "Or I'll—"

Kiran braced himself for the next blow, but Ryan loosened his hold and cocked his head.

Kiran's head clanged, and the sky tilted overhead. But no, the clanging was outside him, real: the tower bell.

Ryan climbed off Kiran. He stood, wiped an arm across his face, and looked out over the valley. "It's too early in the season. Isn't it? Does it usually come this soon?"

With the world still slanted, Kiran rolled onto his stomach, pushed himself up to hands and knees, and heaved himself upright. He felt like vomiting. It hurt to put weight on his left foot. He hobbled over to stand on the edge of the bluff next to Ryan. Below them, the hillside dropped down to the village of Lanath's bare fields and orchards, still blurry in the river mist. Smoke rose from huddled cottages. Centered among the cottages, the temple dome gleamed in the early light. Ser Vetel would be muttering as he waited for Kiran to arrive for work. Beyond the village stretched the beech forest where Kiran's stepfather, Lir, oversaw the harvest of the *nuath* fungus that gave the village its name.

In the tower at one corner of the village wall, the sun glinted off a bell as it swung, clamoring: The first barge of spring was about to arrive.

Sweeping his gaze down the long curve of river, Kiran saw at first only the surge of brown and ruffled water. But there, nosing its way past the second bend, slid the low-crouching barge, its sail hanging limp, oars shooting out its sides like the legs of a water bug. He pointed. "Less than an hour away, I'd guess."

Ryan looked. "Just time enough to get your face washed, flute boy." He gave Kiran a playful punch on the shoulder, then stepped over to the tree where Kiran had propped his flute. He lifted his foot as if to stamp down and snap it in two. "Shall I? Now that you're going to be a soldier and not a flute boy?"

With a half-swallowed cry, Kiran dove for the tree to protect the flute.

Ryan laughed and drew back. "Aw, come on, I wouldn't. That would be just cruel. Because you'll never be a soldier, will you? You'll be here playing that little flute all your life."

He gave Kiran a half salute and took off at a lope down the trail.

Limping as fast as he could, Kiran followed.

★ ★ ★

Kiran slipped through the east gate among farmers the bell had summoned from the fields. Ahead, two children chased a snuffler that ducked its head and kicked out its hind trotters. Kiran followed the children toward the alley that led to his stepfather's house. Just in front of the alleyway entrance, the snuffler upended a woman carrying a bundle on her shoulder.

The woman's bundle burst open, and the snuffler clattered away. With shouts of laughter, the two boys jumped over the fallen woman's legs and bounded after the beast.

Without thinking, Kiran reached a hand to the sprawling woman. When she brushed back her shawl, he stiffened. She was the herb-woman Nora. An evil influence, according to Ser Vetel—one who deceived the poor people of the village by offering worthless herbs in place of his cordials and incantations.

Still, it was only right to help her up. "Take my hand," he offered.

Before she could respond, someone else's bony hand, reaching from behind him, closed in Kiran's hair. The hand wrenched him around until he stood face to face with Ser Vetel, tall and glowering in his long green priest's robe.

"You haven't finished the ceiling stars," Ser Vetel said. "And now our visitors from Catora are here. What will they think of a village that let its temple fall to ruin? Gaping holes in the ceiling! Get back to work."

"But the greeting ceremony!" Kiran protested.

Ser Vetel's eyes narrowed and he gave Kiran's head a shake. "Look at the filth of you. Look at your hands! How will you play your flute?"

Kiran turned his hands over, examining the bruised wrist, scraped knuckles and torn fingernails. "I can play."

Ser Vetel's hand fell to Kiran's narrow shoulder. "Brawling again, and for nothing." His fingernails dug in, and he heaved a sigh. "For the thousandth time, boy, can't you see you'll never make a soldier? There are no flute-playing soldiers, dear boy. And no heroes, either. It's nothing but mud and diarrhea and slops, lice and the stink of fear."

Kiran bit his lip and met the priest's eye. "I swore a vow, Ser Vetel." He moved to grasp the hilt of his wooden sword, but it wasn't there, and his hand wrapped around the end of the flute instead. He closed his eyes and pictured the sword still lying where he had dropped it when Ryan made him trip. *Idiot.*

Ser Vetel gave another sigh and released his shoulder. "I don't know why I waste my time. Get home and wash. Wave at the examiners, then hustle back and finish your work. The ceiling first. After that I want you to run the girls' chorus through their performance one more time." He raised his eyebrows. "For the sunrise song, I want you to play that descant of yours above their voices."

Kiran's mouth dropped open. To play his own composition in front of everyone! In his head he heard it already, a playful line skipping and coaxing, a song of sunrise calling the dew. One last concert before he began his life as a soldier.

Ser Vetel gave him a push. "Go now, and come back to me clean." The old priest turned away.

Kiran took a step toward the alleyway. At his feet, the herb-woman Nora still crouched, sweeping her scattered weed-stalks into a pile. Courtesy made Kiran kneel down to help her scoop the pile back into the center of her bundle so she could tie it again.

"Thank you, Kiran the musician," she said, rocking back on her heels and peering at him with hazel eyes.

Kiran averted his glance. Was she mocking him? She never came to temple ceremonies, so when had she heard him play?

Nora hoisted the bundle back onto her shoulder and stood. "Help me draw the seffidges some water," she said. "The soldiers are packing them back in their shed."

Draw water for seffidges? He had no time for extra chores, and certainly not to serve seffidges. He shook his head and took a step backward.

She gestured toward the well. "The soldiers neglect to give them fresh water. A day gets long with nothing to drink."

Kiran looked around at children shooing chickens back to their coops and young women hurrying from the tailor shop with their arms full of ribbons. Around and among the villagers, the seffidges slouched toward their quarters. Heads low, feet dragging, their long hair tangled and their red-brown skin smeared with dirt, they looked no more than half human. What business was it of his what they drank all day?

Nora said, "We wouldn't treat our cattle so."

Heaving a sigh, Kiran walked over to the pump in front of the temple where he drew water for Ser Vetel every morning. Two buckets lay against the base of the temple dome where it met the pavement. He brought the buckets over and cranked until water splashed over their rims. Without a word he lifted the buckets and followed Nora toward the back of the village, through the poor quarter. Leading him, she picked her way over puddles and heaps of vegetable peelings.

Across a muddy yard, close to the village wall, crouched the long shed where the seffidges slept at night. A soldier posted at the door prodded the line of gathering seffidges to move inside.

The herb-woman veered left and made her way across the mud to a cottage with a fenced-in garden. At the steps she set down her bundle and turned to Kiran. "I know why you're discontented, Kiran. Instead of the sword you yearn for, you carry a flute. Instead of a spear, you carry water for slaves. I'll tell you something that's painful to learn. We don't always choose our burdens; sometimes they choose us. In war or in peace—"

The cottage door opened, and out stepped Nora's daughter Myra, who sang alto in the girls' chorus. She looked surprised to see Kiran. So this was where she lived, next door to seffidges.

Myra descended the steps. Throwing back her dark unruly hair, she took the buckets from Kiran's hands, nodding her thanks.

Nora reached to probe the bruise on Kiran's wrist where he had struck aside Ryan's sword. "What I mean to say," she told him, "is you need not worry. The day will come, and you will be a warrior, Kiran."

Chapter 2

Splashes of blue paint framed the windows of Kiran's stepfather's house, and flowers climbed the outer walls. In the doorway, Kiran's mother waited, her woven hair hanging to her waist in a golden curtain. "Son, come dress!" She held up the new tunic she had embroidered for him. Kiran slipped past her, laid down his flute, and stripped off his shirt. The water bucket reflected his smudged face and light brown hair. He plunged his arms and head in the bucket and washed off the mud from his fight with Ryan. He scrubbed his head with a towel and combed his fingers through his hair.

Before the fireplace, Kiran's half-sister Dara danced from foot to foot, holding dried flowers up to her father, Lir. Like her mother's, her hair was golden, but it had the same wave as Kiran's. She was six years old this year, old enough to travel downriver to Catora for the first time. The importance of it had swelled her almost to bursting. "Papa, do my hair! Kiran, tell Papa to hurry!"

Kiran glanced at his stepfather, who filled the corner of the room. He knew better than to tell Lir anything.

Lir drew his fingers through his beard and chortled. "Kiran here is the one who should hurry. Took your time getting home, boy. I thought that priest of yours had drowned you in his seeing-basin."

With lips pressed shut, Kiran dried his torso, then stooped to wipe the mud from his legs and boots.

Lir continued: "Anyway, why hurry? Let them wait for us, this once." He spun Dara around and began to weave the flowers into her hair. "Ten days early, they come drifting up here. They treat us like seffidges, the way they whistle and expect us to jump. No respect for time and a man's work. Serve them right if we were all as dreamy and slow as our Kiran." He chuckled and tugged on Dara's braid.

Biting the inside of his lip, Kiran turned to his mother and ducked into the tunic. *When I'm a great warrior, he'll stop mocking me.*

His mother straightened the tunic, running her hand along its edges. All winter she'd sewed and embroidered, head bent, not even singing as her needle dipped and glinted in the firelight. Kiran knew how she dreaded watching her two surviving children drift away.

His mother reached up to touch his cheek. "With all my heart, Kiran, I've prayed for you to find happiness here, playing your flute and working in the nuath grove with your. . ." She glanced at Lir and let the sentence trail away. "But now I've decided just to wish for your happiness." She gave a sickly smile, and Kiran set his hand on her shoulder.

"Come with us to the river," he said on impulse. "Come stand with Dara and me."

She looked down, shaking her head in confusion, and Kiran knew he shouldn't have asked. His mother hadn't stepped outside the village walls in nine years.

Without saying anything more, he tied the new tunic and pushed his flute through the belt. At the door, he paused to make a face at Dara.

★ ★ ★

Kiran limped along the muddy cobbles of the village lane, taking care to keep his new tunic clean. The morning sun shone warm on his back. A stream of villagers swept him out the gate, down the main path to the riverbank where the craftsmen and farmers were already arranging themselves by rank.

He pulled up and scanned the crowd for the other sixteen-year-old boys and girls. This was their year, the year they might leave home at last. Over the next few days, a handful of boys would be chosen for soldiers, and a handful of girls would be selected to serve in Catora's grand houses. Only the chosen youth received passports allowing them to move freely about the kingdom. The rest would be tied for life to Lanath, the farthest upriver village, to farm and manufacture and hold the frontier against Savages. Most important of all, they would harvest the beech fungus, nuath, used in religious ceremonies all over the kingdom.

Near the gate stood a cluster of young children dressed like Dara, with flowers in their hair. Catoran law required all six-year-old children of the outpost villages to visit the capital for twelve months of learning their country's songs and history. They lived with relatives or host families, but still there was homesickness. Kiran remembered longing for home so hard that on the return journey it had seemed his own yearning drew the barge upriver toward Lanath.

Toward Lanath and sorrow. Because on the shore, his mother met him empty-handed, alone, her face drawn with weeping. Savages had snatched his baby brother Calef from the apple orchard. His hotheaded father, storming after them without waiting for help, had vanished in their pursuit. Kiran's mother had been left a widow, and Kiran a fatherless son.

That day, standing by the river with his fists clenched and tears running down his face, Kiran had sworn that someday he would become a great warrior and sweep the kingdom free of

Savages. "No, no," his mother had protested. "Not you." She had reached for his hand and knelt to pull him into an embrace. "Not you, my sweet son, my warbler. For you I will find a different life, safer and more beautiful."

★ ★ ★

The tower bell tolled once more, and villagers streamed past Kiran on either side. He caught sight of Ryan waving to him. "Kiran! Over here!"

Warily, Kiran shouldered his way through the throng. Ryan pushed Garront aside to make room for him. "Nursing your battle wounds? They're about to come ashore. Doesn't the barge look bigger than last year? Look at those banners!"

The banners, three golden otters on a field of green, hung over the sides of the barge, trailing almost into the water. The barge rested long and low against the landing, sails furled at its two masts. At a shouted order, six rowers lifted their oars to make a corridor through which the examiners could pass. The rowers were seffidges, their mottled brown skin like smudges of dirt against the festive green and gold. On shore, two Lanath seffidges caught lines thrown from the barge and wrapped them around posts on the dock. Two others scuttled to push a gangplank against the barge's side.

Now the Catoran envoys appeared at the top of the gangplank. In front strode a broad-shouldered man with a long black beard that came to two points. He wore black armor. Behind him crowded three smaller soldiers with short, neatly trimmed beards. Farther back, one bald priest in a green robe herded the group of returning seven-year-olds dressed in green and gold. The black-bearded officer paused at the top of the gangplank to survey the rows of villagers before him. Beside Kiran, Ryan pulled himself to his full height. *So that's it*, Kiran thought. *He made a place for me so he can look bigger and tougher in comparison.* He gritted his teeth in frustration. The crowd was too tight for him to move aside.

The envoys waited as Lir, with slow, ceremonial steps, led a procession of heavy-laden seffidges down the path toward the barge. Lir looked tall and grand with his great bushy beard, his bronze medallion and his fur-lined robe, as befitted the Master of the Harvest.

Tradition required the Master of the Harvest to present official visitors with a first bundle of nuath before they came ashore. Lir's seffidges carried a roll of canvas on each shoulder. Within the rolls, the nuath was bedded in the dark moist soil that kept it fresh until it could be processed into incense and the ceremonial tea that priests drank to bring on visions. At the dock, Lir lifted a bundle from the nearest seffidge and hoisted it up the gangplank. The black-bearded captain stood back, and Kiran craned his neck to see his stepfather lay down the bundle, unroll it, thrust his hand into the black soil, and hold up a strand of thick, rust-colored fungus. The captain accepted it and the crowd cheered.

Then the captain stepped forward to address the villagers. "People of Lanath! I bring you greetings and blessings from King Arluin himself! In this season of peril, I command you to show me the best of your village, so I can bring him a good report."

A murmur swept through the crowd like a wind through corn. Old King Arluin still alive. And peril—did that mean war in the south again?

With no music but the stamping of their own feet, the little band of soldiers marched down the gangplank and up the flower-strewn path. Swinging his head from side to side, the black-bearded captain peered into the crowd, while seffidges carrying nuath rolls to the shore pressed to the side to let the soldiers pass.

Just as the captain approached where the sixteen-year-olds stood, Ryan gave a seffidge in front of him a quick shove. The seffidge stumbled and fell against the leg of the examiner, who drew back with a look of disgust. Dirt and fungus spilled across the path. At once, Ryan leaped into the walkway. "Out of their way, you clumsy beast!" he bellowed. He grabbed the seffidge by his belt, heaved him up and threw him aside to land cowering at Kiran's feet.

Ryan flashed a grin and a salute to the chief examiner. The examiner laughed and Ryan stepped back into line, shooting a look of triumph at Kiran. He had made himself noticed.

Ryan's smile dissolved into a grunt as he doubled over, clutching his side. Myra, Nora's daughter, planted herself between the two boys, her chin jutting out and hands on her hips. In the bright sunshine she looked taller and bonier than ever, all elbows and knees and long chin, awkward in her embroidered dress, proud and smart but surely too graceless to be selected for Catora. Kiran was unsure which sharp angle, elbow or knee, she had just used on Ryan.

"Beast yourself!" Myra hissed. "You cheating oaf!"

Ryan raised a large fist, his face reddening. The girl flinched. With a sick feeling in his stomach, Kiran stepped up next to her.

But Ryan shot a sideways glance at the marching examiners, sucked on his lip, and let his hand fall. Apparently he was smart enough not to slug a girl in front of everyone. Kiran shook his head. How many times had it been drummed into the children of Lanath that seffidges, though lowly and servile by nature, should not be mistreated without reason?

Myra leaned down to help the seffidge rise. The seffidge cringed, the way seffidges always did, and refused to stand. Instead of leaving him to himself, Myra actually knelt down, took his hand, and whispered in his ear. Taking things too far, as usual. By the time she came up with the seffidge, the front of her new dress was muddy and the hem sagged.

The crowd broke up around them; villagers trailed back to the gate in the perimeter wall. Even Ryan, with a last glower at Myra, swaggered off to help his father at the forge.

Kiran waited, groping for something to say to Myra. Why did she always make him feel as if he'd failed to measure up? Even now she was glaring at him in such an irritating way that he blurted, "It's dumb to risk a broken nose for a seffidge."

She snorted. "You saw what he did?"

Kiran nodded. There was a catch in Myra's voice, and he wondered how many herbs she and her mother had gathered to buy the material for that ruined dress.

Myra brushed at her muddy knee, then gave up and straightened. "No one stands up to bullies. Can you imagine if the seffidges stood up to us?"

The question was meaningless, because seffidges had no spirit. Instead of answering, Kiran offered her his arm. But she took a step backward and shook her head. "You should have poked him yourself, Kiran. How can you ever be a warrior when he makes you look like such a weakling?"

Chin high, half tripping over her sagging hem, she left him standing alone in the empty lane.

Chapter 3

Two days later, the five sixteen-year-old boys followed Bulo upriver to face the examiners. Kiran had wrapped some of Nora's crushed herbs around his ankle, and it felt cool and reasonably supple.

Bulo, youngest soldier of the Lanath garrison, was a husky southerner with a catch in his speech and an oddly gentle manner. He had trained the boys in wrestling, archery and use of the sword and spear, but privately he had taken each boy aside and in stammering speech had urged him to avoid the army and stay home in Lanath instead.

On a flat rock by the river, flanked by his three companions, Orda, the chief examiner, stood with his head thrown back, hands on hips and beard flowing down his chest. He waved Bulo out of the way so he could peer at the boys as they ranged themselves in front of him. Kiran felt that measuring gaze bore into him, judging him too small, too scrawny. He straightened his shoulders.

"Well, boys," Orda began, in a voice loud enough that Kiran flinched. "Two of you, that's our quota this year, just two. A shame if you ask me, in a year when we need hundreds more to throw against the southern spears. But you catch a break because your village is a 'vital frontier outpost.' So why don't three of you skip the humiliation and go home right now?"

Again he glared at Kiran, who to his horror felt himself waver on his feet.

Orda grunted. "None of you? Right, here's the first test."

He set them a long footrace, wide around the sheep meadow and through the orchard, to circle the village walls and then return upriver to the base of the waterfall. He dispatched his soldiers to stations along the path to make sure the racers took no shortcuts.

Ryan took his arms out of his tunic and tied it around his waist, and Jovan, the carpenter's son, tied back his hair. Only Kiran took off his boots. He knew the path; it wasn't rocky, and he ran better when he could feel the earth beneath him.

With a shout, Orda dropped his arm, and the boys leaped forward.

It was a cold clear day with high puffs of cloud, perfect for running. Kiran set himself a moderate pace and stuck with it even as the other boys surged past him. It was the pace Bulo set when he ran ahead of them, singing aloud, the pace of a song he remembered his father singing long ago, jogging down to the river with little Calef on his shoulders. In those days Kiran's mother hummed all day at her weaving, and Kiran thought she pulled music and sunlight through her loom.

After the Savages shattered her family, Enya grew silent. Running through the sheep meadow, Kiran remembered that first dark year: the house shadowed and close, bread and firewood short, his mother's hands and voice shaking. Until one day a cardinal sang outside the window, and she sat for a long moment listening. Then she combed and dressed her hair, counted out a pair of coins from the purse that hung by the fire, and walked out to order a flute from the carpenter. As soon as she had taught Kiran how to finger a few notes, she sent him for lessons to Ser Vetel. To pay for the lessons, she made Kiran do chores for the priest. She had him apprenticed almost before he noticed. Kiran grew used to the smell of incense and to how the sweet longing sound of the flute echoed in the temple cavern.

As Kiran ran through the orchard, ducking under low branches, he felt the turned clods underfoot and let a song for picking peaches play in his ears.

After his mother married Lir, the richest man in the village, she began to set money aside. When she had saved enough she ordered an arloc from Catora. Kiran remembered resting the package on his knees, unwrapping the burlap that covered its sixteen shimmering strings. It had taken all day to tune, but when he touched the strings there rose a half-finished skein of chords that glimmered in his mind like a spiderweb on a foggy morning.

Rounding the village walls, Kiran began to catch up with the other boys. He passed first Terrill, leaning against the wooden wall, catching his breath, then Garront, doubled over by the side of the path. As he turned back onto the upriver path, Kiran saw that he was closing slowly on Jovan. Even Ryan, far ahead, looked heavy and lumbering. It was time to sprint. Kiran played the deer hunt song in his head—the herd leaping away through the forest, then a great buck fleeing ahead of the dogs. He tore past Jovan, who staggered in surprise, and was closing on Ryan when he felt his breath coming ragged and his legs turning to wood. He'd made his move too soon.

But Ryan was slowing down now, too; he didn't seem to know someone was behind him. Kiran lowered his head. His fists and knees pumped. Pace by pace, taking great gulps of air, he inched up on Ryan. No music now, just the pain in his ankle and the pressure in his chest as he drove forward. He heard the waterfall ahead, and with a final surge he burst past Ryan, past Orda, until he pulled up in front of a grinning Bulo.

Ryan threw himself onto hands and knees beside him, chest heaving. Then he rolled over onto his back and snarled at

Kiran. "You little sneak." He sat up. "This competition is mine, you understand? Mine. Go for second place if you want. But try to touch me and I'll crush you."

Orda, watching, gave a harsh laugh and turned to watch the other boys stagger in.

★ ★ ★

The next challenge was swordplay. Ryan jumped to claim Kiran as opponent, but Bulo separated them. Not that it made much difference: in two minutes Jovan beat Kiran to the ground, and he had to sit aside and watch Jovan lose his final match with Ryan. In archery, Kiran's arrows fell farthest from the target. For the next task, climbing the cliff by the waterfall, Kiran's lightness and agility took him fastest to the top, and he ignored Ryan grunting just below him. But at the crest, Orda commanded the boys to lift and throw bigger and bigger rocks, and Kiran ran out of strength before the others. "That little pebble too much for you?" mocked the examiner.

Kiran's face burned. He should have worked to build his strength. Lifting a flute or strumming an arloc was no match for Ryan's work at the forge or Jovan's sawing and hammering in his father's carpentry shop.

Then the soldiers led them along the length of the cliff, to the pool above the waterfall. Kiran hated this place. He never felt confident in the water, and whenever the boys swam here, with the sound of the waterfall pounding at his ears, cold fingers of fear groped at him.

Orda set them a task. "Edge out on that log as far as you can. On my whistle, swim to the far bank. Run up and grab a branch fit for a club. Swim back holding it overhead. No dragging it, hear? First one back with a dry club wins."

The boys jostled onto the log. Kiran found himself in the middle of them, taking slow breaths, preparing himself, fighting down his dread. But as Orda raised an arm, Ryan's foot swept behind Kiran's, and Ryan's elbow drove hard into his ribs. Kiran toppled backward off the log. The water closed over him as he tried to take in air, and he came up flailing and coughing.

Ryan leaped into the water beside him, shouted, "I've got him, sir!" and grabbed Kiran by the hair. Kiran struggled to turn and punch him, but he couldn't free himself from Ryan's grip.

Ryan wrenched his head back. "Don't panic, Kiran, I've got you!"

As Kiran started to curse, Ryan thrust his head underwater again, and Kiran's windpipe filled with water.

Orda's whistle sounded, but Ryan still towed Kiran by the hair toward the riverbank. With every stroke he ducked Kiran's head underwater. Kiran had to quit struggling to concentrate on timing his breaths. In a moment Ryan dragged him ashore. Gasping, Kiran hauled himself up to face his tormentor.

But Orda was already shoving the other boy toward the water. "You shouldn't have wasted your time. You're falling behind." Ryan made a beautiful flat dive, skimmed across the water, and started to swim with a strong, smooth stroke.

Kiran doubled over, coughing, until river water spewed from his mouth. None of the soldiers even glanced his way. Nobody had seen the elbow in his ribs. His chest still hurt from that and the water he had taken in. He hated Ryan with all his being, but that wasn't going to do him any good. Grimly, he waded out into the current. With his own awkward, choppy stroke, he set out across the water. He couldn't get the rhythm of it, and he kept gulping in more water. The others, returning, passed him midstream, a lace of splashed water sparkling in their wake. By the time he had found a tree branch and labored back across the river again with the branch held high in one aching arm, only Bulo remained to watch. The other boys and the soldier examiners, in two separate, laughing groups, were already jogging back to the village.

"I'm sorry, K-Kiran," Bulo said. "You're out."

* * *

Kiran stood on a ladder, polishing the star tiles in the dome of the temple cavern. Below him, Ser Vetel fussed at the altar, rearranging flowers and fruits. The old priest had placed incense burners around the circumference of the cavern and taken an extra pinch of nuath powder in his tea. Now his eyes were glazed, but he kept fidgeting, glancing up at the star-studded ceiling and instructing Kiran to move the ladder and keep polishing.

"All right, boy, that's enough. Put away the ladder. They'll be here any minute."

Kiran trudged down the ladder, pulled it from the wall, and carried it into the storage tunnel. Behind him, he heard the heavy temple door creak open and the beat of footsteps crossing the stone floor. He drew back in the darkness and kept silent. After yesterday's humiliation and the crumpling of his hopes, he didn't want to face the examiners again.

"Kiran!" Ser Vetel's voice creaked with annoyance. "Get out here."

Kiran emerged, head low. Trying to look like an obedient, inconspicuous servant, he took his place next to Ser Vetel.

"Is this the boy?" The voice was richer than Ser Vetel's, sweeter than Orda's. Kiran looked up to find the priest examiner appraising him.

"Ser Wellim wishes to hear you play," Ser Vetel said.

Kiran's hand dropped to his flute, and he took a step backward in dismay. What game was Ser Vetel playing? Kiran's mood was all wrong for music: his bitter disappointment would sour the notes.

Behind the priest, Orda raised his eyebrows, sneered, and turned to survey the torches lining the walls.

"Can he play the King's Song?" Ser Wellim asked.

The question was an insult. It was a light and easy melody with a couple of tricky twists at the end. Kiran could probably play it in his sleep. He lifted the flute and played it simply, without the decorations he liked to add when he played for the village children. He wanted to make the song sound insolent, but the music caught hold of him, and he let the final notes echo under the dome for a long time.

The examiner nodded. Behind him, Orda picked at his nails.

"Play your moonrise song, Kiran," Ser Vetel said.

Kiran took a breath. This song, his own, he couldn't play half-heartedly. He closed his eyes and blew the long low tones of twilight, the warm shiver of first moonlight, the skittering of notes as the full moon's light outshone the nearby stars. He played stumbling dark tones as a cloud passed in front of the moon. Finally, the notes grew clear and long again, and he let the song play itself out into quietness.

The quietness lasted. Then Ser Vetel spoke. "He plays the arloc, too. As a beginner."

The examiner nodded, and Ser Vetel waved at Kiran to lift the beautiful instrument from the wall. Kiran knelt and placed it across his knees. When he touched the sixteen strings, they all rang true. This time he played the fields in midsummer, when the grain was high and the children of the village chased in circles to keep the crows away. The arloc was more of a struggle for him than the flute. At times his fingers seemed to plod across the strings when they should be dancing. So he slowed down, made the summer day lazier, and ended the song when he could. He looked up.

The priest examiner nodded. "Untrained, but promising. Not much to undo." He peered sharply at Ser Vetel. "Can he read?"

Ser Vetel looked shocked. "I would never overstep—a mere village boy! What would be the chances?"

The priest examiner smiled. "With flute-playing like that! You must have known.... Naturally, we'll take him."

Take me? Kiran rocked back. *Take me for what?*

"He's a hard worker," Ser Vetel said. It was the opposite of anything he'd ever told Kiran. "Humble, never argues, respectful..."

"And is he clever?"

Ser Vetel hesitated. "Who can say? He's different from the others. Not a fast thinker, but could be a deep one."

The priest examiner laughed. "What do you say, boy?"

Kiran stood up. "Say to what, Your Eminence?"

The priest laughed, and Kiran's ears burned. *Not a fast thinker.*

Ser Vetel leaned forward, and his voice crackled with impatience. "The best music instruction in the country is found in the temple training schools of Catora. If your spiritual ear proves as finely tuned as your musical one, you might become the first priest from the frontier in twenty years."

"Though you're starting late," Ser Wellim said. "You'll have to learn to read with the young sons of rich merchants, bred from the cradle to the priesthood. Half of them tone-deaf lunks who by rights should be wrestlers." He smiled more broadly.

Even Orda grinned, shaking his head. "A good thing he plays," he said with a chuckle. "He sure won't get to Catora by swimming!"

The priest looked horrified. "This is the one you were telling me about? Boy, listen to me. You're a musician, and with training you'll make a priest. But no more consorting with ruffians, do you hear? You don't want a sword to injure your hand, or water to injure your ears. You could lose everything. You are under my orders now, and I forbid you to engage in violence or competition."

"Yes, Your Eminence," said Kiran. In a daze he lifted the arloc and hung it again on the wall. He felt as if he was walking in a dream, his feet hardly touching the floor, as if a heavy pack filled with all his shortcomings had fallen from his back. But when the pack hit the ground it burst open, and some of his hopes flew away, too. *Will I never hold a sword again? But the music. I'll have music.*

Ser Wellim waved a hand at him. "Go enjoy your last evening with your family. You, too, Orda, get out of here. Go curse at some soldiers. I have priestly business with Ser Vetel which only the purified may hear."

As they climbed the stairs, Orda clapped Kiran on the shoulder with sudden friendliness. "What do you reckon, little shipmate?" he asked. "You think they're really talking secrets of the kingdom, or are they just brewing nuath, the old drunkards?"

Kiran yanked his shoulder free and gave him a dark look. Orda only laughed and turned away.

Chapter 4

The tower bell rang as the departing children paraded down to the riverside to bid their families goodbye. First came the seven youngest children, with flowers in their hair; the villagers lining the walk sang and clapped as they passed. Next came the sixteen-year-olds who had been chosen for the journey. There were three girls, Myra among them. The other two kept their eyes demurely lowered, but Myra held her head high and swung her arms as she walked. Ryan and Jovan followed, their boots loud on the cobbles, shiny new swords hanging from their waists. Kiran brought up the rear with the flute in his belt and the arloc slung over one shoulder.

Ser Vetel blessed the children one by one. When Kiran reached him, the old priest gripped his shoulders and said into his ear, "Peace and order, boy. Grow in wisdom. Someday you'll guide the people and thank me for turning you back from the roads of war."

Kiran's mother, trembling outside the village walls, stood with Lir supporting her elbow. She held Dara a long time, and then, as Dara ran up the gangplank to join the other children, turned to embrace Kiran. Her tears fell on his neck.

"You should be happy for me," he said. "This is what you wanted."

"I'm proud of you, Kiran." She wiped her eyes and leaned close again, speaking so only Kiran could hear. "But I've been thinking all week of your brother Calef. His curls, his little round cheeks . . . Kiran, take care of Dara. I know she'll be fine with my cousin, but visit her. Don't let any harm come to her."

He squeezed her tight. "I promise. She'll come home safe."

She pressed her wet face briefly against his.

Lir shook Kiran's hand. "So, you're to be a priest," he grumbled. "Filling people's heads with superstition. Makes your mother happy, I suppose. But if someday you think better of it, come home and I'll set you up in the nuath grove."

Kiran didn't remember noticing gray in Lir's beard before, or those lines around his eyes. Seeing Lir's hand supporting his mother's arm, Kiran had a strange impulse to thank his stepfather, but instead he shook his head. "Ser Vetel doesn't lie."

He stepped backward onto the gangplank, one hand brushing the flute in his belt. He looked back at the walled village, the muddy fields surrounding it, and the bluff rising beyond. As he backed away from his stepfather's warnings and his mother's sorrow, he felt so light he thought he might rise into the air. "I'll put you in my music!" he called, and then he turned and ran aboard.

★ ★ ★

From Lanath-above-the-Falls it was four days' easy float downriver to the Serpent, the roaring chasm where they would moor the barge and transfer their goods to the downriver barge for Catora. The first afternoon they floated with no sail, just one soldier watching the seffidges push a long oar in figure eights off the stern and another keeping lookout in front for rocks or sandbars. In early spring like this the water was high, and they swept along in the heart of the current.

Kiran spent most of that day on deck, watching the forested shore drift by or lying back to watch the clouds. Ryan and Jovan leaned over the side, scouting for fish. The younger children played catch with balls of tied-up grass, squealing with delight whenever one was lost overboard. After their last ball skimmed the water, they squatted on deck beside the cage of blue messenger birds, trying to imitate their chirring calls.

As evening settled, the barge moored beside an island that was little more than a sandbar. Ryan and Jovan waded through hip-deep water to carry the small children ashore. One of the soldiers started a fire, and to the boys' dismay, Orda called for Jovan and Ryan to prepare the meal.

"What?" Ryan protested. "Cooking's for women or seffidges."

Orda barked out a laugh. "And which of them does the army drag along on campaign?"

Kiran decided to work on setting up the tents. The soldier Losar helped him with the first, then left him to struggle on his own with tangled lines and mismatched posts. Myra came over to point out what he was doing wrong until he drove her off with a ferocious look. By the time he'd finally worked it out, the girls were helping dish up the burnt and salty food.

"Why do we stay on an island, Kiran?" Dara asked him after dinner, as she crawled onto his lap.

"Here on the island no wild thing can get us."

"You mean like wolves?" She shivered deliciously. "Can Savages get us?"

He twirled a finger in her curls. "Savages haven't attacked a barge in years and years. Most people say they've moved over the mountains and beyond the desert." He wondered. If the Savages had fled for good, maybe his dreams of vengeance could never have come true, even if he had become a warrior.

"Do Savages have babies like us?" Dara asked. "I'd like to see one. If we see Savages, Kiran, you should catch me a baby so I can tame it."

"Maybe." He loosed her curl and it sprang back into place. "Did you know that some people say our servants, the seffidges, used to be Savages once, in our great-grandparents' time?"

"But seffidges aren't cute. I don't want one of them." She set her face in a pout. "I want a real one."

Kiran laughed. "Well, you won't see one tonight, so hush up and go to sleep." He wrapped a blanket around her and carried her to the children's tent, but when he tried to set her down, she clung to him. She had never slept away from home or family before. So Kiran scooped out a place for the two of them in the sand under a bush.

He lay with one arm around her, looking up at the glittering trail of the Sky Serpent swimming across the night sky. The stars were the Sky Serpent's scales, shaken off as he swam. Every night he swam across the sky to woo the Moon Lady; every month he nourished her back to health and hope before she wasted away again in her sorrow that they couldn't stay together always. *Lies*, Lir called the old stories; but Ser Vetel said each one had a deeper meaning, the way music has a structure beneath its surface. And now the meanings would open themselves to Kiran.

His way lay spread out before him as mysterious and glittering as that wide path of stars above his head—a life of music, ceremony, and learning. He breathed the night air, still sweet with smoke from the dying fire. Beneath his back the island itself seemed to drift downstream.

★ ★ ★

At mid-afternoon on the fourth day, Orda set the rowers to pulling in long slow strokes against the current. Dara ran over to Kiran. "Why are we slowing down?"

"We're almost at the Serpent," he told her. "Listen. Can you hear it?"

Over the splash of the oars came a low, hissing roar. At the Serpent, the river plunged in linked and sinuous six-foot drops, impassable by barge. Upriver barges moored on the near side of it, and all the goods had to be carried on a detour through the rocky woods to Serpent Camp, below the cataract, where the downriver barge awaited. The Serpent kept Lanath-above-the-Falls isolated from the rest of the kingdom. Kiran crouched on deck, explaining it to Dara until she grew impatient and ran away to watch a kingfisher plunge into the water.

The seffidges hauled on their oars, and the barge veered into the shallows along the left bank, where Orda's soldiers tied it to two iron rings anchored in the rock.

"Children and girls wait here," Orda commanded. Jovan and Ryan jumped ashore, but when Kiran moved to follow them, Ser Wellim laid hold of his sleeve and drew him back. Kiran whirled around to object.

Ser Wellim spoke in a cool voice. "You were not called on, young man. You will help the young ladies see to the children." When Kiran made a sound of protest, the priest frowned. "Remember, obedience and service. You are not some hooligan adventurer, you're a young scholar."

Biting back his frustration, Kiran withdrew to stand at the far side of the barge. Myra threw him a look of sympathy, then turned to get the children involved in a hopping game.

Twenty minutes later, Orda returned, scowling. "Bandit trouble. No sign of the two guards we left to watch things. And someone's looted the trunks. Tools, weapons, half the food missing."

Bandits! The children's eyes flew wide. They turned to each other in a thrill of delighted fear.

Ser Wellim raised an eyebrow. "More soldiers deserting? I thought you said those two were reliable. And the downriver barge?"

"No sign of it. Still at Pomel, I suppose."

"Never mind," Ser Wellim said calmly. "Let the seffidges unload and the children run around on shore. No doubt the barge will arrive by nightfall."

★ ★ ★

As the seffidges, grunting, heaved the baggage ashore, Kiran led a band of girls and children along the path that wound down between the edge of the forest and the thundering falls. The roar of the Serpent drowned out the little ones' chatter, and spray rose over the rocks to settle in their hair.

The path led into Serpent Camp, which looked as if a windstorm had just swept through. Tents had collapsed, pots were strewn across scattered fireplaces, and empty chests lay on their sides with their locks hanging askew. Ser Wellim was still upriver consulting with Orda, so Kiran joined Ryan and Jovan to heave the tents upright and stow the empty chests. For once the two of them accepted his help without comment or mockery.

Ryan worked with furious impatience. "I hope the bandits come back. Let them just try. We'll give them such a battle!"

When the camp was orderly again and the seffidges had piled Lanath's cargo alongside the lower mooring place, the boys paused to drink at the pool below the falls. Close to shore, fish wavered against a smooth pebbled floor, but farther out, the water boiled and churned beneath the thrashing Serpent.

Kiran doubled back along the path and climbed across the rocks for a closer look at the Serpent. Knees unsteady, he edged out over a boulder slippery with spray. A sound of rock grating on rock made him turn, and Ryan stepped past him to stand overlooking the cataract. The river writhed in the chasm between the rocks, dropping, bucking, ejecting jolts of water. "Look at it," Ryan said. "Wouldn't it be something to go down it in a canoe!"

Kiran shuddered, and Ryan laughed. "I know I'm crazy," he said. "But I need some adventure. Finally out of Lanath and all we do is sit on a boat. If only the bandits try to raid again tonight! Tell you what, let's go down and take a swim. Let's see who can get closest to the Serpent's tail."

Kiran snorted. "You think I'd swim with you, after you tried to drown me?"

"Drown you!" Ryan gave a hoot. "I was doing you a favor, pal. You'd be a lousy soldier, but you might make a halfway decent priest." He jumped to his feet. "Suit yourself, flute boy. I'm going down."

* * *

Ryan and Jovan swam below the cataract while the smaller children, under Myra's watchful eye, splashed and paddled close to shore. Kiran paced, feeling discontented and out of place. Finally he leaned against a tree beside Myra and muttered, "What are we doing here, anyway? You and me?"

She looked up in surprise. "You'll be a priest, of course." She caught his eye and frowned, touching her bushy hair. "Oh, I see. You mean, how'd someone who looks like me get picked along with beauties like them?" She nodded at the two other girls where they sat on the rocks, tossing pebbles at the swimming boys.

Kiran flushed. "I didn't mean that."

"Didn't you? Well, I'll tell you. It seems Catora has a lot of rich young mothers who want help with their children, and help bringing new ones into the world. Turns out all those nights I spent helping my mother wrap up brand new babies count for something after all."

"Is it true you give them nuath?" Kiran asked. It was one of Ser Vetel's complaints: Nora fed the sacred fungus to unpurified women.

Yes," Myra said. "Just the stringy part. It dulls the childbirth pains, and if they chew it slowly, they don't hallucinate." She stuck out her chin. "Oh, sorry. I mean they don't have sacred visions."

★ ★ ★

After supper, as the firelight cast dancing shadows on the tents and canvas awnings, Orda strode up and down, cursing the missing barge, while the other soldiers told jokes and guzzled beer.

Finally Orda planted himself in front of the fire. "I've decided," he said. "Downriver barge or not, I think we can trap some bandits. If they're spying on us, they've seen us unload. Now we march back to the barge and make a show of going aboard. Ryan, Losar and Jovan, you guard the barge and the children tonight. Don't worry, nothing will happen. The bandits are only after our cargo. The rest of the company will sneak back here and stake out the camp. With luck the bandits will take the bait and we'll see some action. Now, torches! Lots of noise! Move!"

His face pale in the firelight, Ryan begged for a chance at his first battle, but Orda told him to shut up. Then, with a clatter of boots and false drunken laughter, Orda led the troop of soldiers and passengers back up the track to the upriver barge at its mooring. Ryan marched beside Kiran, his eyes cast down and his boots clumping his disappointment.

Aboard the barge, Orda commanded Kiran to play old river songs, and the soldiers sang out in rollicking tones. Then Ser

Wellim suggested he choose something softer, and he switched to one of Ser Vetel's songs for teaching star names. The three girls sang along, their voices so sweet and true it was hard to believe any harm could come in the night.

Under cover of the music, Orda ordered his men to remove their boots and creep ashore.

"Now, Losar," Orda said quietly, with one foot on the gangplank. "Push offshore a bit. I want a stretch of water between you and shore. Let the seffidges sleep on deck so the wind carries their stink away. You take the first watch, and let the boys relieve you at midnight. No griping, lads, you'll get more sleep than we will." He turned to Kiran. "Keep up the music for an hour."

He slipped ashore, and darkness swallowed him.

Chapter 5

Kiran played for another hour, while most of the passengers drifted off to sleep below decks. Ser Wellim was one of the last to stand and stretch. "I'm sorry to disappoint you all," he said dryly, "But don't expect excitement tonight. The bandits won't attack with so many soldiers around. Orda's just using this as an excuse to train his men."

Dara stayed on deck for a while, sitting on Kiran's lap as he pointed out the stars and told her legends about their lives on earth. Finally she, too, got tired and went to curl up in the bow with Myra, who never slept below; she had laid out two big blankets.

With Dara gone, the only sound came from Ryan, who had traded with Losar for the first watch. Ryan clomped up and down, slamming his heels into the deck so loudly that Kiran wondered how anyone below could sleep. A glance at Ryan's thunderous face warned him not to say anything.

Kiran settled amidships with his flute resting on his knees, listening past Ryan to the night sounds of water, whirring insects and peeping frogs. The seffidges, all in a heap in their filthy rags, muttered and ground their teeth in their sleep. Focusing on the Serpent's rush and roar, Kiran set his back against the cabin and played his flute too softly to be heard.

***

Something woke him: a splash, a choked cry? He still sat in the shadow of the cabin with his hand closed around the flute. The heap that was Myra and Dara lay undisturbed, forward by the starboard side of the barge. No one was pacing the deck—he couldn't see Losar or the boys. And then there came a snorting and scuffling. Could that be Losar?

Kiran thrust the flute through his belt and crouched to peer around the cabin toward the stern. A dark lean figure stood urging the seffidges over the side. He grunted at them in what sounded like their own language. Kiran started up in surprise, and the figure looked back at him. In the moonlight Kiran caught a glimpse of a bare, fierce face, half-shaven head, sharp nose and glinting eyes. He felt a shock of recognition, but then it was gone, and he was sure he had never seen the face before.

But the Savage had seen him, and with a low command he pushed another seffidge over the side—there was no splash—and took a silent step toward Kiran, brandishing a knife.

At that moment there came a shout and the sound of footsteps running along the path.

It was Ryan, calling, "Get up, turn out! It's Savages attacking! Jovan, Losar!" What was Ryan doing on land? Ryan seized the mooring rope and jerked it to draw the barge closer to shore. Kiran stumbled. The Savage dropped his knife hand and vaulted over the side after the last seffidge.

In a running leap, Ryan landed aboard the barge with sword drawn. The barge swung out again into the stream.

For a moment only Kiran and Ryan stood on deck, facing each other across planking oddly empty of seffidges. But then, ululating, three Savages climbed over the stern. Whooping, they rushed at Ryan, who stood his ground with his sword raised. Kiran backed away, groping behind him for some kind of weapon. His hand fell on a long oar that hung in a bracket under the lip of the barge. Kiran whirled to tug it free. Jovan appeared beside him, sword drawn, his face white and hair wild.

The oar came free and Kiran staggered backward, lifted it high and turned. Ryan and Jovan stood shoulder to shoulder, trying to hold back the tide of Savages. Amidships Ser Wellim lifted his head out of the cabin and froze in place.

A cry from the bow made Kiran swing his head around. To his horror, he saw a Savage heave a small wriggling bundle over the side. A slim figure launched itself at the Savage. "Let her go, you beast!" Myra shouted. She pounded the Savage with her fists until he struck her and she collapsed on the deck.

Kiran tried to swing the oar around to knock the Savage down, but he couldn't balance its weight, and it slammed against the cabin wall. With a wild glance in his direction, Ser Wellim withdrew his head into the cabin and pulled the hatch shut.

Kiran dropped the oar and started forward without it. He bumped against Jovan, who was falling back, swinging his sword wildly. Before Kiran could cross the deck, the Savage hoisted Myra over the side. He kicked a blanket after her, looked back to survey the deck with a fierce grin, and leaped over the gunwale himself.

Kiran bolted to the spot where he had jumped.

Three canoes drew away across the black water, across the trembling tongue of the Serpent, heading for the opposite bank. In the closest canoe, three Savages struggled to wrap a blanket around Myra as she thrashed and cursed. Propped against the side of the canoe, another rolled blanket spilled golden hair from the top. The canoe rocked, and Kiran caught a glimpse of Dara's white face and pleading eyes.

He set a foot on the rail. Behind him sounded the grunts and clash of battle. If he leaped now with all his strength he would land not far behind Dara's canoe. While Myra struggled, he might slip his sister overboard and swim her to shore. But if he misjudged, the cold black water would deliver them both to the sucking current of the Serpent.

His heart pounded in his ears, and doubt tore at him. The dark water swirled below.

Myra's flailing made the canoe bob and turn. Then one of the Savages lifted his paddle and struck the thrashing figure twice, hard, and she fell to the floor of the canoe.

Kiran felt the barge shift under him. He glanced back. Ryan and Jovan, holding the Savages back with the long oar, were being pressed back toward him. Shouldn't he jump down to fight with them? Kiran looked out at the water again. The girls' canoe was pulling away. He balanced on the railing, torn. Surely he couldn't swim fast or far enough to reach them now.

Feet pounded the deck behind him. He twisted around to look. A club slammed into Jovan's face, and Jovan toppled backward, knocking Kiran from the railing.

Kiran shot out an arm to catch himself as he fell. His hands caught at the gunwale and his body slammed into the side of the barge. His feet hovered above the water. Kicking in the air, he heaved with all his strength to get his left arm up on the railing.

The club swung down on his arm, and in an explosion of pain he lost hold. He plunged into the water. Cold and darkness engulfed him.

In a rush of bubbles he flailed upward. His left arm, hanging useless, felt like an animal's paw. He broke the surface only long enough to catch one gasping breath before the current tumbled him down again.

He kicked and fought, but the surging water roared in his ears as the Serpent swallowed him. Water pressed against his chest and eyelids. The roaring maelstrom spun him head over heels. He couldn't find the surface, couldn't tell up from down. The Serpent thrashed its coils, whipping him from side to side.

His legs and shoulders slammed against sunken boulders. His shattered arm cracked against rock. At the new shock of pain he gasped in a great lungful of water. The current sucked him deeper, and lights burst behind his eyelids.

Then the water spat him out. His head broke free long enough for one rattling breath. The river pulled him under again, but its grip had loosened. He swept through the darkness, battling his way to the surface again and again.

At last an eddy swirled him into quiet water. He kicked his way into the heart of the stillness. He had come to the edge of the river. His good hand grabbed onto a handful of reeds, and he hauled himself forward into the muddy shallows.

From the way he had come, he heard the sound of cracking wood. He twisted around to peer upriver. By the light of the quarter moon he saw the barge poised halfway down the Serpent, caught between two rocks, water pouring over its middle. Then abruptly it broke free, plunged down the last cataract, shuddered, and veered downstream. He staggered to his feet and waded back into the water, hailing. But he glimpsed only a rush of confused movement on deck before the barge was past him, running downriver, receding, gone.

Chapter 6

When the pain in his arm and side broke through his numbness, Kiran found himself sitting once more in the shallows. He stood, shivering so violently it was hard to keep upright. Grabbing hold of reeds with his good arm, he dragged himself toward shore. His foot struck something soft and he stumbled, falling to his knees on a thick mass that bobbed under his weight. When he reached down, his hand clutched a tangled beard, and a shaft of moonlight shone coldly on protruding eyes that stared sightless at the sky. Kiran started back in shock. Orda, dead.

After a time he knelt in the water and, fighting down his horror, prodded the body with his good hand, feeling for a wound. His fingers caught in a cord twisted tight around the captain's throat. So a Savage had sneaked up on Orda and throttled him before he could fight, before he could even cry out a warning. Whoever killed him must have shoved his body into the river.

Kiran crouched beside Orda's corpse, shaking, wondering if the Savages still lurked nearby. His teeth chattered and he knew he had to get out of the frigid water. Still, he didn't want to leave the body drifting like a piece of trash. He tugged on the captain's tunic, but the waterlogged body hardly budged and pain wrenched at Kiran's chest where it had smashed against the rocks. In the end he had to leave Orda behind and make his way ashore alone.

His left arm was useless. Below the elbow it was a reddish purple mass, still swelling. Now that he was out of the water, the arm throbbed almost unbearably. It must be broken. At least no bone was showing through. He would deal with it later.

Peering around in the faint moonlight, he saw that he had come ashore on the left bank of the river, in the quiet water not far below Serpent Camp. With heart pounding and breath coming in short gasps, he made his way upriver toward the silent tent silhouettes. He slunk through the trees, keeping to the deep shadow, but he could make out no movement in the darkened camp. Cradling his injured forearm against his chest, he crept closer. Dark man-sized humps littered the ground. Fear clutched at Kiran and he waited, clasping a tree. Finally he called out softly but no answer came. He entered the clearing, dreading what he would see.

It was two of the soldiers who had stayed with Orda, one with a spear wound in his chest, another sprawling with his head at an odd angle and blood matted in his hair. In front of a tent he found the third, throat slashed, lying in a sticky pool of blood. The skin of their faces was already cold to the touch. Kiran called into the tents, but he knew already there was no one else to find.

At the edge of the forest he sat shivering on a fallen log to think. Orda and three soldiers dead. Ryan, Losar, and Jovan fighting on the barge, perhaps dead. All the seffidges gone. Myra and Dara stolen. Ser Wellim, the other girls and children still on the barge, if it hadn't sunk.

And the downriver barge, the one that had gone to Pomel? Had it been attacked too?

He needed dry clothes. The tents lay open, the pile of supplies by the riverside toppled, but the Savages hadn't had time to take much. Kiran found his own trunk and managed to pry it open. Within lay the clothes his mother had folded for him so carefully. Sinking to his knees, he buried his good hand in the soft woven cloth and pressed it to his forehead. He had promised to watch over Dara. Her face still looked back at him over the Savage's shoulder, pleading. Armed with nothing but fists and curses, Myra had attacked the Savage. Kiran had hung back. He had hesitated, unwilling to leap after them, afraid of the water, afraid of drowning. He had failed his mother, lost his sister.

Coward. The word stabbed at him like a Savage's spear, rushed in his ears like the crushing water of the Serpent, like the throbbing in his arm. He wanted to crawl into a tent and hide his head under a blanket to muffle the sound.

But tomorrow the downriver barge might come, full of apples and eager recruits from Pomel. Kiran would show them the soldiers' bodies, show them where the Savage canoes had headed across the river. Only he could help them recover Myra and Dara. So he had to take care of himself.

First, dry clothes. He reached to loosen his belt and was bewildered to find his flute, cracked lengthwise but not shattered, still stuck through it. He laid the flute aside, but tugging the wet tunic off over his battered chest and broken arm was unbearable. Tears started to his eyes. He let the sodden tunic fall back, stumbled to the edge of the water, and vomited. His ribs screamed.

The pain was more than he could bear. He moved among the scattered baggage and abruptly knelt in front of one of the nuath rolls. Nuath. He remembered Myra's words. Chewed slowly, it dulled pain without bringing hallucinations.

Kiran probed the end of the nuath roll with his right hand until he managed to pull one fungus free. He shook most of the dirt free and bit off a small piece of the trailing end. The taste reminded him of rotting wood, like the smell of damp leaf mold on the forest floor.

Gradually, as he chewed on the spongy mass, the throbbing in his hand and side grew blurry. He changed into dry clothes, then searched through the soldiers' luggage until he found a knife. For a moment he stared stupidly at the battered flute, the roll of nuath, and his swelling arm. Then he cut the cord that held the nuath roll tight. Holding the nuath's canvas wrapping between one knee and his teeth, he sawed a strip of it free.

After another mouthful of nuath, he probed his forearm. One bone, at least, still seemed whole. He set the flute against the other bone, wrapped the canvas strip around it several times, and then wrenched it snug and tied the cord around it with his right hand and his teeth. The flute end protruded beyond his elbow.

He stood up, swaying. Somewhere above the Serpent and across the river, beyond his reach, the Savages must have pulled their canoes onto the bank to flee through the forest, dragging the girls along. Unless they had already killed them and thrown their bodies aside. He shook away the thought. No, the girls were alive, and tomorrow the downriver barge would arrive. Maybe.

He wanted more than ever to crawl into one of the tents and fall asleep. But the Savages might have left some clue at the upper mooring, site of their attack. Kiran dug out another handful of fungus and stuffed it in his pocket. In the dark shade of the forest, he made his way back up the trail that led from the mooring, past the low blowing roar of the Serpent that had tried to swallow him. The image came to him of a giant reptile rearing, swiveling its head side to side as its flickering tongue tasted his fear on the air. He shook his head. Not completely free of visions after all.

As he approached the edge of the woods, he smelled water and imagined he heard moaning. No doubt just the wind, or wavelets lapping at the shore. He crept to where the trees fringed the bank and stepped into the open, calling out, "Who is it?"

A dark hump on the sand before him leaped up. Moonlight glinted off metal, and the creature before him bellowed and charged. It was Ryan, and as Kiran sidestepped, raising his splinted arm to ward off any blow, he saw that Ryan's face was stained with tears.

★ ★ ★

Ryan braked and lowered his sword. "I thought you were dead." He wiped the back of his hand across his nose and stood trembling, his face white.

"Everyone else is," Kiran said. "All the soldiers."

"Don't you dare tell anyone." Ryan's face twisted. "Else I'll tell them how you jumped."

"What are you talking about?" Kiran demanded. "Tell them what?"

"The Savages ran away," Ryan said. "After they knocked Jovan's face in, and you went over, there was a whistle and the two guys I was fighting jumped ashore. One of them started sawing at the mooring rope, so I jumped after him, but he cut through the rope and ran off to his canoe. When I turned around, the barge was already floating away. I couldn't reach it."

"You should have swum for it," Kiran said brutally. "You're such a great swimmer. You let them go over."

Ryan looked sick. "Did you see them? Are they all drowned?"

Kiran peered at him. His thoughts moved slowly, as dull as the ache in his arm. "You're not even hurt."

Ryan darkened. "You saw me fight. I only wanted to fight."

Ryan's hammering gait along the path sounded in Kiran's mind, and he pictured Ryan's heroic leap into the battle. Light glimmered. "You ran to warn us. You weren't already there. You abandoned your post."

Ryan let his sword fall and covered his face with his hands. "I wanted to be in a battle. Orda said they'd never attack the barge. I waited in the woods behind Orda's men, ready to jump in if something happened. And then there was a rustling, and little choking sounds, and when I looked up there were shadows struggling with the men, and I was too late, so I ran back to wake you all, but you were already under attack. The barge broke up, didn't it, Kiran? And they're all dead."

Kiran picked up Ryan's sword. In another life he might have triumphed at Ryan's shame. Instead he was hiding a dark failure of his own. He parted the air with the sword, and Ryan took a step backward, as if afraid Kiran would strike.

"The barge survived," Kiran said. "It took some water, but it was still floating when it passed me. Ser Wellim and the girls and children were down below."

Ryan pulled himself straight. "Then we have to go after them."

"No." Kiran sliced the air again with Ryan's sword. "They'll meet up with the Pomel barge, or sink. There's nothing we can do for them. But the Savages took Myra and Dara in one of their canoes. That's who we have to go after. You have to take me across the river."

Ryan's mouth dropped open. "You're imagining things."

"Take me over," Kiran said. "Rescue two captives and get your honor back. I can't swim, not like this." He waved his splinted arm. "But you can tow me the way you did before."

"What happened to your arm?" Ryan touched it and Kiran pulled away. "Serpent, it's broken. You need a better splint than that!"

"No time," Kiran said. "Take me across."

"Two of us against a band of Savages?"

"Take me across."

Ryan thought for a moment, then held out his hand. Kiran gave him the sword, and he fastened it back to his belt. "Agreed, but I'm the soldier, right? And I say we need gear."

He led Kiran back to Serpent Camp, where he supplied them each with a long knife and a pack of food. Kiran dug out more strands of nuath to stuff into his pack, but he refused Ryan's offer to re-splint his arm. "We have to catch up with them."

Ryan tied three thick tent posts together and dragged them into the water. On top of them he fastened Kiran's pack and his own. "Go on, wade in," he told Kiran. "Hold onto the raft."

Kiran draped his arms over the poles and pushed into the water. Even with the poles under his arms, it was hard to make himself plow into this river that had twice tried to drown him. But Ryan struck out across the water with his sure splashing stroke, tugging Kiran along. In the dark water, with the spray of the Serpent raining down around him, Kiran kicked his legs in rhythm with Ryan's.

On the far bank, Ryan pulled him ashore and helped him settle the pack over his good shoulder. Now, in action, Ryan had become sure again, swift and silent. Without speaking, he led Kiran through the darkness, along the riverbank and into the woods to climb along the winding course of the Serpent. Kiran stumbled after him, too battered, cold, and exhausted to speak, glad to have someone to follow. He was surprised Ryan could find his way at all, until he realized that the darkness had frayed around the edges: dawn was on its way.

They scouted along the upper bank until Kiran found gouges in the sand where canoes had been dragged into the woods. In the early light they made out bare footprints and broken stalks of underbrush, and then a path thin as a deer track leading into the woods.

Ryan stopped and turned to Kiran. "You have to be ready," he said. "Savages don't take captives."

Kiran pretended not to understand. "Then why take the seffidges?" He was still trying to figure that out.

"Maybe they wanted slaves. But they don't take regular people. They kill them. They slice them open and leave the entrails to scare off anyone following. Like they did with your father. Everyone knows that."

Kiran shook his head. "I don't believe it." But he did believe it. He felt his knees lock, reluctant to carry him forward. "I'll go alone, like my father," he said.

"Don't be dumb, Kiran. I'm just saying prepare yourself." Ryan swung around and continued leading the way in the early light. Kiran followed, Orda's dead eyes swimming in his head. But he saw no bodies, no blood, just scratch marks of dragged canoes in the pine needles and occasional broken twigs that made him think of Myra thrashing in her blanket.

Five hundred yards into the forest, Ryan pulled up, pointing.

Four canoes lay overturned under the bushes at the side of the path. Kiran drew close and lifted the edge of the first one. With two good arms, Ryan helped him tip up each canoe to look beneath it. Kiran thought they might find some trace of Dara, a hair ribbon, perhaps, or even a strand of golden hair. But they found nothing, only paddles, carved with jagged lines like lightning bolts along their shafts.

Kiran sat back on his heels. His neck prickled, piercing his fatigue and the dull blur of the nuath. If the Savages had carried the girls farther than this, then surely they didn't mean to kill them. They might be only an hour ahead, or even waiting nearby, resting with their burden. Straining in the morning quiet, he heard nothing but a jay's call and the creaking of trees. Ryan stood before him, looking thoughtful, pulling a paddle through the air as if he were midstream.

Kiran cast about to find the path. But without the dragged canoes marking the forest floor, the track was harder to discern.

He moved toward a break in the underbrush, but after a few steps lost his certainty, tried another direction, and pulled up just as uncertain. "Come on, Ryan, give me a hand."

Ryan kept paddling the air. "Savages disappear into the woods. We'll never find them. If we did, two of us alone would never overcome them. But they've left us canoes, Kiran. We can go after the barge."

"No," Kiran said. "Help me spread out from here. We'll find the track, I know it."

"Two girls," Ryan said. "Or a barge full of children. Come with me, Kiran. We'll carry a canoe down below the Serpent, load it with supplies, and paddle like mad." His voice grew thick with pleading. "Listen, if you can't paddle with one arm, I'll do enough for two of us. That barge won't get far without us. Think of it hung up somewhere, and the forest crawling with Savages."

For a moment Kiran imagined rushing down a swift current with only a thin skin of wood between him and the water. Why was Ryan so keen on doing that? *He abandoned his post, that's why. Guilt's driving him, just like it's driving me.*

Kiran couldn't afford to be understanding. He let a sneer into his voice. "You're afraid of the Savages. One little battle, and you're turning tail."

Ryan flushed and shoved the paddle under the nearest canoe. He gave Kiran a look of hatred, moved past him, squatted to examine the underbrush, and crept forward again.

Kiran followed, his chest and arm aching. He hoped Ryan was as good a tracker as he bragged of being at home. At this rate, the Savages would be pulling farther away.

After a short distance, Ryan straightened. "Look, Kiran, two paths here. Which way do you want?"

When Kiran hesitated, Ryan spoke impatiently. "Which way? You take one, I'll take the other. Follow it for a mile or two and try to see if it's been used in the last day. We'll meet back here before the sun's above the first branches. Got it?"

Kiran nodded. They separated, Kiran taking the left fork. True, there was a path now, one Kiran could see, but whether it had been used most recently by Savages or animals he couldn't tell. He walked with silent, crouching steps as the path climbed away from the river. Half an hour later, it crossed a patch of bare granite that skirted the bottom of a cliff. A hollow in the cliff rock was scarred with the black of old fires. The rocks were cold, but among the old ashes he saw the clear imprint of a shoe. Myra's? Excitement rose in him. A cooking spot like this must mean the Savages passed often. He turned back to collect Ryan.

He waited at the fork in the path as the sun climbed. Maybe Ryan had found something of interest, too, and followed his path longer than planned.

A pair of squirrels scrambled overhead. As time passed, Kiran's uneasiness grew. What if Ryan had fallen, or what if he had stumbled into a camp of Savages? Should Kiran go after him or keep waiting? Could Ryan have meant a different rendezvous? Couldn't be. But eventually Kiran followed the faint track farther back to the hiding place for the canoes.

Only three canoes remained. Fresh scuff marks on the ground showed how the fourth canoe had been dragged along the path. Kiran gave a bellow of rage. At a furious run, his breath coming in short stabs, he tore along the path to the riverbank, then followed the drag marks all the way around the Serpent to the lower river. The Serpent's roar drowned out his shouts. Empty, the pounding river ran on. Ryan, the betrayer, was gone.

Chapter 7

Kiran kicked at the shallow water, cursing himself with clenched fists for having trusted Ryan. Even worse than his fury was the shiver of fear running down his spine. Ryan had left him injured and alone in Savage country, separated from supplies and shelter by a cold river. Kiran's notion of rescuing the girls had seemed crazy enough before. Now, without Ryan, there was no hope at all.

He stood ankle deep in the water, swaying with fatigue. His arm throbbed.

Finally he splashed back to shore, took off his pack, pulled out another strand of nuath and chewed. His pain and fury dulled. Suppose the barge from Pomel returned. He could lead its soldiers on a raid against the Savages, but only if he knew which path they'd taken.

Starting back at the canoes' hiding place, he set out to explore both branches of the path, Ryan's and his own. But as dark settled, he knew it was no use. The paths trickled away in the underbrush until he lost them. Even in this small task he had failed. In despair, he crawled under a bush to sleep, starting awake every time a branch cracked or a wolf howled in the distance.

At first light he woke with the cold certainty that the barge from Pomel was gone for good. Which meant no barge would pass this spot for at least a month. If he wanted help for Dara and Myra, he would have to fetch it from Lanath.

First he should swim the river for more supplies. The raft Ryan had used to tow him was gone, but with his good arm he hauled a log to the edge of the lower river and waded in.

When the water reached waist high, he leaned on the log, but it rolled, ducking him. He sputtered, choked, and flailed back to his feet. Cold seeped into his bones, and he couldn't force his legs to walk deeper. With his broken arm, the rib pain that made his breath come short and the cold water lapping his sides, he felt he was already drowning.

In the end he turned back. His failure to cross the river rang within him like a death sentence. With no clear path, half a bag of food, a dwindling supply of nuath, and only a knife for a weapon, he turned his steps upriver.

★ ★ ★

The people of Lanath thought of the river as a thin chain linking them to the civilized world, while the forest brooded around them like a circle of wolves, poised to attack. Beyond the cleared fields and sheep meadows of the village, trees grew close and tall, filtering out the sunlight. The village people ventured into the forest only in hunting parties or to scout out the giant beech groves where the nuath fungus grew.

Fighting his sense that the forest was watching him, Kiran trudged through the pine forest, pushing branches out of the way until their gum coated his hand. In the afternoon he crossed a series of dark boggy meadows smelling of rot. The mud released his feet with a sucking sound at each step.

When the pain in his arm grew too strong to bear, he chewed a bit of nuath until his tongue felt thick and the pain had dulled again. It was hard to tell how far upriver he had come, how many days he would have to walk. He set one foot down, then the other.

At night he pulled leaves into a pile around him and tried not to think of wolves.

Twice a day he ate something from his pack, a few mouthfuls of dried meat or fruit. His stomach clenched down hard on the meager food. He drank from the river, squatting on the bank and scooping up cold water by the handful.

Even through the nuath blur, the forest surprised him. Flashes of color caught his eye—a blue jay's wing, the red crown of a woodpecker, tiny yellow flowers pushing up around the roots of an oak tree. On the third day, a sharp, tart smell reached him, and he walked through an abandoned apple orchard. Who had planted it, and when had they left it forgotten, a hundred yards back from the river? The hard, shrunken apples were too sour to swallow.

By the fourth day he hit a kind of rhythm, striding forward in a fog of nuath and hunger. He was too exhausted for fear. As long as he kept the river to his right, he was heading toward Lanath. But at dusk, as he passed beneath the branch of a maple, a rustle almost too faint to hear made him turn his face upward.

A blow fell on his neck and shoulders. Kiran's knees buckled and he fell. A snarl sounded in his ear. The creature on his back reached out a claw and slashed fire across his cheek.

Kiran lurched to his feet, his mind moving slowly. He tried to shake the thing off. When that didn't work he flung himself backward against the trunk of a tree. With a yowl the creature twisted its body and leaped away, a thick-bodied phantom in the moonlight. A wildcat. He'd never seen one before.

It had meant to break his neck. He fled from it, crashing through the underbrush, running upriver. How had he let the forest lull him? Like Ryan, the forest meant no good. Blood dripped down his cheek and dried. That night he built a flimsy barrier of pine branches under a hanging rock and huddled behind it until sleep came. Every hour or two he awoke, sweating in spite of the cold, to hear an owl's low haunting demand or the mad lonely cry of a loon.

Each day took him farther from Dara, and each day he found it harder to walk. His breath rasped, his cheek burned, and every cough stabbed his chest. Only scrapings of food remained in his pack. Without weapons he couldn't kill any game. The season was too early for berries. Sometimes he saw a birds' nest overhead, but he couldn't climb for eggs with only one arm. His only chance was to reach home with his news before he starved. The weaker he felt, the harder he pushed. A distant buzzing filled his ears. He wondered if the wildcat had been a hallucination. His leather soles wore through.

On the seventh day, he ran out of food. He turned the bag inside out and ran his mouth over it like a snuffler, searching for crumbs. Even the nuath was gone. His feet were so heavy he seemed to be laboring up a sand dune, sliding backward through the shifting ground. Toward evening a thin rain began to fall. By the time it was too dark to keep walking, he was soaked through, coughing and shivering. He crawled under a rhododendron, filled his empty food bag with pine needles for a pillow, and waited dully for sleep to interrupt his misery. He half hoped that morning, and the need to push on, would never come.

A few hours later he started awake to the light of a full moon streaming into the forest clearing. The light was so bright and strange that he wondered if the Moon Lady had descended to guide him into another world. When he stood, he found his body burning with fever. There was no lovely maiden with silver tresses beckoning to him as the songs promised. Instead he saw pine needles on the forest floor picked out in golden light, and mushrooms glimmering.

With his heart hammering and the way lit before him, he decided to walk. The blisters on his feet rubbed against the remnants of his shoes so badly that he threw away the shoes and walked barefoot over the glowing floor. The moonlight played over the ground like the shimmering notes of a flute. But in his head he heard nothing. What if his arm healed poorly and he could never play again? But that was all behind him anyway. By crossing the river with Ryan he had left his boyhood apprenticeship behind. Like his father, he had chosen the path of the warrior.

At the thought, a surge of pride lightened his step. He was a warrior. Even if he died here in the forest, he would die a warrior. He walked faster. As his feet planted themselves on the wet pine needles, music played in his head at last. It was the moonrise song, but with something foreign about it, a new verse maybe, one he had never heard before, the nighttime walk through the forest. For a time the music seemed to carry him, but as he walked on and exhaustion reached its long hands to drag him down, he heard another strain of music, something darker, a lower tone, as if a second flute had arrived to tug the song apart, to summon sorrow and loss. In a kind of delirium he stumbled through the sound, wondering if anything could ever weave the sounds back together into one.

Toward morning, he found himself passing through beech forest, dazed to see the thick smooth trunks. Scuffed dirt around the base of the trees where snufflers had been rooting tripped up his feet. He reeled between the trunks of the beech trees, tugging himself up a ridge. Near the top, he heard voices. Coming through a stand of firs at the spine of the ridge, he surveyed an expanse of beech grove spread out before him. Red-brown men crawled out along the high branches, digging at the fungus that grew in the cracks, letting it drop to the village men and the soldier watching below.

Kiran stumbled forward. His feet tripped each other as he hurtled down the hill, and his voice grated strangely in his ears. "The barge! Get help! Savages attacked the barge!" From the trees, the seffidges turned their dull eyes in his direction, and then he saw that the soldier running toward him was Bulo. Kiran sank to his knees and burst into tears.

Chapter 8

The rough wool of Bulo's tunic smelled of sweat and cookfire smoke. As Bulo carried him, Kiran heard the slap of running feet against cobbles, and children's voices shouting.

Then Bulo planted Kiran's feet on the ground, and Kiran lifted his head to see his mother erupt through the door of their cottage. With a cry of dismay she rushed forward to throw her arms around him. He gasped at the sudden pain in his arm, and Bulo swept him back up and into the kitchen.

Kiran's mother hastened to prepare a cot by the fire. As soon as Bulo laid him down among the fleeces, Kiran felt himself drowning. He clawed his way onto his side and leaned over the edge of the cot, coughing, coughing, unable to stop. Only when all his air was gone did he fall back, gasping, sweat drenching his face and chest. His mother's horrified face hovered above him. Beyond her, the thatch of the roof swam across his vision.

There was a commotion at the door—Bulo chasing curious children away—and Kiran turned his head in time to see Lir burst through the opening. With two strides the Master of the Harvest reached the center of the room and took Kiran's mother in his arms. Only then did he approach Kiran.

He loomed over his stepson, his black eyebrows pulled together. Then he drew up a stool and settled on it, leaning toward

Kiran with his forearms on his knees and his huge hands hanging down. He said, "You look half dead. I've sent for Ser Vetel."

Kiran turned his head away. How could he face his stepfather, with Dara gone?

"What happened, son?"

Kiran found breath enough for short sentences. "We camped at the Serpent. Some on the barge, some on land. Savages attacked in the night. They stole the seffidges. They took Dara and Myra in a canoe."

Lir cursed. Behind him, Kiran's mother crept forward and placed a hand on his shoulder. Lir pounded his fists against his forehead and groaned.

Kiran tried to continue. "I . . ." He choked. His voice wouldn't say the words. *I was too scared to swim after them.*

Lir lowered his fists onto his knees. "Finish."

"I—got knocked off the barge. I went over the falls. Then the barge came loose. The Savages cut it. I saw it go over." He stopped to catch his breath, trying to keep his facts straight. "They killed the people on shore. Orda and three of his men. Jovan—he was aboard. Ryan—" He stopped. He didn't want to talk about Ryan. "The other girls and children were down below. So was Ser Wellim."

"The barge went over the Serpent?"

Kiran nodded.

"It sank?"

"Not right away."

"I have feared," Lir said, his face pale. "I have feared, ever since the messenger birds came home, nine days ago." He beat his head again with his fists. "Why did I let her leave us?"

He threw himself to his feet and took long strides around the room. Kiran's mother ducked past him to kneel by the cot, holding a bowl of soup. She wept, the bowl shaking in her hands.

Kiran tried to lift himself on his good elbow. His mother slid an arm behind his neck and lifted his head just enough that she could tip the bowl into his mouth.

He sipped the warm, meaty broth that had cured him of everything from colds to spotted fever since he was a tiny child. A thought surfaced and he struggled to sit all the way up. "They didn't kill them," he said. "Master Lir, I followed the track. The Savages didn't kill Dara. That's why I came back. We can take the guard and find them."

Lir stopped his pacing and jumped back to crouch at the bedside, bumping his wife so that her bowl sloshed its contents down the front of her dress. His hand gripped Kiran's good shoulder. "Is that true?"

"After a couple of miles I lost the path."

His stepfather's big hand squeezed Kiran's shoulder and released it. Lir opened his mouth to say more, but just then Ser Vetel bustled through the door, led by his beaklike nose. Following after walked a young boy carrying a satchel. How many times had Kiran accompanied the priest, lugging that bag, and watched him sit by some ailing person to murmur soothing words and pour out cups of healing cordial?

Lir dipped his head and stepped aside for Ser Vetel, whose eyebrow twitched, because Lir usually made no secret of his disdain for priests and their ceremonies.

Ser Vetel perched at the bedside, asking questions, clicking his tongue against his teeth and shaking his head at the answers. He reached across Kiran to unwrap the injured arm. Kiran gritted his teeth against the pain, and he heard his mother gasp. He glanced down at his arm, which was swollen and discolored. Ser Vetel drew Kiran's flute out of the wrappings and held it up between two long fingers. It hung at an angle. A crack ran along its length and it was stained with old blood.

Ser Vetel dropped the flute into the fire. Kiran jerked in protest, but the old priest's glare silenced him. Ser Vetel beckoned to the new boy—Tad, the potter's son—and pulled a small brown bottle from the satchel. With a muttered prayer, he held it to the light, then poured the contents into Kiran's mouth.

The cordial seared Kiran's throat and warmth spread along his limbs. He sank back into the fleece. Then his eyes flew open and he fought to lift his head.

"The captain," he said. Even to himself the words sounded slurred. "Get Captain Morol—Master Lir, get him—so we can plan our attack."

"Delirium," he heard Ser Vetel say as the waters of sleep closed over him.

★ ★ ★

Time slid and roiled like the river. The river had slithered its way into him, filling his chest. No matter how he coughed and writhed, he could never find enough air, until the sweet heavy cordial flowed down his throat and set him floating between consciousness and sleep. Somewhere on the riverbank, Lir's voice and the priest's rose and twisted in argument. From a distance, Kiran heard himself address the captain of the guard, answering questions with a thick tongue. From the river where he floated, Kiran chased fleeing Savages through the woods with an army at his back. He floundered in a mud pit, unable to pull his legs free, as a Savage fled with Dara kicking over his shoulder. Time and again he stood frozen on the rail of the barge, poised to dive, as black water boiled beneath him and the canoe pulled silently away.

Once he woke to the sensation of someone wrenching his arm apart. Heavy hands pinned his shoulders and legs. Bulo and the blacksmith, Ryan's father, pulled his elbow and wrist away from each other. He screamed, then heard a grating sound. "Good," said a woman's voice, and the men let go. In a whisper, the pain that had accompanied him since the Serpent was gone. He fell asleep.

Later he woke to find a woman who was not his mother bathing him. He closed his eyes and as she squeezed water onto his face, he remembered. She was Nora the herb woman, Myra's mother, who doctored sick animals, women in childbirth, and seffidges. She had Myra's hazel eyes. He felt her wipe the sleep from his eyes and he opened them again.

"I had the men re-set the bone," she said. "The carpenter made you a wooden sleeve." She lifted the blanket for him to see. Two troughs of carved wood clasped a dressing on his arm.

Kiran said, "Myra is alive."

She nodded, her eyes wet. "Your father told me."

His head swam with confusion. "You mean my stepfather." He tried to focus, so he could tell her more. "Myra fought. She attacked the Savage who grabbed Dara. That's why they got her. The other girls stayed below."

Nora stood perfectly still, one hand holding the dripping cloth. He continued: "The Savages wrapped them in blankets—Myra and Dara—and threw them in a canoe. Three Savages paddled the canoe, but Myra fought, so they were slow. I was at the side—I could have jumped in after them, but I—" His voice broke, but he pushed on. "I was afraid."

"To jump into the canoe?" she asked.

He fingered the jumbled blankets. "Into the water, to swim after them."

There was a silence, and then he felt the cloth run along his hairline and dab at his neck. "Only a fool would do that," she said. "You couldn't catch up with a canoe. If you did, how could you pull three Savages from a canoe without drowning two girls who were wrapped up and terrified? You walked a week to get help for them."

He looked at her again. She was crying openly now, her tears falling to mix with the water of her cloth as she washed his chest. Her tears seemed to rinse him, to seep into him and release something that had been holding his breath constricted.

He asked her, "When did they send out the soldiers? How will they find their way without me to show them?"

She shook her head. "No one has gone. Your stepfather storms around telling people to prepare for war, but Ser Vetel preaches in the temple that you're too delirious to know what you're saying, and the captain of the guard says if the Savages are on the prowl he needs all his men here to protect the village."

"I'm not delirious."

She smiled. "Not since I poured out that cordial Ser Vetel had your mother give you every time you woke. Now you're getting apple cider."

He wrinkled his forehead. "Ser Vetel was poisoning me?"

"It helped your coughing. But now your chest has air again. I think he's letting you sleep while he and Captain Morol decide what to do. Master Lir isn't waiting. He's provisioning boats with food and weapons."

"Where's my mother?" He tried to sit up.

Nora held him down with one hand. "She's at the market. She's grateful you're too sick to go anywhere, Kiran. I think she hopes you'll sleep until any danger has passed. Try to stand if you like, but when we hear her at the door, lie down and close your eyes."

Kiran nodded, and Nora took his good elbow. With his feet planted on the brick floor, he levered himself up. The room swayed. Just as he decided he would like to lie down again, Nora pushed him back, and footsteps sounded on the threshold. He stretched out on the cot.

Through eyelids opened just a slit, he saw his mother enter with a basket of vegetables, which she dropped on the table. "Is he sleeping?" she asked, her voice tight.

"Enya, forgive me," Nora said. "I know the priest tells you not to let me come. But your husband has asked me to make sure the arm mends straight."

Kiran's mother let her gaze slide to the side. "I thank you for straightening his arm, Nora. May the gods support us both, for we each have lost a daughter. But my son is here and safe. I beg you not to help revenge and raiding lure my last child away."

Nora bowed her head and stepped backward.

All at once, Kiran couldn't stand it. They were all deciding for him, ignoring what he had dragged himself so far upriver to tell them. Where were the screech of weapons sharpening on the grindstone and the stamping of men making ready for war? He stirred his legs and groaned, as if he were just waking. He sat up and opened his eyes. "Mother," he said, "bring me soup. I'm hungry and my legs are weak. I need to go talk to Ser Vetel."

Chapter 9

In the end, Kiran's mother sent for Tad, the potter's boy, to bring him to the temple. The boy took Kiran's hand and led him down the lane, his wide brown eyes staring at Kiran as if he were a hero or a madman. Kiran was annoyed to have a guide, as if he hadn't walked to the temple on his own every day for nine years. But his legs wobbled after the time in bed, and soon he set a hand on the boy's shoulder for support. He took the stairs to the temple cavern carefully, holding onto the wall.

Ser Vetel stood at his desk in the half-lit interior, examining a paper covered in signs. When he saw Kiran he sprang up and bustled to meet him, his hands held out before him. "Kiran, dear boy, I rejoice to see you well enough to walk." His glance darted side to side, and his tongue ran over his lips. "Tad, bring Kiran a stool. He has walked too far."

The stool rocked on the uneven floor. Kiran worried at how dried up and fragile Ser Vetel looked. At a time like this, the villagers needed his guidance. Village priests not only taught music, mythology and history, they were wise in the ways of the Savages, and advised the garrison captains.

"Your Serenity," Kiran asked, meeting Ser Vetel's piercing gaze. "How will I save my sister?"

The old man examined him. "How sure are you, Kiran, about what you saw? It was night; you almost drowned. Is this not some nightmare that led you astray when you woke and found yourself alone?"

Kiran closed his eyes. Moonlight, the river, Savages slipping away. He could hardly distinguish memory from the visions of his sickness. What if the attack had been a dream, and even now Dara was dancing in the plazas of Catora, missing her brother's music? But how could he believe such a thing? He remembered her eyes burning into him from across the water.

He shook his head. "The Savages attacked. Orda and three others are dead."

Set Vetel sighed and turned away. "And yet war would be folly, when we are isolated here, the king lies dying—Oh, yes, make no mistake, he is dying—and the south is in rebellion."

He swung back around and peered at Kiran. "We can't throw peace away on what's already lost."

The priest's words made no sense to Kiran. He felt light-headed. "But Dara. We have to go after Dara."

Ser Vetel's forehead wrinkled, the picture of concern. "We need to know the truth about Dara. I have waited for you to be well, child. I need you to help me. Your mother has brought me one of your sister's toys, but your eye and hand will help, because you were the last of her loved ones to see and hold her. Come here. Tad, fetch water for the basin."

As Tad brought buckets of water from the underground spring, Ser Vetel led Kiran toward the wall, where a bronze basin stood on a pedestal. For a fee, Ser Vetel used this basin to see the faraway loved ones of villagers too impatient to wait for the messenger birds to bring dispatches from the capital.

Kiran held Dara's doll in his hands. It was her second favorite—a much-mended doll with beads for eyes and wool for hair.

"Close your eyes," the priest told him. "Hold the doll and think of your sister. Lift her up in your mind."

Dara, thought Kiran. *Dara.* Dara holding his hand on the island sandbank, asking for a Savage baby. Dara wrestling with a snuffler on the hearth at home. Dara wishing him good night their last evening on the barge. But other images intruded. The shouts of Savages, a paddle thwacking against flesh, the sudden cold splash—

"Now!" Ser Vetel said, and pushed Kiran's head into the basin. Kiran hadn't taken enough of a breath. Ser Vetel's long fingers held his head down. Cold smothered Kiran's face, and fear tore his chest. He waved his good arm.

Ser Vetel's fingers caught in Kiran's hair and pulled his head out of the basin. "Good. Now go and sit."

Kiran backed away, shaking the water out of his eyes and hair. He found the stool and sat, gulping air. Cold rivulets crawled down his neck. Ser Vetel hovered over the basin, weaving a pattern with his hands and mumbling a prayer. Abruptly, the old priest fell silent and bent forward to peer into the water.

When Ser Vetel raised his head he let out a long sigh. He held out his hands to Kiran, shaking his bowed head.

"Oh, child, child, it is as I feared. I saw her clearly. They are dead, Kiran. That girl Myra tried to break away. An arrow for her, Kiran, and a"—he winced—"a club for your sister. Her skull!" He shuddered. "I saw their bodies laid out side by side on the ground."

Kiran jumped to his feet. "No!"

Ser Vetel laid an arm over his shoulder.

"But listen, Kiran. I saw the Moon Lady, leading them hand in hand up the lane of cool light to their new home in the sky."

Kiran remembered the moonlight waking him, his last night in the forest. The Moon Lady had visited him but not shown her face. Was that the very night she had led his dead sister away?

He stood in the center of the temple, under its winking sky. His shoulders shook, but no sobs came. So there was to be no marching out from the village, no rescue.

Ser Vetel pulled Kiran close against his bony chest. The scent of incense clung to his robes, and his breath smelled of the nuath that brought visions. He stroked Kiran's head. "Go home now, child, and rest. Send your mother to me. I will visit you this evening and bring medicine to help you sleep. Tad, take Kiran home."

* * *

Harsh sunlight made Kiran squint as he trod with heavy feet across the village. Halfway down the lane to his house they encountered Lir, striding forward to meet them. "Kiran, so, you are up!" His hand fell on Kiran's shoulder, and he said to Tad, "Thank you, boy. I'll see him home."

Tad took one look up at the imposing Master of the Harvest and backed away.

Lir released a bark of laughter with no humor in it. He bent to look closely at Kiran. "You're pale again, son. Is it pain or something the priest said?"

Lir's never treated me so well before, thought Kiran. *Always before it was 'boy.' Now it's 'son,' again and again.* He opened his mouth to say, "Father," but the word wouldn't come. To speak at all was a struggle. "I'm—It's bad. Dara—Dara and Myra are dead." And with a coughing sob, the tears came.

Lir didn't move to comfort him as the priest had done.

Kiran wiped his sleeve over his eyes and faced his stepfather. Lir glared at him, his eyebrows drawn together. "Come with me," he said, and abruptly turned away.

Kiran had to scuttle to match his stepfather's long stride. They left the village by a path that led through the cornfields. At one point, Kiran stumbled and had to catch at Lir's sleeve. Lir looked at him sharply, then muttered, "Sorry," and proceeded more slowly. He stepped along a path heading to the beech grove. But once they were out of sight of the village, Lir paused, pointed out a redbud bush, and slipped behind it. Kiran dared not ask where they were going. His legs dragged, and his breaths came in short uncomfortable gasps.

The path took them toward the river, to a place where a sandy bank met a shallow backwater. Several sets of footprints crossed in the damp sand—prints of his stepfather's long feet in their pointed shoes, the mark of a large boot, and the splayed bare footprints of seffidges.

Lir lifted the branches of a flame leaf bush, revealing a beached rowboat with three pairs of oars. Bundles and casks filled its bow and stern, and ropes and packs lay beneath the seats.

Kiran waited until he had caught his breath. "Only one boat?"

"I've prepared others up by the dock. Only one boat is hidden."

"I don't understand."

"They're dragging their feet, Kiran. The garrison and that fake priest of yours. Too risky to leave the village undefended, they say, if Savages are on the prowl. Unwise to move without orders when the king is dying. Have to wait for reinforcements from Catora, they say." He ground his teeth. "I'll tell you what it is, son. Two girls don't matter as much as shipping the nuath out on time." His eyes narrowed. "While I work to provision boats they assign all the free men and even seffidges to build a new barge with a deeper nuath hold."

Kiran's anger flared up but then died away. "It doesn't matter. It's too late now."

Lir grabbed his good shoulder and shook it. "Aren't you listening? All they care about is nuath. They'll say anything to keep the manpower here."

Kiran twisted out of Lir's grip. He wished he could believe Ser Vetel was wrong. But Ser Vetel was the wisest man in the village, the only one who could read and see far in the basin, the one who knew history and the ways of Savages. Against all his wisdom Lir had nothing to offer but stubbornness.

And hope. Kiran said slowly, "What are you going to do?"

"I've demanded a council meeting tomorrow. I'll appeal to the people of Lanath to send a proper rescue expedition. If they refuse . . ." He shrugged. "You and I and a couple more will make the journey alone."

Wind rustled in the trees overhead. Kiran thought of the arloc playing the stately thrum of men preparing for war. A shiver ran down his spine. His real father had charged into the forest after a stolen child and never returned. Now his rich stepfather would make the same journey, and he wanted to bring Kiran along.

Kiran straightened his shoulders and nodded. Something was choking him, and he didn't trust himself to speak. He swallowed and nodded again, and Lir clasped his good hand.

★ ★ ★

They waited for evening, Kiran dozing in the rowboat, before they made their way back through the woods onto the beech grove trail. On the path, they slipped in among Lir's workers, who were herding the seffidges home to their shed behind the cow barn. Kiran caught their rank odor. What would the Savages do with the seffidges they had stolen? What heavy dull work did they need carried out in the forest?

Kiran walked by Lir's side, pushing himself to keep pace. His head still just reached Lir's shoulder. He saw how the men looked up to his stepfather. It was not just his size or his band of office, not even his wealth, Kiran thought. Lir had something else. He made decisions, and he acted.

"Father," Kiran said under his breath. He closed his eyes and tried it out loud. "Father."

Lir stopped and stared at him.

Kiran trembled. "I have to tell you something. When the Savages stole Dara, I . . ." He looked at his feet. It sounded so stupid. "I didn't swim after her. I was afraid."

Lir's eyes flashed. "That priest made a weakling of you. But I see you fighting free of it, son." He laid a hand on Kiran's shoulder. "Let's get home."

Chapter 10

At mid morning, Kiran prepared to follow his stepfather to the beaten earth yard under the watchtower, just outside the southwest corner of the village wall. Women were not invited to council meetings; Kiran's mother clutched his hand at the doorway, her eyes red and watery. Ser Vetel had visited her last night to bring his condolences, and for long hours afterward, Kiran had heard his mother's voice and Lir's rising in argument.

As they walked, Lir drew him close. "They may ask you to speak, though you're only a boy. Once you do, get out of sight. If this doesn't turn out as we hope, I'll meet you at the boat as soon as I can slip away."

A group of four women stood at the edge of the council ground, under the witness tree. "What are they doing here?" Kiran asked.

Lir gave a grim smile. "They're all willing to tell how your priest looked into his water basin and told them false things about absent people. If that old fraud tries to convince people the girls are already dead, I'll call them to testify. And I told him so, the old vulture. So I don't think he'll try it."

"You'd call women?"

Lir shrugged. "Whatever's necessary."

Now the village men gathered, looking askance at the gathering under the tree. Lir sent Kiran to wait with the women. One of them was Nora, who nodded at him. "You have color, Kiran. You look awake."

He said, "I spat out Ser Vetel's cordial. Why are you here? What are you going to say?"

She snorted. "I'll tell them how Ser Vetel looked in his bowl and told me my Morgan would live after his fall. And how years ago he told me my brother was coming to serve as captain of the garrison."

The other women chuckled and nudged one another. Kiran felt uncomfortable. It wasn't seemly for women to criticize a priest. Then he pictured his own mother, waiting meekly at home.

The men formed a wide circle with the witness tree touching one edge. With a clash of metal and clatter of boots on stone, the Captain of the Guard marched into the circle, accompanied by three of his men. One of them, Kiran saw, was Bulo, who stationed himself with his head thrust forward and his mouth set in a stubborn expression. Then came Ser Vetel, with Tad trailing after him. Kiran felt a pang of jealousy. Ser Vetel had never brought *him* into the center of a council meeting. He had always had to linger at the outskirts with the other boys.

The head councilman, an old farmer with a receding chin, raised a hand. He had a tremor and his voice quavered as he asked, "Who has petitioned this meeting?"

Lir stepped forward. "Men of Lanath! For the first time in nearly a decade, Savages have attacked our people and our goods, at the Serpent on the river. As you all know by now, they killed four soldiers of Catora, stole our seffidges, and abducted two daughters of our town. It is for times like these that we support a garrison. I call on you, Captain of the Guard, to assemble a war party with no more delay!"

"If the Savages are on the prowl, who will protect Lanath?" the head councilman asked.

"All able-bodied men can form a militia. Let fifteen or twenty join the war party, and the rest remain home to take turns guarding and working the fields."

The councilman's voice grew more querulous. "How will we bring the harvest in? How will we meet our nuath quota?"

Lir made a gesture of impatience. "Other men, boys, seffidges, will toil in the forest. We'll do our best, and make up for it next year."

At this point, Ser Vetel slowly waved his hand. "All this commotion rests on the testimony of the boy," he said. "Where is he?"

Nora gave Kiran a nudge and, trembling, he stepped into the ring.

Ser Vetel asked him, "Tell me, Kiran, tell us all, how did you break your arm?"

What was he asking that for? "I . . . I fell off the boat, Your Serenity. I went through the Serpent, the great rapids."

Ser Vetel raised his eyebrows. "And you came through clear-headed? And then you saw these Savages run off with your sister?"

"No, Your Honor, that was before! I saw them before I fell!"

Ser Vetel put his head on one side. "This frightful vision made you fall, or the fall caused you to see strange things?"

A couple of men in the crowd laughed. Kiran felt his face grow hot. "The Savages attacked! They killed Captain Orda! I found him floating in the shallows."

Ser Vetel raised his eyebrows, and his voice grew gentle. "Boy, boy! Who knows you better than I? Water has held its terrors for you ever since you fell off your father's fishing boat when you were three years old. Don't you remember the strange tales you told me just two weeks ago after Ryan had to rescue you above the falls? What was it you raved about? Bears carrying off one of the boys?"

The crowd of men hooted with laughter. Their shouts beat at Kiran's ears, confusing him. "I saw—" he began.

Lir broke in. "Then where's the barge? Why hasn't it returned?"

Ser Vetel lifted his hand again. "Much is still unclear, but I have foreseen that a message will arrive this very morning. No doubt it will answer many of our questions. We should all be scanning the sky." He waved his hand in a broad gesture, and a few of the villagers turned and raised their eyes.

"By the Serpent, he's right!" shouted one man, pointing.

Winging its way from the riverbank came one of the blue-winged messenger birds trained to fly between Lanath and Catora. Its wings rippled against the cloudless spring sky.

Ser Vetel nodded to Captain Morol, who called to one of the soldiers on the tower. The soldier reached up a gloved hand to let the bird land on his wrist. In front of them all, he cut the thread that tied a strip of parchment to the bird's leg and tossed it down to the captain, who passed it to Ser Vetel.

"Word from Catora," the priest said. He unrolled the bit of parchment and peered at it.

The villagers waited. Kiran felt himself relax. Ser Vetel was wise after all; he had known the bird was coming. And now, through the secret writing, he would learn the truth.

The priest frowned and muttered to himself as the villagers watched. At last he nodded, wiped a hand over his face, and cleared his throat. The villagers held themselves absolutely still.

Ser Vetel said, "I read:

"Greetings, brother Vetel.

"I write in warning, with news of near disaster."

A murmur of consternation arose from the crowd.

"Yet be assured that nearly all of us arrived at Catora safely..."

Relief, confusion, village men turning to one another with questions.

". . . despite one grave misfortune. As we camped above the Serpent, with the barge moored as usual and the girls and children safely aboard, Savages attacked the camp. Our soldiers fearlessly drove them off . . ."

The crowd stamped and exclaimed.

". . . but I regret to tell you that as our soldiers and young recruits battled two Savages aboard, the boy Kiran, for whom you and I had such hopes, panicked and cut the mooring rope. In the struggle to control the barge, our valiant soldiers turned aside from the Savages, who succeeded—alas!—in slaying two passengers, the child Dara and the young girl Myra, before making their escape.

"Before we could secure it, the loosened barge went plummeting over the Serpent. Luckily, the boys Ryan and Jovan managed to grab hold of two oars. Though you will scarce believe it, they aimed the barge in such a way that it survived the trip. Only Kiran fell overboard and was lost. We never found his body, and I pity him, but he endangered us all. As for the girls, we gave them full funeral rites in Catora, and sent them to the Moon Lady with solemn ceremony. Please convey my deepest regrets to their parents, concealing the boy's shame if you can, and salutations to all the other families of Lanath's children. Build another barge without delay, and guard Lanath well against Savages."

Faces in the crowd, dark with anger, turned toward Kiran.

"That's not true!" he protested. "Savages killed Orda, they took—"

The crowd's roar of anger drowned out his words.

Nora tugged on his tunic. "Duck down and touch the tree!" She grabbed the arm of one of the women, who had turned to Kiran with a face contorted in anger, and pulled her around to face outward, shielding him. "Lies," Nora hissed to the woman. "Remember all his lies."

The woman gulped and nodded, and the other women closed ranks around him. But the crowd roared again, and Kiran heard one man yell, "Out of the way, woman! He killed your daughter!"

Then Kiran heard Lir's voice rise in a roar of its own. "Priest, I have had enough of your lies!"

Peering between two women's shawls, Kiran caught a glimpse of a dark blue robe swaying in the middle of the ring as Lir made his argument. His voice rang out. "Yes, priest, I challenge you. Who knows what these scratch marks on parchment really tell you? Men of Lanath, my son Kiran walked a week through the forest to warn us. How many of you could have walked so far, wounded, without food or weapons? Is that the act of a coward?

"Now who of you has the courage to listen to truth and rescue two young girls from a gruesome fate? Men of Lanath, if you are true men, follow me to the boats!"

Kiran stretched to his feet and craned his neck. As Lir finished his words with his arms raised high and swung around to leave the circle, Ser Vetel nodded at the Captain of the Guard. The captain grabbed Lir by one arm and jerked him backward. Lir planted his feet and shook himself free, but at once three soldiers surrounded him, their swords drawn.

Lir looked straight toward the witness tree as they grabbed his arms again. "Meet me at the boats!" he yelled again. "At the boat! The boat!" He struggled to free himself, thrashing and kicking. One of the soldiers struck him in the jaw with the hilt of his sword, and Lir staggered.

At last Kiran understood. While the crowd turned, transfixed, to watch their leading citizen thrash and curse like a schoolboy, Kiran slid backward through the skirts of the women and sidled into a cornfield. With his head low, he ran between rows of corn. When he reached the edge of the woods, he sprinted full out, until the searing pain in his chest slowed him to a jog. His breath came in short gasps. Behind him, he heard Lir's voice still thundering above the roaring crowd.

Part Two:
The Cedar Flute

Chapter 11

Kiran lay all day under the flame leaf bush, in the shade of the rowboat, while hunger gnawed his stomach and his fractured arm itched in its wooden sleeve. He shook with fury at what Ser Vetel had done. One lie with the basin last night, another with the bird today. How many other lies had the old man told him over the years?

Kiran had always marveled at how Ser Vetel wrote and deciphered the mysterious marks permitted only to priests. Like the basin, writing offered a way to know what was happening at a great distance. And now to learn that both were used for lies! Why?

How long could the old man hide the truth Kiran had told? No word would reach Lanath from Catora until the villagers built a new barge to travel to Serpent camp. But maybe the bargemen from Catora would play along with the lie. Then the villagers wouldn't learn the truth until the younger children returned from Catora next year. But maybe no one other than Kiran had seen what happened to Myra and Dara. They were lost; who cared or remembered how? Maybe lie would pile upon lie until the truth meant nothing. Kiran's head spun as he lay waiting for his stepfather to come.

Hours passed, and Lir did not come. Maybe he would never come. He might be locked in the guard tower, injured, even dead after his struggle with the soldiers. Then there would be no expedition, no redemption, no one even to comfort Kiran's mother as she wept over Ser Vetel's latest version of her son's cowardice and her daughter's death.

A squirrel rustled overhead, and then the quiet of evening fell over the forest, intolerable in its peacefulness. Kiran felt he could jump out of his skin. Waiting, not knowing, was more than he could bear. Should he try to slip back into the village in the falling darkness? If no one was looking for him, he might slink to the guard tower and learn what had happened to his stepfather.

If Lir was imprisoned, Kiran's mother would need him. He pictured her opening the door a fraction, letting him slip into the kitchen warmth and the smell of bread rising by the fire. No matter what she believed he had done, she would forgive him, her last remaining child.

But Lir had fought like a wild beast so that Kiran could escape. He had shown Kiran the boat and taken the village's fury on himself so that Kiran could reach it. The knowledge settled in Kiran's stomach that his stepfather had invited the soldiers' blows because he believed his stepson would have the courage to act. To act, even alone.

With an aching chest in the fading light, Kiran examined the boat's contents. Bows and arrows, hatchet, rope, chests of food, flints for starting a fire, blankets. Enough provisions for three or four men. But no other men were coming.

The choice he had been avoiding lay clear before him. He could return to the village to live in safety and shame, swallowing Ser Vetel's lies. Or he could journey downriver alone. Maybe, with a rope and hatchet, with an adequate supply of food, he could find the path that had eluded him before. He could follow the Savages to the heart of their country and then—who knows. Steal his sister and Myra under cover of darkness? Die, probably. He shivered. Die, and follow the Moon Lady into the sky. Unless she was a lie also.

He stood and wrapped the rope from the boat's bow around his good hand and over his shoulder. He leaned into it, scrabbling with his feet at the leaf-littered ground. The boat shifted. He inched it forward, groaning, until it lodged against a root and stuck fast. He moved alongside the boat, set his back against it, and levered it sideways, then returned to the bow. Already he was worn out, and he had moved it only a fraction of the distance to the river.

He looped the rope over his shoulder again. But just as he dug in his legs, a hand fell on his shoulder, and he cried out.

The hand spun him around. He looked up into the face of Bulo, broad and grim in his heavy helmet and leather armor.

Who would have thought that Bulo would be the one to arrest him? Kiran hung his head in despair.

Bulo gave his shoulder a shake. "I'm c-coming, too," he said. "You show the way."

Kiran's head shot up. "You're coming? And my—the Master of the Harvest?"

Bulo shook his head. "In the g-guard tower. He h-h-hurt one of the soldiers. He's raving like a madman. They'll never let him g-g-g—" He lifted his hands, defeated by the work of speaking. But he tossed his bundle into the boat, seized it by the bow, and heaved it backward, over and through the bushes. Kiran ran to push on the stern. The boat lurched out of the bushes and down the sandy riverbank. Bulo stood to one side and slid the boat into the water. He handed Kiran in and scrambled after him.

With an oar, Bulo pushed at the bank until they floated free and then settled himself amidships, his back to the bow, and began to row in long, slow strokes. His scowl eased, and in the darkness Kiran caught the reflection of moonlight on his eyes and teeth. He might even be grinning.

Bulo was crazy to leave the village. Once, years ago, the guards had hauled a deserter back from the river and hanged him on the witness tree. Kiran's mother had forbidden him to watch with the other children, but a week later, Ser Vetel had made him follow along when the soldiers cut the swollen, blackened body from the tree and discarded it in the woods to be gnawed upon by wolves. Kiran remembered the smell.

He shuddered. "Why did you come, Bulo? Are you deserting?"

Bulo made a noise like a snarl. "That b-bird. That messenger bird. I know him. He has a b-brown patch on his wing."

"Yes?"

"I f-fed him in the shed last night. That bird didn't f-fly from—from—" He shook his head in frustration.

"You mean . . . someone took him out today and let him fly home just in time for the council?"

Yes!" Bulo exploded.

★ ★ ★

They floated day and night.

Bulo rowed for hours at a time, adding his strength to the current that drew them downriver. When he tired, he crouched in the bow, keeping one oar ready across his lap to fend off snags and sandbanks. Kiran watched the bank, trying to track how far they had come, listening for traffic on the river in case they had to hide. Or else he rummaged in the chests for food and cut off hunks of bread and cheese for Bulo, or passed him the cider jug.

At the bottom of one of the chests, wrapped in a bit of cloth, he found a flute made of cedar wood. When he pulled it out he sat back on the floor of the boat in amazement. Turning it in his hands, he could see that it was brand new. The unpolished wood had a reddish grain and the finger holes were sharp and unworn. Lir must have had the carpenter make it just for this voyage. A gift for Kiran, to replace the one he had used as a splint.

Kiran pictured the trip Lir had wanted, four boats filled with soldiers and the men of the village. He, Kiran, would play for them as they rowed. His stepfather had planned for it. He felt a choking sob in his throat. *He's proud of me*, he thought. *He's proud of me and my music.*

Kiran had trouble bending his left arm sharply enough to hold the instrument to his lips. The fingers on his left hand were stiff and awkward. He blew an open note. The flute was pitched a note lower than his old one, and the tone was different, hollower. More melancholy, maybe. But none of that mattered. Kiran navigated scales and trills. He played the old songs in short stretches until his arm ached too much to continue.

As they floated, Bulo's speech began to grow easier. He hummed along with the flute music as he rowed, and sometimes he added words, so that his speech came out in a kind of sing-song current that ran smoothly past any hidden snags. He sang to Kiran that he came from a farming family down south, and that he had never wanted to be anything but a farmer, with his animals in the barn and his fields full of corn. But the army came through one day as he was wrestling a cow free from a bog, and they drafted him on the spot for his strength.

He had hoped to be posted back to his hometown, where he could keep an eye on his widowed mother and his sisters, but instead he was shipped to Lanath. Away from the sun-drenched valleys of his youth, stranded in the whispering forest of the north, he found that his tongue couldn't form well round the words, and he grew stupider every year.

"But that Myra," he said. "I could talk to her."

★ ★ ★

Mid-morning of the third day, Kiran heard the distant roar of the Serpent. He warned Bulo, and they brought the boat to the bank upstream of the spot where the water began to swirl and plunge. They hauled it up the bank, over the pebbles and well into the woods. Bulo sent Kiran back to brush over the marks they had left so that anyone following would be unable to track them.

When Kiran came back, he found Bulo filling their packs. Two casks and a food chest hung from a tree to await their return. Bulo prepared a huge pack for himself, with food and cooking gear and blankets, and a smaller one for Kiran.

Each of them carried rope and a knife; Bulo hung an axe and sword from his belt as well. He took only one bow, because Kiran couldn't pull one, but he gave Kiran a quiver of extra arrows.

Kiran scouted downstream until he found the path the Savages had taken. He led the way along it to show Bulo the place where the three remaining canoes lay hidden, but when he found what he was sure was the spot, the canoes had disappeared.

Bulo squatted, ran his hand over the bent leaves of the ferns on the forest floor, and nodded.

By noon they reached the fire-scarred patch of granite where Kiran had turned back the first time. Bulo followed the trail, and when it thinned to almost nothing he paused, took a few steps backward, and searched to the side. A half-broken fir limb hung akimbo, and when Bulo pushed it away he revealed a branch path veering toward the cliff face. The two of them slipped through. Here the path was clear, and it led in a series of switchbacks up the steep, wooded slope.

They came out on a broad shelf of granite above the fire site and looked back the way they had come. A dip in the forest showed where the path cut and wound its way from the river. Distant water glinted, mist rose from the Serpent, and the great green forest billowed away to the river and far up into the hills beyond.

Two tracks led away from the lookout site. The scuff marks and indentations on the left hand side were fresher, so they took that side and ducked into the forest again.

Sunlight winked faintly through the shadows of the fir trees and squirrels chirred questions, then tore away overhead. Treading after Bulo in silence, Kiran pushed branches out of the way and tried to push aside his fears. The sweet smell of fir brushed his nostrils, and he imagined flute tones, low and breathy, painting the forest.

Something hooted in the forest in a tone he hadn't heard before. Bulo's head lifted; he heard it, too. It was higher than an owl's tone, and now it added a hiccup.

Bulo's hand closed on the hilt of his sword. He looked back at Kiran and nodded.

Kiran's heart beat faster. He pulled out his dagger. Without even a bow, what use would he be in a fight?

As they crept forward, the hooting subsided.

Then, ahead of them, a flash of yellow and brown shot diagonally across the path. A shout of laughter sounded, and then, again, someone darted across the path, going the other way. Bulo held up his hand. The hooting came again.

Bulo said, "Let's t-try to ta-ta—Not fight."

"Talk?" asked Kiran.

Bulo nodded, pushing Kiran's dagger aside. The big man waited and Kiran realized that Bulo, with his stumbling speech, could never parley. It had to be Kiran. He hesitated. *Maybe if I played my flute*, he thought wildly. *Even Savages might understand.*

No, he had to speak. Kiran shot a look at Bulo and took a step forward. "Uh, can we talk to you?" He forced himself to make his voice louder. "Whoever you are, we're looking for two girls. We don't want trouble. Can you help us?"

A rustle of leaves, and a small figure appeared in a patch of sunlight. For a moment Kiran's heart leaped at the sight of golden hair. But of course it wasn't Dara; this was a boy, ten or twelve years old, with a tangle of hair and a slim body clothed in skins.

As Kiran stepped toward him, a hand held out in appeal, the boy dove into the forest. Fifty yards farther down the path, he re-emerged. Crouching, ready to flee, he peered back at them.

"Come back! Talk to us!" called Kiran. He wondered if the boy knew the language of Catora. He was no Savage; his skin shone pinkish-brown, little darker than Kiran's. But instead of answering, the boy flitted away again, and Kiran and Bulo picked up their pace to follow.

The path reached a clearing cut through by a gully. Two long, shaved half logs lay across the gully. The wild boy glanced back at the start of the bridge and waved at them. Kiran crept toward him, his hand held out, calling as if he were trying to tame some wild animal, a deer or snuffler. He could see the boy's white teeth and blue eyes.

The boy turned and skipped across the bridge, then backed away, beckoning.

Kiran and Bulo came forward to examine the gully. It was only about twenty feet deep, with a small rush of water at the bottom, no real barrier to cross even if the logs weren't there.

"He wants us to follow him," Kiran said.

Bulo nodded, and stuck a tentative foot onto the first log. It rocked under his weight.

"Let me go first; I'm lighter," Kiran said.

Bulo shook his head. He stepped onto the plank, while the wild boy skipped backward, nodding and beckoning. Bulo edged forward, balancing his heavy pack.

Something rustled in the woods behind the boy. "Watch out!" Kiran yelled. At the same moment, the boy whirled around and shouted in dismay. From the woods behind him, an arrow shot toward the log bridge, and then another. Bulo twisted aside, but the second arrow grazed his shoulder, and as he recoiled, his foot slid and he toppled off the bridge.

"No!" cried Kiran, starting forward.

Bulo cried out, flailing, and his body crashed on the rocks. Kiran threw himself down to look over the lip of the gully. Bulo lay with his back in the stream and one leg folded under him at a grotesque angle. He struggled to lift himself onto his elbows, and he shouted at Kiran, "Back! Get away! Run!"

Kiran hesitated. On the opposite bank, the boy, no longer laughing, ran toward the edge, and three men came out of the woods, bows drawn, to stand around him. In sudden fury, Kiran lunged toward the bridge, but the notched arrows swung to follow him, and he knew he would be struck down before he reached halfway across.

The boy spoke in a hoarse, frightened voice, still high enough to sing in the girls' chorus. "Go away. If you leave, we won't kill him."

Behind him, the three men waited, their thick arms holding the bowstrings, three arrows aiming at Kiran's chest.

Kiran hesitated. These men must be bandits, and they wanted Bulo, not him. As at the barge, Kiran could be the only one to escape. He could walk away, back to the cache of food and supplies by the river. And then what? Someday a barge would come, and he could go home. He pictured the long days of waiting by the river. He remembered Bulo's humming and slow, singsong stories as they floated down the river.

From the gully, Bulo moaned.

Kiran turned his back on the bandits and, grabbing a root with his good hand, lowered himself into the gully to join his friend.

Chapter 12

At a cry from one of the bandits, the two others scrambled into the gully after Kiran. One seized his arm and spun him around to put him in a chokehold. The other struck him hard across the face and kicked his legs away. They dropped him face down in the wet gravel next to Bulo, one of them setting a heavy foot on his back.

When he writhed, the sharp-edged stones beneath him ground into his belly and thighs.

"Tie him up," the man above them ordered. Kiran felt his arms jerked back. A cord yanked tight around his ankles, while a second rope grated against his wooden sleeve.

Beside him, Bulo groaned. He said, "You should have run."

The harsh voice rapped out above them. "Bring him up."

One of the men grasped Kiran by the hair while the other boosted his bound legs from below. His body jerked and swayed as they hauled it up the side of the gully. At the top, they flung him down at the feet of the yellow-haired boy and the man who was giving orders. Kiran twisted to land on his good side.

The man scowled but beside him the boy gazed down with a brow wrinkled in concern.

"Why didn't you go home?" the boy demanded. When Kiran didn't answer, the boy turned to the scowling man. "What did you shoot for? I was bringing them to be recruits."

The man growled. "Your father let you come on a hunting trip and you pull something like this. These two are not volunteers. The soldier kept his helmet on, this one's a runt, and neither one's carrying a peace flag." He kicked a toeful of dirt at Kiran's face. "Your father will have my head off! Why did you let them see you? Best thing we can do now is toss this one back in the gully and let them both rot."

Kiran spat out what dirt he could and pulled his knees up, readying himself to spring at the bandit.

A shadow crossed the boy's face. "We can't do that, Ram. Is that what you do? I thought the rule was no killing unless we're attacked."

The man spat. "They were following you."

"That's my fault, not theirs! We can't kill them for that. Let's take them back a way and untie them. They can go home."

"Same difference, for the big one at least. He'll never make it out with a busted leg. Best drop a rock on his head right now."

"No!" Kiran jerked his body to get their attention. "Let us go. I'll get him out!"

One of the armed men drew back a boot to kick him but the boy held up a hand and the man stepped back with a grunt.

The boy looked down on Kiran curiously. "What did you come here for?"

Kiran ground his teeth. "I came to find my sister, who was stolen by Savages from the river."

The boy frowned and nodded. He looked abruptly older, thought Kiran, as though he were girding himself for a fight.

"Why did you wait so long?" the boy asked.

It took Kiran a moment to understand and when he did, his heart thumped. So this boy knew how long it had been, knew the girls had been kidnapped. "Where are they?" he demanded. "How can I find them?"

"Where's your raiding band?"

Kiran shook his head. "Just us. Bulo and me, Kiran."

The boy jerked. His voice caught. "Say that again—your name."

"Kiran. Kiran of Lanath."

The boy beckoned to the leader and they drew aside. Turning his head in the dirt, Kiran saw them arguing furiously until finally the man threw up his hands in assent.

The boy came back. "We will take you with us, Kiran of Lanath, if you swear not to struggle, escape or report to anyone what you learn."

"What about Bulo?"

The boy looked in appeal to the man Ram, then asked, "Who does he fight for?"

Kiran thought. He was sure these men were outlaws, with no allegiance, living to prey on people of the kingdom. "He fights for nobody. He came as my friend."

The boy let out a sigh of relief. "Then we'll take him, too."

★ ★ ★

Loosely blindfolded but no longer bound, Kiran made his journey comfortably enough. The boy outlaw let Kiran rest a hand on his shoulder as he walked. He felt the narrow, muscled shoulder bounce and shift as the boy turned to talk to the men or gave a little skip over some obstacle in the path.

Bulo, he could hear, was having a much harder time of it. Lashed to a litter made of branches, he was carried by the impatient, stumbling men who took turns lifting and dropping him. Kiran heard Bulo try to talk to them, but between his stutter and his groans, he didn't make much headway.

They camped for the night in a pine grove. After some discussion, the boy lifted Kiran's blindfold but bound his arms again so that his shoulders ached and he figured he'd never fall asleep. The boy warned him not to speak a word to Bulo and then curled up by the fire. In sleep he looked so smooth-faced and innocent that Kiran thought with a pang of Dara sleeping on the deck of the barge. Even his hair, with its golden brown curls, reminded him of Dara's.

In the morning, Kiran woke in the cold dew and the boy loosed his arms and retied his blindfold. He led him along the path again, peppering Kiran with questions about life in his village, people's houses and work, what they wore, what songs they sang. When Kiran began to sing the Dawn Song, the boy said excitedly, "Oh, yes, I know that one!" which surprised Kiran, because he had always heard it was a song that belonged only to Lanath, invented by the priest who had served before Ser Vetel.

Their path wound steadily higher. The soft woods path gave way underfoot to a firmer track across rock and at times the boy guided him to take large strides across crevices. The air grew colder, too, and brighter around the edges of the blindfold as they climbed.

Soon more men came to join them and take turns carrying Bulo so they moved more quickly. Voices questioned the boy and eventually hands seized Kiran by either arm. They led him across the rock, then shoved him up a passageway that seemed to climb between two rock walls. The hands pushed him, not roughly, into a stone-floored space. He stumbled onto his knees. Behind him, the boy's hands untied the blindfold.

Kiran knelt in a stone storeroom of some kind, with burlap sacks on all sides. One of the sacks near him was open and spilling grain. The boy came around to stand in front of him, hands on his hips. "Welcome to our castle, brother. I'll go and tell my father you're here." He ran off, leaving Kiran under the watchful eye of a long-limbed man with a mournful face and a racking cough.

That word *brother* struck Kiran like a blow to an arloc string, resounding even after the boy withdrew. As a brother all he had ever done was lose people—first little Calef, whom he'd hardly had a chance to know, and then Dara, snatched from his care. Why should a blue-eyed outlaw call him brother?

"Where's Bulo?" he asked his guard. "The big fellow, where did they take him?"

The gaunt fellow coughed and wiped his mouth with the back of his hand. "They took him to the armorer, I reckon, to have his leg pulled straight. Don't worry; they're good at pulling strong men straight. Wish they were as good at clearing a weak man's lungs." He gave a grin, showing crooked yellow teeth.

Kiran decided to risk another question. "So, you're the famous bandits?"

The gaunt man laughed. "Could say. Or you might say we're all fellows as been robbed ourselves. We're outlaws, I'll give you that."

Kiran took a breath. "And do you know the Savages, where they hide out?"

At that moment the outlaw boy burst in, practically dancing with excitement. "He wants to see you, Kiran of Lanath. Oh, wait till you see him! We have to put the blindfold back on, but it's just for now. Norbal, my father says to bring them both some food." Kiran ducked his head and the boy tied the strip of cloth around his eyes again, then led him out, up what felt like steps cut in the rock face, around a turn and through a door.

"Let me see him," said a voice, deep and thrilling. A voice made for singing, Kiran thought; a voice you could build a choir around.

The boy's hands turned him toward the voice. "Shall I take his blindfold off now, Father?"

"Yes, and then go. Go wait with the other one, the soldier."

Kiran ducked and felt the boy's light fingers lift the blindfold away. He looked first at the boy, who raised those blue eyes to him, serious now, even apprehensive. Then the boy tucked the blindfold into his shirt and slipped out the door.

Kiran stood in a room that was half cave. Wooden walls rose behind him but at the far corner of the room, above the hearth, two walls of granite stretched toward the sky in a high chimney. The whole room seemed to be straining toward something it could never reach. Kiran's eyes dropped from the chimney to the man who sat in a chair by the hearth.

"Come closer," said the man in that deep voice. Once again, something in that voice called to Kiran so that for a moment he wanted to run across the space between them and throw himself at the bandit leader's feet. Instead he took a cautious step forward, then another. The bandit sat half hidden in the furs that lined his chair. Stiff brown and gray hair shadowed his forehead and his drawn gray cheeks. Gray-green eyes searched Kiran's face from beneath the ledge of his brow. He seemed to crouch like a wildcat ready to strike.

Watching him, Kiran felt his heart leap with recognition and knowledge. It was impossible, it could not be, but hope pulled him and he took two more steps toward the man.

"Do you know me?" the man asked.

Yes, yes! Kiran wanted to shout but he knew it was stupid, he must be wrong, he couldn't voice even to himself what he thought he knew. And he couldn't afford to make a fool of himself in front of the bandit king. He shook his head. "No, sir."

The man passed a hand over his eyes, then set his hands on the arms of his chair and hoisted himself up. The furs fell away from his lap. He grasped a staff from beside the chair and labored forward.

"Kiran," said the man. "I would know you still, though it had been nine times nine years. I remember the day you floated away on that barge with a crown of beech leaves in your hair. Boy, come and embrace your father."

Kiran stood frozen as the man approached, hauling himself forward with the staff. That voice, of course he knew it, his father's voice singing the Dawn Song at nightfall as Kiran fell asleep in the corner. But this man was so small and twisted, so gray. One leg was bare, wrapped about the thigh with a wide cloth bandage. A greenish-gray stain seeped through the bandage and as his father approached, a sickly-sweet odor caught Kiran's nostrils. He fought off the urge to gag and held himself stiff as his father pressed him close. The side of his face felt the bones of his father's chest and he pushed away.

His father stood back, leaning on his staff, and waited. *No doubt I have disappointed him already*, thought Kiran. Suddenly he was filled with anger. *What do you know of me, old man, to be disappointed that I don't call you father? For eight years I saved the name of father, held it back from Lir, waiting faithfully, as if my real father would come back. For eight years I lurked in the background in my own house, a disappointment to my big stepfather with the loud laugh. And here you were hiding and stealing all the time, and look at you, puny and stinking. Is this what I will become?*

He forced the words out, forced himself to say something. "Why didn't you come back?"

His father swung his head away as if it had been struck and Kiran knew he had injured him again. His father shrugged and gave a short humorless laugh. "Yes, why didn't I come back? Why not ask them, your whore of a mother and that rich man she clung to the moment I was gone? Why not ask that priest and the captain of the guard who sent their soldiers to drive me away with their spears dipped in poison?"

"What?" Kiran shook his head in anger. "What are you saying?"

"I followed him, your brother Calef. None would come with me. I tracked the Shelonwe who stole him through the falling snow to their village high in the foothills west of here. When I found them, I put aside my weapons and walked right in among them to demand they give him back. And what a deal they gave me! Three years of servitude and then they'd set him free. I offered single combat, but no, nothing would do for them but to make me a slave."

"Shelonwe?" Kiran asked in bewilderment. "What are Shelonwe?"

"You call them Savages, but they proved no worse than your men of Lanath. Three years of labor I gave them, three years filled with kicks and curses, and then they kept their word. Yes, Kiran, Savages kept their word and gave us food and clothes and weapons, and sent us home. We walked down the paths to Lanath, my five-year-old son and I. We came to the gate at nightfall and the guard wouldn't let us in. Oh, no, they sent for the priest, and the captain who came and met with me and told me to go—they would take the boy but not me because my time in that village was over, my wife remarried, my name forgotten."

Bitterness dripped from his voice; he turned his back on Kiran and hobbled to the bed that stood against the wall. He lowered himself onto it and turned his head to the wall.

"Never mind," he said. "Send my son to me. Send Calef."

"Father," Kiran said. The man didn't stir.

Again, Kiran felt anger move within him. "I was there," he said. "I would have come with you. Why didn't you send for me? Why didn't you fight them?"

"Oh, I fought them. I said my wife must come to the gate to see her little son. I thought they were lying, that she loved me, that she would come. But she sent a message with the ring I gave her when we wed, saying she must be dead to us as we were dead to her, for she had a new baby now and a new husband, to replace the ones she had lost. And then I went wild inside and swore I would see her and plead with her one more time.

"I hid Calef in the forest and just before dawn I scaled the wall by the guard tower. But they were waiting for me, five of them, with spears and arrows. They drove me back into the forest and then they hunted me. One of them speared me in the thigh and they left me in the forest to bleed to death. Ah, but what do you care about that? I see you wrinkle your nose at me and flinch away instead of honoring me as a father deserves!"

Kiran took a step forward, feeling the hot rush of tears. "What you say is terrible! I—"

His father interrupted him. "Yes, the truth is terrible, and lies are so pretty. Go away now, boy, for I am ill. I asked you to send my son."

A silence fell. Throbbing, it filled the room. The tears dried on Kiran's face.

Finally, he turned and found his way across the dirt floor to the door. No guard waited outside. He crossed a patch of bare cracked stone among pinnacles of granite as if he were walking through the courtyard of a castle whose foundation was falling away.

Chapter 13

Kiran found Bulo propped with closed eyes on a cot in a room built under a stone overhang. His leg, wrapped in wood and cloth, lay thrust out before him and his torso was uncovered except for a bandage that ran around his chest and shoulder. Bulo's white face and bare chest glistened with sweat. Calef, who sat on a stool beside him, jumped up as Kiran ducked through the door.

"Did you see him, Kiran?" he asked, his voice bright with excitement. "Were you surprised?"

"Yes," said Kiran heavily. "I was surprised." He crouched next to Bulo's cot.

The wounded soldier opened his eyes and gave Kiran a weak smile.

"You knew," Kiran accused him.

"I guessed," Bulo said. "Who wouldn't, seeing the two of you together?" He nodded toward Calef. "B-bless your good fortune, Kiran. It was worth it. You've found what was lost." He closed his eyes and grimaced as a wave of pain ran through him.

Kiran laid his hand on Bulo's shoulder. *I wish I had some nuath for you.*

Calef tugged on Kiran's sleeve. "What did Father say?" The younger boy bent and peered into his face. "But you don't look happy. I found you, I brought you—I have a brother!" He pounded Kiran on the back.

Kiran shook him off. "He practically cursed me. He wants you. You better go to him. He's not in the greatest mood."

A cloud came over Calef's face. "His leg gets so bad sometimes. When the pus pours out of it like that, it's as if—I don't know, he throws up, he says the pain is like an animal gnawing on him and howling in his head. I wish I'd found you sometime when his leg was good."

Bulo lifted himself on his elbows, wincing. "How did he g-get the leg wound?"

Calef looked at Kiran. "It happened when we went to Lanath. They used a poisoned spear."

Kiran started up in fury. "That's a filthy lie!"

Calef drew back in surprise and Bulo caught at Kiran's arm. "Calef," he said, "g-go and see your father."

When his brother was gone, Kiran strode around the room, beating his arms against his sides. A hollow ache in his chest made him groan and gnash his teeth. Bulo watched him, then reached out and tapped the stool beside him. Kiran slouched over to sit down.

Bulo said, "Your father and b-brother, that you thought were dead, are alive."

Kiran grabbed his head in his hands. "But they're not—"

Bulo waited.

Kiran dropped his hands. "Everyone's lied. I bet my father's lying. He said—he said he came home and—" He felt too ashamed to say it but Bulo waited. "And my mother sent him away. He called her a—"

Bulo touched his arm again. "Don't say."

Kiran stood up and paced once more around the room. He snorted. "A poisoned spear! Who's ever heard of poisoned spears?"

Bulo stirred and Kiran shot a look at him.

"Kiran, we . . . I never told you b-boys because it's not heroic. When we're standing in defense against a v-vicious enemy, we're t-t-told to roll our spear tips through the mushrooms that grow on manure piles."

Kiran's jaw dropped. He clenched his fists, digging his fingernails into his palms. What a fool he'd been. Priests, soldiers, they were all liars. There was no honor in any of them.

After a minute Bulo said softly, "I'm sorry, Kiran. But he's alive. I never m-met your father. Tell me about him."

Kiran glowered at him, then turned his head aside and fought to let his fists loosen. He closed his eyes to help him cast far back in memory. "He sang all the time and he carried me on his shoulders. He took me fishing. No one in Lanath was a better hunter. When Calef was a baby, he used to throw him so high in the air it scared my mother."

Kiran remembered the spring in his father's step, how he had always seemed younger and lighter than all the other fathers. Once he challenged a group of men to race across the rooftops of the village. One of them—was it the potter?—fell through a weak spot in the thatch right onto the dinner table of a sheep farmer.

Bulo nodded. "And now?"

"He's like a mangy cat, gray and shrunken, snarling in a corner."

"Yes, that's bad." Bulo paused. "But my father is really d-dead. I saw him waste away and then I helped my mother bury him in the orchard. Yours is still alive."

Kiran shook his head. A dead father was better than a stinking, bitter father who hated him.

Bulo shifted on the cot and grimaced. "Look, Kiran, with my leg and your arm, we may be stuck here for a while. This is your chance to g-get to know your brother."

Kiran thought of Calef dancing backward along the trail, luring them forward. He remembered the shape of Calef's shoulder under his hand. Calef, his mother's lost child, alive and lighthearted here in the wilderness. Calef, whom his father loved.

Kiran set the stool against the wall and sat on it, his head resting in his hands. He tried to picture his family restored, back in Lanath, sharing bread at the table by the hearth. His father's bow hung by the door, his mother's loom stood by the window. He and Calef laughed about some fishing expedition as they slurped at their soup and his mother chided them for their manners.

In the picture Dara sat cross-legged by the fire, combing her doll's hair and singing to it. At the sound of her voice, his father turned to scowl at her. Then his mother scooped Dara up onto her lap, spreading a shawl to shield her daughter from her husband's frown. She turned her back to them and carried Dara to the door. The door opened and Lir Coman stood there in his fur-trimmed cloak, waiting to take Dara from Enya's arms. But instead of handing Dara over, she hesitated on the sill, Enya, wife of two husbands, torn between her sons and her daughter, caught on the threshold, unable to come or go.

Kiran pressed the heel of his hand to his forehead. *She would choose Dara*, he thought. *And the family would still be broken.*

A loud groan from Bulo broke into his thoughts. Bulo tossed his head from side to side, his jaw clenched and new beads of sweat dotted his hairline. "Serpent curse me for a whining weakling," he said. "Forgive the noise but this be-hellioned leg is killing me. I wish you'd play for me, Kiran. Play me back to the river, please, can't you?"

Kiran was in no mood to play but he could hardly say no. He pulled the cedar flute from his belt. When he blew into it, the hollow tone seemed to echo the emptiness he felt. His breath swirled around inside it the way the water curled back on itself in the shallows. It was a strange, lonely sound, different from the sweet tones he was used to. Before long he found himself trying to bring the strangeness out, to play the rills and backwaters.

He was still playing when Calef came back. The younger boy crept to the foot of Bulo's cot to listen. Kiran's arm ached in its heavy cast and his fingers felt thick and clumsy, as if they were wrapped in wool. The memory of his father's anger burned in his chest. But as he blew and the clear, plaintive notes rose from the flute, he felt the coil of bitterness wrapped around his heart begin, ever so slowly, to unwind.

★ ★ ★

Were they prisoners? Kiran wondered over the next few days. Or was he just waiting for Bulo to heal? He felt weighed down by a guilt he didn't understand. Where did his duty lie now? His real father lay here, lurking in a cave. Did he still owe anything to the mother and stepfather who had lied to him? Did he even care what happened to Dara, so spoiled and petted, with her golden hair? And what about Myra, of the sharp tongue and sharp elbows, who hadn't hesitated to fight a Savage with bare fists?

All he knew for certain was that he couldn't leave Bulo until he knew he was safe.

He was never alone: Calef followed him everywhere and one of the bandit men always lingered in the background. Norbal came out of his storage cavern, coughing and wheezing behind them, or else the bowman Ram, who had shot Bulo, followed them at a distance, eyes shadowed beneath his bristling eyebrows.

Calef wanted to take him everywhere, show him everything. Kiran carried news of what he saw in the camp back to

Bulo who lay all day with his leg propped on a barrel. Kiran told him about the storehouse, the forge, the chickens, the carpenter's shed, the kitchen. "What, no c-caves of bandit gold?" asked Bulo. "It sounds like a regular village."

The second day, Calef led Kiran to the peak just south of the camp, nodding to a man who stood sentry there. From the crag they could see all the way to the ocean, far to the southeast. Kiran's breath caught at his first sight of the ocean in nine years. And that smudge of white must be Catora, seven days' float below the Serpent. The path of the river curving east and south appeared like a fold in the blanket of trees before him. One branch folded just to the south of them. "Right down there is Pomel," Calef said. "We trade with them all the time."

"Pomelans trade with bandits?"

Calef laughed. "Father says we must never steal from the Pomelans and must always remember to bring them things they need. They're so close, they almost know where we live. They could betray us. Shall I show you what we trade with them?"

He led Kiran down the slope to a mountain plateau covered in dark green. When they drew close enough, Kiran saw that the green came from the leaves of low woody plants. Calef drew back their dense leaves and showed his brother the cluster of berries growing at the bottom of each twig. "Mountain berries!"

Kiran put one in his mouth, puckered and spat.

Calef laughed at him. "Can't you see they're still green?"

Kiran gave him a hard look. "What good are they?"

"You've never heard of mountain berries? You have to wait till they're purple. People use them to preserve meat. And they make the best jam. Pomelans squeeze them into the cider they send to Catora. But they keep it a secret so the soldiers won't know they're trading with us."

Beyond, in a mountain meadow sloping down to the west, a flock of longhaired goats grazed on the long grass. "This is our summer pasture," Calef told him. "We come up here for four reasons: for the mountain berries, for the grass, to trade with Pomel and to take turns at the lookout where we just were."

"Looking for what? Fat barges, stuffed with goods?"

Calef grinned. "Yep. Or people running for the mountains to join us. A lot of things we won't steal."

"What kinds of things?"

"We don't steal food. No nuath either. Father says it makes people weak. Sometimes a band goes down where the rivermen are camping at night to steal weapons. I stole some cooking pots once."

"Pots?" Kiran shouted with laughter. "You're a fearsome bandit and you steal *cooking pots*?"

Calef's cheeks reddened. "We didn't have a blacksmith then."

★ ★ ★

The fourth morning, Calef and the grizzled carpenter brought Bulo a pair of crutches, freshly hewn and smelling of pine sap. Bulo ran his hands over their surface. Then he struggled upright and positioned the crutches at his sides. "Ready to go," he said. "I want to see everything."

But in fact he had a hard time making his way over the rocky ground, hauling his wooden cast along. Calef led him around the camp, introducing him to all the bandits, talking non-stop. Bulo greeted each person, leaning over his crutches to shake hands.

Watching, Kiran felt the pull of resentment. People liked Bulo. They nodded at him, talked to him. He fit right in. In no time he'd forget all about Myra and Dara. Kiran didn't want to tag along after him, making friends with bandits—bandits whose leader stank and snarled and sent him away.

Instead he pulled out the flute and ran his hands along the wood. Norbal hung nearby, nodding at him. Kiran blotted him out by closing his eyes. Leaning against a rock by the carpenter's shed, he lifted the flute to his mouth and sounded a breathy note. The crag above the bandit village came to his mind. He tried to find the sound of the wind battering it in winter and the river below.

Before he knew it, Calef was tugging at his tunic, urging him to come to dinner. Kiran opened his eyes to see some of the bandits squatting nearby, listening to him and grinning.

Now that Bulo was stronger, they ate their dinner with the rest of the bandits, twenty men at two ramshackle tables in a clearing in front of the kitchen. Calef always went to the front of the line and filled two plates, one for himself and one for his father. He carried the two plates up the narrow rock path to where the bandit leader's sickroom lay out of sight and he only returned to sit by Kiran at the end of the meal.

Kiran and Bulo slurped their soup and gnawed on chunks of meat, with Norbal and Ram flanking them. Their guards, Kiran thought. But Bulo talked cheerfully. "So this is just your summer campground?" he asked Norbal.

"Yup. Winter up here'd freeze your toenails off. Come fall, we take the goats back down to our valley. Heck, most of us stay there all the time. Farming and fishing, keeping our families. That's where our sheep and cows are."

"Sounds like a regular village," Bulo said.

"Yup. The Village of Exiles, we call it. A hidden village for all the people who ran away."

Across the table, a tall man with chestnut hair combed straight back from his forehead thumped his fist on the table. "Shut up, Norbal."

"Take it easy, Yaysal. I didn't tell them where to find it."

The man stood up and shifted his muscled shoulders. He glared down at Bulo. "That's my deer you're eating."

Bulo nodded up at him, his eyes wary. "And we thank you for it, brother."

"Thanks are lovely, but how will you pay us back? Men should earn their keep."

Norbal let out a loud wheeze. "They're guests, Yaysal."

Yaysal placed his hands on the table between Bulo and Kiran. When he leaned across the table toward Norbal, Kiran smelled the sweat-stained goatskin of his tunic. "We don't keep guests, Norbal. Men here work. Even you."

"Back off. Corbin gave the okay. Besides, they bring music. Did you hear the boy play?"

"Is that what you call that moaning and hooting?" Yaysal sneered. "I thought that was just your lungs gasping again." He turned to Bulo. "You eat a lot. You look strong. We can use you."

Bulo said, "As soon as I can walk, the boy and I have a job to do. Then he'll go home, and I'll come back to work off our debt."

"Oh, no," Yaysal said. "No soldiers leave this camp. Can't be trusted."

"I'm a deserter," Bulo said evenly. "I can't go anywhere in the kingdom."

"Unless you bring your captains a spy report about the bandits above the fork. That'd get you back in the army, I bet."

Bulo shook his head. "I want to stay here. I'll follow you to the Village for Exiles. I want to farm."

"Not until you've shown your mettle. You kill a couple of soldiers first."

"No," Bulo said. "That I won't do."

Across the table, Norbal stood and took a breath. But before he could speak, he fell into a coughing fit. When he finally stopped, he gasped out, "Yaysal, you're not the chief. Sit down."

"Yet." Yaysal pulled away and swaggered the few steps to his place. Before he sat down, he fixed Norbal with his gaze. "When I'm chief, I'll clear the band of weaklings and invalids. But as you say, I'm not the chief. Yet."

Chapter 14

When Kiran closed his eyes at night, his head rocked as if he were suspended on a swaying bridge. Behind him lay his life in Lanath, the sweet smell of incense, the weaving voices of the girls' choir, the colors on his mother's loom in the firelight. Ahead lurked the Savages in their muttering forest. Somewhere in that forest cowered the figures of Dara and Myra. He couldn't picture their faces.

Even at night with his eyes closed he couldn't make himself take the final steps across the bridge. His legs wobbled. He pictured his father's years of slavery with the Savages. His father who didn't want to see him. He remembered his father's gray face, the stink of his wound, his voice sending Kiran away. The memory smoldered like a handful of coals at the pit of his stomach.

What made it worse was his sense of trouble brewing in the camp. Bulo, on crutches, dragging his heavy leg behind him, didn't see it. He spent his days with the carpenter, chisel and file in hand, trying to learn a new trade. For Kiran it was different. He followed Calef to milk the goats or scour the mountainside for dead branches for the kitchen fire. Along their way they often came across huddles of men who looked over their shoulders and stopped talking as they passed.

Calef, oblivious, chattered all the time. He told Kiran about his life among the Savages. "I hardly ever saw Father. He worked but they let me play. They taught me how to catch fish with my bare hands. Once I caught a bird in a snare and kept him tied by a string around his leg but he got away. I wanted to be a Child of the Forests and Mountains forever but my skin was too pink so I got some mud and smeared it all over my face and arms to be reddish brown like them."

"You speak their language?" Kiran asked.

"*Yol,*" Calef said. The rest of that morning he would only speak the Savage language, with its odd sounds like pebbles rolling together in a streambed.

Morning and evening, whenever they were back at camp, Calef went to check on their father. He ducked his head sideways and excused himself. Then he scrambled up the narrow rock stair that wound back from the dining area. He disappeared behind the tall rock that stood like a sentry in front of the opening to the cave where Corbin lay.

As Kiran waited for his brother to come back, he leaned against the rock wall and played the flute. Some of the outlaws nodded at him as they walked past. The flute sounds wove among the smells of the cook fire. He tried to play the sound of smoke or the sound of the river winding far below between the trees. When he grew tired of the new sounds, he played folksongs.

Sometimes one or two of the men came up to him and hummed songs of their own in a rough, tuneless way. Kiran played along, tried to fish out the real notes from their grunting attempts until they nodded and said, "Yeh, you got it. That's it there. No—no—not like that, it's more like—" and they worked it out.

When Calef came pattering down the steps, Kiran always looked up, his heartbeat quickening for a moment. But the boy saw his face and slowed his steps. His glance slid away. He never said, "Kiran, he wants to see you."

Other men climbed those stairs during the day, going to confer with their chief. At mealtimes the sentry rock loomed over them as if the outlaw chief were watching them, judging. But there was grumbling.

"What's he still chief for?" one man said, nodding up at the rock as he carried his soup bowl to the table one evening. He set down the bowl, wiped his nose with the back of his hand and settled into his place on the bench. "Sure, he was strongest once. Straightest bowshot, fastest sword."

He glanced sideways down the table at Kiran and lowered his voice. But not low enough. Kiran saw Yaysal at the next table raise his head and fix his gaze on the speaker.

The man wiped his nose again. "Used to be the sickness came on him just a few weeks a year. But now he don't even come down and talk to us. Not since that one"—he nodded in Kiran's direction—"came with his soldier friend." He sniffed. "Like as if Corbin's gone to ground." He tipped his soup bowl and took a long slurp.

The smaller man hunched beside him shook his head. "You shut up. I don't hold with talking down the chief. Didn't he gather us together? Take in all us runaways? Help some get their wives? Teach us to fight? Didn't he make peace with the Savages? Team us up to plant crops and build houses back at the winter village?"

"I'm not saying he didn't. I'm saying he's not doin' it no more. What're we all here for? No trading, no raids. Next barge's due any day and no plans made."

The other man chewed on his lip. "Yeah, you're right on that. Corbin never did hang back so much before."

At the other table, Yaysal's eyes glinted and he turned back to his meal.

★ ★ ★

"Bulo, we've got to move on," Kiran said that night, once he heard Calef's soft snore. He was lying on his back on the floor next to Bulo's cot. "We can ask Calef to show us the way."

Bulo's voice came slowly. "It'll be another month at least before I can really walk. And I'm hoping—well, I'm hoping by then we'll have some friends here that'll come along and help us."

"They won't come. They're at peace with the Savages."

Bulo was silent.

"We can't keep waiting, Bulo! I can't stand it! We sit here stuffing our faces while who knows what happens with the girls? Besides, I'm not a stinking bandit."

"They don't seem much like bandits to me," Bulo said mildly.

Kiran felt something boiling up inside him. "If you don't want to do it, Bulo, if you're scared the Savages will kill you, just tell me. Just hang around that carpenter and then run off to be a farmer!" He thumped his wooden arm cast against the floor and rolled over onto his stomach.

Bulo stirred and Kiran heard the thump of his cast on the floor. He flinched but Bulo just sat on the edge of his cot, looking down at him. "I can come along on my crutches, Kiran, if that's what you want."

Kiran gulped. "It's not. It's not what I want."

"I can talk to some of the men tomorrow. You need to speak with your father."

"I can't." Hot tears sprang to his eyes. He swallowed. "He doesn't want to see me."

There was a long pause. Finally, Bulo's cot creaked as he lay back down. "Sleep now, Kiran. It'll all come clearer in the morning."

Kiran let out his breath. He unclenched his hands and tried to let his muscles loosen.

As he drifted toward sleep, he realized something and he sat up to say it. "Bulo, you don't stutter at all any more."

* * *

The next morning, when he came skipping down the stairs from visiting their father, Calef jumped the last three steps. For once, he looked Kiran in the eye. "I think he's better today. Kiran, he hears your flute. He says he likes to hear it."

Kiran felt a leap of hope. *This is the moment. I should go up there right now.* But three men, Yaysal in front, were already leaping up the steps.

Calef challenged him to a race up the slope to the crag.

Kiran was fast but Calef was light and quick and had the advantage of using both hands to help him scamper up the rocks. He was already standing by the lookout laughing when Kiran reached the top. Kiran gave him a shove and then looked past him at the mist rising from the river.

"Company," said the sentry, pointing. "Barge headed for Serpent Camp. Looks like it's packed with extra men. They'll unload the next couple of days before they head for Pomel."

Kiran's heart thudded painfully. He felt a twist of shame in his gut. They would find Orda still bobbing in the shallows and the other soldiers at the edge of the camp, unburied, foxes or wildcats gnawing on their bones.

He asked, "No upriver barge?"

"No. Probably haven't finished building their new one."

Calef said, "We should run and tell my father."

The sentry shook his head. "No need. Yaysal was here at dawn. He's got some big plans."

Calef's head whipped around to look at him, his eyes wide.

The sentry grinned and clapped him on the shoulder. "Be happy, little brother. Maybe you'll see action at last."

All day long the camp was quiet but Kiran could tell that Calef was anxious. He had promised Kiran that he'd show him how to catch a fish with his bare hands today but now he didn't want to go down to the stream. Instead he hung around the kitchen peering into pots until the cook smacked him a few times with a spoon. Once he ran up the steps to his father's room but came down again right away. The chief and his lieutenants were discussing what to do and they had chased him off.

In the afternoon, they went to linger near Bulo in the carpenter's shed. The carpenter had chiseled out a set of rough wooden bowls and he let the boys sit in the yard, filing them smooth. Kiran held his bowl in the crook of his injured arm and held the file in the other hand. How long since he'd broken the arm? He counted back. Twenty-nine days. One full turn of the moon. Less than that, only twenty-one days, since Nora had set it right. Not time yet to loose the fitted leaves of the wooden cast. And the carpenter had bound Bulo's leg only nine days ago.

As they sat at dinner, eating rabbit stew and summer greens, Yaysal stood. The outlaws fell quiet before he even had time to lift his hand. "Men," he said. "Two barges parted at the fork this morning. That means one will camp at the Serpent tonight and one will moor halfway to Pomel."

The men jostled and muttered. Yaysal shook back his hair. "I see you all wondering why we haven't left yet. You know it takes most of the night to reach the Serpent."

Without rising, the blacksmith said, "Sit down, Yaysal. You know very well, because you were there when Corbin gave his orders. The chief wants us to let the Serpent barge pass this time. No robbing. He says it will be piled with soldiers on alert because of the Savage attack last month. He doesn't even want to attack the Pomel barge. He wants a group of three, the quietest scouts, to sneak down and check it out. See what the guard is like, for future reference. No pilfering. Not one spoon."

Yaysal grinned, showing his eyeteeth. "How do you like it, men? Summer's begun. We watch these barges go by, practically sinking under their filthy wealth. And we just let them pass! That's not what I came up here for."

Norbal said, "Don't bother stealing anything for me, Yaysal. Trading's good enough for me. I have what I need."

The carpenter grunted from his seat nearby. "Same here. Good tools, plenty of wood. No soldiers or officials breathing down my neck. Sit back down, Yaysal."

"I say no!" Yaysal strode to the pile of weapons leaning on the rock wall and seized his sword belt. He drew his blade and waved it in the air. "I'm sick to death of caution and excuses! Do we let a sick man lead us into weakness? This time I'm going to tell you *my* plan."

Across from Kiran, Calef started up from his seat but Norbal clapped a hand on his arm.

"This is how it starts," Yaysal said. "You loyalists go to the Pomel barge, scout it out like he said. Make a little noise to keep the soldiers on their toes. But keep out of sight. And the rest of us slip down to Pomel itself. Bring 'em some goats and some berries, whatever else you like. Morning comes and five of us knock on their gates like usual and tell 'em there's time to trade before the barge comes. Get 'em to let us in, trade and drink and have contests all day long." He turned to Kiran. "You can earn your keep, come along and play that flute of yours for 'em."

Kiran waited, his stomach clenched.

One of the men said, "I don't get it. What's different, besides the partying?"

Yaysal grinned again. "Night comes, we seem to be falling down drunk, we fall asleep in the lanes. But as soon as their torches are out, I whistle and we leap up. Kill a sentry or two and throw open the gates. Then all the others waiting in the woods come pouring in and we sack the town."

There was a shocked silence, except among Yaysal's close companions, who turned their heads, scanning their companions' faces for their reactions.

Norbal stood. "You're crazy, Yaysal. Pomel has our sworn protection."

Yaysal curled his lip. "Not my sworn protection. Not yours. Only Corbin's. And he's out of the picture now."

Beside Kiran, Calef slipped his legs free of the bench and crouched in the shadow of Norbal. *He's going to run and warn our father.*

Yaysal leaned forward, his hands braced on the table. He lowered his voice. "Think of it, men. Women. Hard cider. Fat cows and snufflers to drive over the mountains."

The blacksmith thumped his fist down on the table, making his plate jump. "No. It's mutiny."

A few men, scattered around the tables, stamped their feet and banged their mugs on the table. "Women! Cows! Hard cider!" Kiran recognized the chanters as Yaysal's friends. The men beside them shuffled uneasily.

In the confusion, Calef made a dash for the granite stair. But one of Yaysal's companions, sword in hand, lunged out of the shadows. His sword slashed across the entry to the stairway; he advanced on Calef, sword tip tickling the boy's belly.

Tense silence fell.

Kiran stirred to make a stand beside his brother but Norbal's hand, surprisingly strong, gripped his shoulder. Norbal stood.

"I'd like to speak," he croaked.

Heads turned toward him as he fell into a fit of coughing. His chest heaved and saliva dribbled down his chin.

Finally, he wiped his mouth with the back of his hand and Kiran thought he saw a glint of teeth. A grin. Norbal was playing for time.

"I don't get it," he gasped at last. "We go in there, slaughter a bunch of soldiers, haul away some female mouths to feed and supplies for just one winter. Then what? What about next year, when we have no place to trade?"

Yaysal scowled. "I wouldn't harp on useless mouths to feed if I were you."

Norbal shrugged and smiled.

"Norbal, you think too small." Yaysal swung around, glaring at all of them, his hand on his sword. "All of you think too small. Sickly leaders are making women of you! This is what we get out of it, Norbal the Puny.

"In the chaos after we burn the town, we destroy the barges with axes and fire. We cut off all commerce between the capital and the outposts. That way we show our strength and attract new recruits. New outlaws come swarming to the mountains. In two years' time, maybe less, we bring the kingdom to its knees.

"Then all the injustices we've suffered will be redressed. You men who lost your farms can hang the landlords and reclaim your homes. You who fled the law courts can see your wives and children. You young men who left the army can claim your sweethearts. You can put to the sword all those who lorded it over you."

His voice boomed across the tables. The men leaned forward, shifting their shoulders, a hungry look in their eyes. One of the men beside Kiran began banging his cup on the table. Those seated nearby took up the rhythm, thumping their cups down hard and stomping their feet. Voices rumbled under the clatter, building like a wave rolling in toward shore. Men jumped to their feet. "Yaysal! Yaysal!" one of them shouted and the rest took up the name.

Bulo prodded Kiran's ribs and pointed. At the top of the narrow steps above the dining area, Kiran's father leaned on his walking stick. He stood waiting, a slight, dark figure, while the men below poked and hushed each other. Then, with halting gait, he began to descend.

Chapter 15

One hand on the wall, the other planting his stick on each stone step, Corbin labored down the stairs. All around Kiran, the men broke off their shouting to watch. The swordsman at the bottom of the stairs turned toward him, his blade glinting. Kiran's breath caught in his throat. What was his father going to do? He had no weapon. Would he challenge Yaysal? Make the men take sides?

Halfway down, Corbin paused and leaned back against the wall. "Friends, continue with your meals." He waved his stick at them, grinning. "Don't worry, all looks aside, I'm not going to tumble down these stairs. Go on with your dinner."

The men who had left their food half eaten in their cheering for Yaysal now looked back and forth from Corbin to their plates. Some scratching their heads, some letting their mouths hang open, they picked up their spoons.

Except for Yaysal. He strode to the bottom of the stairs and drew his sword to stand shoulder to shoulder with his companion. Shoulders squared, he threw back his head and thrust out his chin as if looks alone could drive Corbin back to his cave. "We've made a decision, Corbin. We've had enough. Tonight we set out to raid Pomel and you can just stay out of the way."

"I heard something about that," Corbin said, smiling down at him, as if approving the cleverness of a favorite child. He swung around to survey the seated men. "Let's talk about the plan." He limped down the remaining stairs as if he couldn't see the two swords pointing at him. Kiran took in a sharp breath. But at the bottom of the stair, his father just brushed the swords aside as if he were walking between pine branches. Yaysal and his companion let the swords fall to their sides.

They can't touch him. He wears his bravery like armor.

Corbin circled around to lean on the end of the first table, where he could sweep his gaze over both sides, looking each man in the face. "In the towns and villages," he said in his rich singer's voice, "people tell stories about vicious bandits in these mountains. They demand that the army march up here and exterminate us. Now it sounds like some of you have fallen for the talk. You've convinced yourselves you're vicious bandits."

He picked up his stick and hobbled the length of the tables, nodding to each man. "Why don't the king's men come after us? Because they have better things to do. Enemies on the southern border, spies and smugglers in the coastside towns. And they know the bandit stories are untrue. Oh, they lose a few supplies but nothing serious. And they know we take a lot of troublemakers off their hands."

He indicated a couple of the men, who flushed as their neighbors laughed and poked them. "We take in deserters, debtors, rabble-rousers, runaway husbands and young folk whose parents won't let them marry. We help a lot of problems disappear. Think about it: mysterious bandits are cheaper for the kingdom than prisons and a lot less trouble than malcontents. As long as we don't threaten their livelihood or their power, as long as they hear nothing about us but rumors, they leave us alone."

He completed his circuit of the tables, nodded to Yaysal and stood again at the table head. He dropped his voice still lower. "But make no mistake, my friends. Sack a town, kidnap women, kill soldiers, burn barges, and the army will mass at the forks and swarm up the mountain after us."

Yaysal took two steps and stuck his face right up next to Corbin's. "Just let them!"

Corbin gazed back at him without flinching or drawing back. With an oath, Yaysal twisted away from his gaze and climbed onto the table, his heavy boots kicking tankards and dishes aside. "What's to be so afraid of? Who can threaten us here in this castle? We have food and weapons. We command the heights. We'll slaughter them by the tens and hundreds!"

"Maybe so," Corbin said quietly from behind him. He took a step to the side so he could better see past Yaysal to the men at the tables. "Let's think it out. If we kill a hundred soldiers, what do we gain? A hundred dead bodies to pollute our mountain? Their weapons? We already have plenty of weapons. What else do you men want? You've built yourselves homes in the valley. You have your own farms and herds. Some of you have wives and children there. No taxes, no army service, no overlords."

He began once more to circle the line of tables and the men swiveled in their seats to watch him. "True, we lack some things. Weavers. Spices. Priests to run the sky ceremonies." He paused behind Kiran. "Music." He rested a hand on Kiran's shoulder and Kiran felt a thrill run all the way down his arm.

"But two years ago we lacked more. Why are we richer now? Because every year more runaways find their way west over the mountains and our scouting parties meet and guide them. Every year our lives get better and our need for thieving decreases. Look how much we've gained by not murdering and raping."

The men shuffled their feet, fidgeted, murmured to each other. The ones at Kiran's table nodded and shrugged.

Yaysal gaped at them. Then he raised his hands to get their attention. But the blacksmith stood up and held a hand out to him. "Come on down off of there, Yaysal. You're messing up the food."

Yaysal glanced around. On all sides, men shook their heads at him or averted their eyes.

Corbin waited while he climbed down and then leaned on his stick and spoke again.

"Lying up there in my little cave, I've been thinking, friends." He took a breath and let it out slowly, taking time again to look each man in the eye. Kiran met his father's burning gaze. For a brief moment, it probed him—and then it moved on.

"Calef tells me the goats are fat already," Corbin said. "Another week and we can harvest the mountain berries. I know summer in the mountains is cool and pleasant and free of bugs but I propose we leave early this year."

A stir of disapproval rippled around the tables. Voices near Kiran grumbled. "Why should we run away? This is our place. The hell with the army!"

Norbal elbowed Kiran and winked. He shoveled a huge forkful of food into his mouth, stood, and coughed as hard as he could, spewing his food across the table. When men turned to him in disgust, he wiped his mouth and said, "You know what I miss? I miss those fat fish down in the valley stream." He rubbed his belly and licked his lips. The men around him laughed.

At another table a short man rose to join in. "I miss my wife's juicy kisses and her big fat—" His neighbor jabbed him before he could say more and pointed at Calef. The man flushed and sat down.

But now more men jumped up to say what they missed and why now was the time to leave the stone castle and head for home. Kiran looked around in amazement. Half a meal ago, these same men had been crying out for a bloody attack on Pomel. Now they were cheering a plan to retreat to the valley.

Corbin leaned on the end of the table, watching. Then he spoke again. "The army will swarm up here, seeking the Shelonwe who attacked last month's barge. To keep our castle secret, we should leave no sign that we've been here at all. It will take careful planning. I'd like to meet in the cave with my captains. Victor?"

The blacksmith stood.

"Yaysal?" The rebellious bandit hesitated, then nodded, a look of confusion on his face.

"And Bersin." A bald man with a bull neck pushed himself to his feet.

"Calef, you, too, come give me a hand up the steps."

★ ★ ★

"He's a master," Bulo said, back in their room. "He had them in the palm of his hand. Did you see them after? Every man with a brighter eye."

Kiran felt his father's grip on his shoulder. "Yes." For a moment his dreams had all fit together—music, courage, honor. "That's more how he used to be."

Calef came scampering in. "He sent us all out except Yaysal."

Bulo asked, "When do we start?"

The "we" resounded in Kiran's ears. Bulo wanted to throw in his lot with the outlaws.

Calef jumped up and down. "Tomorrow! We start packing tomorrow. I have to take down the log bridge and we have to brush out the paths and plant bushes to hide them and take apart the furniture and knock down the doors, and—"

"Sounds like you're not coming back."

"We're not going to be bandits at all any more. We'll send a team for the berries and lookouts to help the runaways, that's all. Oh, and traders." He turned to his brother. "We're going to have our own country, our own whole secret country. And no king!"

"No king, eh?" Bulo said. "Your father won't take that on? I bet that Yaysal would like to be king. King Yaysal the First."

Calef shook his head. "Father won't let him. He'll—" A shadow crossed his face. "Unless his leg goes bad again. He changes when his leg goes bad. The poison goes through him and he gets all dark and hopeless—and then I don't know what will happen."

Bulo said, "I guess I'll just have to come along and be his bodyguard. His farmer bodyguard." He laughed, a sound like sunlight falling through leaves.

"And Kiran, he says you can be our musician. He says a new country needs music. You can teach me to play, too."

Kiran felt a thrill of excitement run down his arms. His fingers tingled. Instead of studying in the temple caverns of Catora he could play in the pastures of a new village, a new country. Instead of tracing the painted stars of a cavern ceiling, he could lie out at night as the real Sky Serpent shivered and sparkled overhead.

But there was Dara. And Myra.

Bulo was watching him closely. He said, "I haven't forgotten, Kiran. I'll come with you to the Savages, the Shelonwe. All this about a new country, that's just a dream."

Kiran looked at his feet. "No, Bulo, you should go be a farmer. Hey, you should leave right now. You and Norbal, it'll take you forever to walk there." He took a deep breath. "Me, I'll talk to my father."

Chapter 16

In the watery light of first morning, Kiran climbed the stairs to his father's den. This time the room smelled clean. Corbin sat up in his cot, with one leg thrust out in front of him, so much like Bulo that Kiran's confidence grew. Calef already crouched at the foot of the bed, chattering, and Corbin was smiling.

When he saw Kiran, Corbin held up a hand to silence Calef. Grabbing hold of the stick that lay beside his cot, he stood.

Kiran advanced. His tongue was thick and clumsy, and he didn't know what to say. Halfway across the room, he stopped and bent his gaze to the floor. "Father."

His father labored forward to meet him.

Kiran forced himself to look upward into the weathered face and probing eyes.

"I've come to ask your help. My sister Dara was taken by Savages and I want to take her back."

Corbin's eyes flashed. "First of all, they are the Shelonwe, and no more savage than those who slaughter and enslave them. Second, what do I care for Dara? She is no kin of mine."

Kiran's heart sank.

His father reached out and touched his shoulder. "Better you should come with us and make your home in a new place."

Kiran remembered Lir holding his shoulder, too. He looked away. His stepfather's voice seemed to say to him, "Save my daughter." His father's said, "Forget her, come away. Come away and have a home at last."

He closed his eyes, wavering. The dark water boiled below him.

He took a breath and met his father's gaze. "No. I will follow the path you took nine years ago and enter the Savage—the Shelonwe village. Won't you send some men to help me? It's not just Dara. There was another girl, my age, brave enough to attack the—the man who took my sister."

Corbin peered at him. For a moment Kiran thought he saw respect flicker in his father's eyes. But then the bandit chief shook his head and limped back to his cot. "We're at peace with the Shelonwe. We don't interfere with their affairs, nor they with ours."

"Just a show of force, a bargaining party."

Again his father shook his head. "Kiran, you've seen the men. They're on edge. One muttered insult, one hand falling on a weapon and there will be slaughter. I won't allow it."

Kiran spoke bitterly. "So you'll let me walk in there alone."

Calef leaped to his feet. "Let me go with him, Father! Just to show him the way and talk to the Shelonwe."

Corbin turned to study him while Calef bounced on his toes.

"How much of their language do you remember, son?"

Calef danced around him, pleading with such an outpouring of words in the Shelonwe language that at last his father smiled and touched his mouth to quiet him. When he spoke, it was only to Calef.

"Don't stay the night in the village or they might claim you back as one of them. You may not lift your hand against any one of them, or your life or freedom will be forfeit. Do you understand?"

Calef nodded.

"Warn your brother that the Shelonwe will charge dearly for what they have taken. And if by chance he frees the captives through any ruse or act of war, he's not to lead the Shelonwe back here to vent their rage."

"Yes, Father."

"And Calef, I expect you back in three days."

Kiran listened, anger and bewilderment churning inside him. Here was his baby brother offering to help while his father, with all his power, his men and weapons, refused.

Corbin turned back in his direction. "Kiran, you go to do a man's task but you will not find yourself greeted like a man. Even if you succeed, you may find no gratitude or welcome, no home you can return to." He hesitated, as if he meant to say more; instead, he thrust out his hand.

Kiran looked down at his father's hand, resentment seething within him. *Yesterday you looked like someone I could follow. Now you might as well curse me as expect me to take your hand.*

He turned on his heel and as he left the cavern, he heard Calef scampering to follow.

★ ★ ★

Bulo implored them to let him come along, hefting the pack he had prepared, showing them his strength. "Look, Kiran, I ran from my post to rescue two children. If you two kids go off alone, that makes me twice a deserter."

Kiran's anger spilled over to engulf Bulo, too. "Then you should have kept your balance. You're no use to me with that leg. You're too slow and Calef has to be back in three days. We're going alone."

The Beechwood Flute

* * *

Before first light, before Bulo could catch them with one more argument or come swinging after them on his heavy crutches, Kiran and Calef slipped out of camp. Calef darted through the forest, sometimes chattering and sometimes gliding forward silently. Once in a while he dropped abruptly to sit in exhaustion against a fallen log. But just as Kiran paused beside him, lowering his pack, Calef jumped up again, ready to move on.

He asked about Myra and Dara. "Dara is like you, a little bird twittering all the time," Kiran told him. "She likes to make houses for her dolls in the grass. Myra has a long face like—" He stuck out his chin.

Calef laughed. "Is she your twin?"

"What do you mean? She's not even my sister."

"Well, of course not." Calef looked puzzled for a moment, then struck his head with the palm of his hand. "Oh, I remember. Father told me: Lanath people don't have twins."

Then he explained. "With the Shelonwe, every boy or girl gets assigned a twin, a *filoni*, as soon as possible after they're born. A boy gets a girl and a girl gets a boy. Then they grow up together. They learn to do everything together, fishing, hunting, mending, cooking, taking care of babies, all the time until the girl is old enough to have babies of her own. Then she leaves for the women's house and learns how to run everything and lead the village. The boy is left to do his hunting and fighting all alone. After three years the girl chooses. She can choose her old twin as her husband and then he has to marry her, but if she doesn't want him, she can choose someone else, if he's still free. Some girls never marry but they can still become leaders of the whole village."

"That's crazy," Kiran said. "Women running everything? With us, women stay home and do the work and if they lose their husbands, they lose everything." He thought of Myra's mother, Nora, poor and hardworking, living at the back of the village near the seffidge quarters.

"A boy who lived in the Shelonwe village died of a fever when I lived there." Calef looked wistful. "Then his twin's mother chose me to be her daughter's new *filoni*. For a year we fished and fought and slept together. I feel sad when I think about her. After I left she had to find a new twin all over again, maybe a brand-new baby."

"So you didn't live as a slave?"

"I lived as a Shelonwe. I am a boy of three people: Lanath, which I don't remember; the Shelonwe, who are shadows in my memory but speak in my dreams; and my father's people, the free people beyond the mountains."

"And Father?" asked Kiran with sudden anger. "Did he live so well, too? As a Shelonwe, not a slave? Is that why he stayed so long? Did some woman choose him to be her twin or husband?"

Calef looked at him sideways. "Were you also struck with a poison spear, Kiran?"

"What are you talking about?"

"You're so angry. If a Shelonwe boy doesn't learn to think before anger, his twin won't choose him and neither will any other girl. Then he'll be only a warrior and never have a real home. Our father was a slave. But even so, he was calm like the Shelonwe, until we went to Lanath and the poison got him."

He has passed that poison on to me, thought Kiran. He said, "While our father was away, our mother thought he was dead, so she chose another man, a rich man who loved her. And that, I think, is the poison that turned our father." A wave of longing washed over him. If only his mother had known, had waited.

Calef shook his head at the mysterious ways of grownups. "You should tell the Shelonwe that Myra is your *filoni*. Then they'll understand why you came."

★ ★ ★

That night they ate dried fish and berries by the winking fire. After they washed their hands in the stream, Calef asked for music and Kiran played some of the first folk songs he had learned, children's songs, without embellishment. Calef had told him they would reach the Shelonwe village by noon the next day and his mind filled with images of childhood and home—the Harvest festival, snufflers digging for potatoes in the field, small boys chasing crows away, himself standing in the temple, blowing notes while Ser Vetel tapped out the time.

In late morning, they came to the edge of a leafy, sun-dappled clearing and Calef signaled a halt. "We're close now. You wait here while I go before you to talk. Oh, Kiran, I hope they'll just let the girls go and then you can come home and stay with us. I think that's what will happen. But don't let them find you before I come. Stay quiet."

Before Kiran could ask how long he would be, Calef slipped across the clearing and disappeared into the woods beyond.

Chapter 17

Kiran waited in the rustling forest. Sunlight sprinkled through the trees. At this time of year the villagers would be shearing the sheep in Lanath, seffidges holding the animals down, boys gathering the greasy, soft wool as it fell. He thought of the breeze rustling through the half grown corn and the smell of bread fresh from the oven. Ahead of him lay the dark unknown of the Shelonwe village. He trembled with a sudden wish to leap up and run for home. Instead, to steady himself, he crouched and placed the palm of his good hand flat against the forest floor.

At last Calef appeared, bright-haired and quick, calling to him as he crossed the clearing. "Come on, Kiran, you can enter the village. I told them you're Dara's brother and Myra's *filoni*. You'll get to meet Labwa-onwe, the chief. She's calling the men who stole the girls. Leave your weapons behind."

Kiran stowed everything among the bushes but the cedar flute, which he kept stuck through his belt. With hesitant steps, he followed his brother. In a thousand paces, they topped a rise and descended into a village of long low houses built of woven branches. Tall, dappled people dressed in skins gazed at them as they passed and a pack of small children scampered after them.

A man, erect and haughty, waited for them outside the door of one of the buildings. He shooed the children away and lifted a flap of deerskin at the doorway to let them enter.

Light fell through the woven branches of the walls, making a diamond pattern on the floor. On a shelf at the back of the room sat a wrinkled, gray-haired woman flanked by two women closer to the age of Kiran's mother. Two young men, each with one half of his head shaved, stood against the walls. Their faces bore the fierce, hungry look he had seen in the shadowy figures that night on the barge.

The elderly woman spoke and Calef turned to Kiran. He gestured to one of the two men. "That one is Gulik-onwe, who owns the girls. Labwa-onwe asks if you know the other one."

The second man stepped forward. His skin was a burnished red and brown, his nose sharp and his eyes glinting green. He gave Kiran a disdainful smile.

Kiran saw in his mind's eye the sharp face of the Savage handing seffidges over the side. "I saw him on the barge."

"She says before that."

Kiran shook his head. "I never saw any Savages before that."

The man let out a sharp laugh and spoke in Kiran's own language. "I was the seffidge Set, who ran away."

Kiran looked at him in disbelief. He had heard of the seffidge who went mad three summers ago and fled into the forest. The soldiers sent to chase after him returned a day later, saying they had found his body torn and half devoured by wild animals. Kiran even vaguely remembered who it was, the seffidge called Set, who worked in the nuath groves. Lir valued him because he was sure-footed high in the branches, though on the ground he was surly and slow.

This could not be the same man. Set was a seffidge, squat, stupid, stinking, his skin a mottled grayish brown. This was a man, proud and quick. Kiran found himself shaking his head.

The man rocked back on his heels and looked down his nose at Kiran. "Now I am Setolo-onwe of the Shelonwe and I have taken the task of freeing my people, those you call seffidges."

What was he talking about? "Freeing them?" Kiran scoffed. "You mean stealing them from those who give them food and labor!"

The man who called himself Setolo stepped to the door and lifted the flap. Six men filed in and lined against the wall to stare at Kiran. They were muscular, straight, their skin brown. Their hair was cut ragged and short. Their fierce green eyes flashed at Kiran, then slid away, then returned again. Peering at them in the half light, Kiran saw traces—a scar on this one's shoulder, a bald patch on the side of that one's head. The knowledge sank into him that these proud men were the same skulking seffidges stolen only a month ago from the barge.

It didn't make sense. Everyone knew that seffidges were degraded men, unable to live on their own, fit only for labor. Seffidges crouched and cringed, held themselves low and never looked a real person in the eye. He couldn't understand it. Was it the air of the mountains that had somehow transformed them?

The chief said a few words and the six stolen Shelonwe nodded and filed out. When she spoke again, Calef translated for Kiran.

"Labwa-onwe says that your twin and your little sister are captives of Gulik-onwe, a man without a wife. He tells her he won't give them up."

The man standing next to Setolo stepped forth from the shadows. Two scars slashed down his right cheek. At the sight, Kiran felt the claw marks on his own cheek burn. He remembered what Calef had told him about the angriest men not being chosen as husbands. Gulik stood with a look on his face so sullen and dark that Kiran shuddered to think how he might be treating his captives.

Now Setolo spoke and so did the women standing to either side of Labwa-onwe. Gulik argued, his hands flailing. Calef, watching, translated in a low voice to Kiran.

"The woman on the left argues that it is wrong to keep slaves. Shelonwe only make someone a slave who has committed a crime, like murder. The woman argues that the girls are not criminals. But the others say they are criminals because they live off the labor of slaves so they do not deserve to be free. And Gulik says he fought for them and stole them, so they are his."

Setolo spoke again and though Gulik argued bitterly, Labwa finally seemed to take Setolo's side. Gulik took a step back and let his head fall forward in a gesture of submission. Labwa nodded at Calef, encouraging him to speak.

"Setolo says the Shelonwe will give the girls back and set you free in return for all the seffidges of Lanath. Oh, Kiran, this is the right answer! You won't have to be a slave like our father and all the people can live in their own places!"

Kiran tried to picture it. He imagined an exchange ceremony, with villagers cheering and music playing in the background, at the border where Lanath touched the forest. He saw himself walking toward the village with Myra and Dara at his side, while in the other direction came the file of seffidges, blinking and bewildered, their heads turning from side to side, their arms swinging low to the ground.

But with no seffidges left in the village, who would climb high into the treacherous beech trees to gather the nuath along rotting branches that could crack at any moment? Who would haul heavy logs for the houses, row the barges, dig latrines, labor in the pits where the nuath was stored until it was ready? None of that was work for real men. And in Lanath, harvesting the nuath came first, before all else. Without the holy fungus, the kingdom would have no wisdom to guide it. And without seffidges, the nuath harvest would surely fail.

A desolate certainty settled at the depths of Kiran's stomach. The councilmen of Lanath would never agree to give up their seffidges.

But he didn't have to tell the Savages that. He could try to deceive them long enough to win freedom for the girls. He told Calef, "Tell them to let me take the girls to Lanath. Once I get there, I'll send the seffidges out."

Calef's eyes widened and Kiran realized that even his own brother didn't believe him. Still, Calef relayed the message, his voice earnest and pleading. The woman chief answered in a slow deliberate cadence and Calef turned back to his brother. "Labwa-onwe says Setolo and I must go to Lanath while you stay here. I'll talk to the villagers and when we bring the seffidges back, the Shelonwe will free you."

Kiran shook his head. "Lanath will never believe you. They'll chase you off, maybe even shoot you." He swallowed. "Besides, you promised to go back to our father."

"Let me try, Kiran."

"It's no use."

Calef protested, but the former seffidge Setolo was already relaying Kiran's answer. There followed a long discussion, with Gulik gesturing sharply and Setolo arguing in even, measured tones until finally Labwa directed Calef to speak to Kiran again.

Tears shone in Calef's eyes. "This is what Labwa-onwe says. You may work for the freedom of your twin and your sister. For your twin, one year. For your sister, one year for every year of her age. Six years."

Kiran's stomach turned, and his knees felt unsteady. "It's too long!"

Labwa-onwe spoke again. Gulik scowled and objected, and Setolo backed away from her, shaking his head, but she was firm. For a moment Kiran hoped that his sentence would be shortened.

"Labwa-onwe says the attackers on the barge were never supposed to capture slaves, only to free Shelonwe people. Setolo led the raid and Gulik disobeyed him. And Gulik treats the girls badly. So Labwa-onwe gives the girls now to Setolo, who does not want them. I think he'll be a kind master. You are to go to Gulik to replace them. He will be your master until you walk away to freedom. Labwa-onwe says you may go now all alone or in one year with your twin or in seven years with both girls."

Kiran looked from face to face before him. Calef's face, his forehead wrinkled in concern. The steady, haughty gaze of Setolo. Labwa-onwe, waiting with her lower lip thrust out, and Gulik, sneering, his face contorted in anger.

Even as Kiran decided, despair pounded him and roared in his ears like the waters of the Serpent.

He said, "I accept. Seven years."

Chapter 18

Gulik stepped up to Kiran and struck him once across the face, hard. Then he shoved him out the door, cursing. The blow throbbed in Kiran's ears. *Seven years, seven years.* One moment he had stood before them as a man and in the next he had become a slave scuttling before his master's rage.

Calef ran alongside as Gulik shoved his captive forward. Tears streamed down Calef's face. "Let me go to Lanath, let me convince them!"

Kiran kept his head down. "It's no use. Go back and tell our father he has his way. Now I'll suffer as he did." Bitterness clenched his chest.

Gulik shoved him again and he fell to his hands and knees. The sky itself seemed to press him lower to the earth. Maybe his father had felt this same sense of sky and forest closing in, that day eight years ago. Only Corbin had had no Calef to translate for him, or to trot along weeping and pleading for some way to help.

Kiran pushed himself back to his feet and squared his shoulders, trying to pry open the fist of bitterness choking him. Even as Gulik pushed him again, he managed to change his tone for Calef's sake.

"Go back, little brother. Your freedom has been bought already. Look how our father paid for it. Honor him. Go back."

Calef hesitated.

Kiran twisted around to see him. "Come again in a year for Myra."

Calef nodded, then abruptly turned and darted away.

★ ★ ★

That first day, Gulik set Kiran to weeding. He took him to a field five minutes' walk from the village on a south-facing hillside and swept his arm to indicate the whole field. He showed Kiran what plants he wanted him to pull up and then went to lie in the shade of a tree and watch. It was simple work, something the children of Lanath often helped with, and Kiran steadily set to, trying to make his mind stoic, focusing just on the patch of earth in front of him. Squash leaves lay green and healthy on the earth and he cleared around them.

After a while he grew thirsty and went to the stream for a drink but Gulik leaped up, cursed at him and drove him away. Kiran protested, touching his throat and letting his tongue hang out to show his thirst but Gulik punched him.

Thirst tormented him. In early afternoon, a passel of children came laughing down the slope to the field, bringing Gulik what smelled like meat and berries wrapped in leaves. One little girl ran to bring a packet to Kiran but Gulik's sharp order called her back. Gulik came to crouch near Kiran, eating noisily while the children splashed in the stream. Afterward the children carried buckets of water up to the field and poured it into the furrows, where it soaked quickly into the ground. Kiran reached pleadingly toward the little girl who had tried to feed him and with a quick apprehensive look over her shoulder, she emptied her bucket's contents over his cupped hands. He buried his face in his hands, slurping greedily.

In the late afternoon, Gulik stretched, grimaced and summoned Kiran to follow him into the forest, where he pointed to a fallen branch. He made Kiran drag it back to a fire pit in the village and then showed him the fingers of both hands. He wanted ten more branches but Kiran, hungry and exhausted, decided to pretend he hadn't understood. He turned away and as he did so, he remembered how seffidges in the beech grove did that sometimes, how they grew suddenly deaf when Lir ordered them up a tree riddled with fungus and how Lir raged at their stupidity.

Gulik didn't fall for it either. Snarling like a wolf, Gulik jumped at him, knocking him to the ground. With his fingers buried in Kiran's hair, he ground his slave's face into the dirt and then leaped up and kicked him in the ribs. Kiran tried to roll out of reach but Gulik yanked him up again by the hair and, with a curse, pushed him back toward the woods.

Leaves shivered in the breeze overhead as Kiran lurched among the trees in the fading light, clutching his side, spitting out dirt. More repulsive in his mouth than any dirt was the humiliation he couldn't spit away.

The afternoon light was fading, and when he rested a hand against a tree trunk to look back, the Shelonwe village was already out of sight. He could flee right now. Less than one day gone and he knew he could never last as Gulik's slave.

He'd made his choice that morning blindly, eyes closed, believing that the choice would be like diving off the railing, a one-time plunge, with no going back. But now he saw stretching ahead of him an ugly road with too many forks to count, all through seven long years. How many times could he choose to remain a slave? And as soon as he chose otherwise, as soon as he veered aside, the deal would be off and Dara would never be free.

The tree bark was rough beneath his hand. This moment, right now, was all he could vouch for. Temptation to quit might come every day. But at least for today he'd fight it off. He ground his teeth, grabbed a huge bough and bent his back to haul it to the village.

By the time he dragged in the tenth branch, Gulik was singing a wild song and waving a joint of meat in the air. Seeing Kiran, he reached with a stick into a pot on the fire and fished out a mass of boiled entrails, which he flung at Kiran's feet. Two of Gulik's dogs leaped for it at the same time that Kiran bent to scoop it up. All three of them yelped in pain from the heat of the food and scuttled backward into the shadow. Kiran tossed a length of intestine from hand to hand until it cooled enough to eat, then wolfed it down and ended by licking grease off his burned hands.

After the meal, as Kiran crouched in the shadows, keeping his head low but watching the villagers pass back and forth from the cookfires to their houses, Gulik came for him. He yanked the flute from Kiran's belt—Kiran had forgotten it was there—and examined it, then handed it to Kiran and jerked his chin, barking an order.

Kiran lifted the flute to his lips. His mouth was dry, and he had never felt less like playing. He blew a long, breathy note and let the flute fall, but Gulik muttered and shook his fingers at him. For some reason, he wanted more. What could pacify a Savage? Kiran chose a song that children sang at the winter festival when they were begging their mothers for cakes. Gulik nodded in time to the music, grinning.

When the song was over, Gulik took the flute out of his hands and pushed it back through Kiran's belt with a satisfied nod. *He figures he owns that, too,* Kiran decided, and the thought made him feel sick, as if he had done something shameful.

Before Kiran could withdraw into the shadows, Gulik grabbed him, turned him around and wrenched his good arm behind his back. He tied Kiran's wrist to the elbow of his casted arm. Then he pushed his slave to a kind of low shed that stood behind one of the long houses. Gulik opened the door and shoved Kiran into the squawking and stench of a pen for the village fowl. Turkeys flapped up gobbling around Kiran as the door swung shut behind him. Stooping under the low roof, he lumbered toward a corner, where he sank painfully against the wall, his body heavy with gloom.

Something scuffled in the far corner and a voice that seemed to be trying for firmness spoke out. "Who is it?"

"Myra?"

Then Dara's voice. "I told you that was him playing, I see him, it's Kiran!" Dara's small body flung itself toward him. She threw her arms around his neck and pressed her cheek against his. With his bound arms, he couldn't embrace her, but the soft roundness of her cheek made him glad he'd come. In the faint slivers of firelight that found their way through spaces in the brush walls, he saw Myra's shape move closer, too.

"I thought everyone had forgotten us," she said. "But Dara kept saying she saw you on the barge. She said you would come and save us." And suddenly she, too, flung herself down next to Kiran and buried her face against his shoulder, weeping.

He hesitated, unable even to pat their shoulders, not knowing what to tell them. Wisps of Dara's hair brushed across his face and he tried to blow them away. "I can't save you," he said at last. "I came alone and I can't save you, not right away. But at least I came."

"You've saved us already," Myra said in a choked voice. "You don't know. They told me my twin, my *filoni*, had come. And then a woman named Ranga, Setolo's wife, came to where we were working and said she would be our master now and no one would beat us or bother me the way Gulik did."

"Bother you?" Kiran asked uneasily, not wanting to hear.

Even in the darkness he could tell Myra had turned her face away. "That first night, where they left the canoes, he threw me on the ground and attacked me, but his brother Setolo stopped him. He said it's against their laws." She reached to pull Dara away from Kiran, onto her lap. She sat smoothing the younger girl's hair, speaking softly over her head. Her voice trembled. "So now all he does is paw at me, slobber on me. His horrible breath! And each time I pushed him away, he cursed and said he would make me his wife or else work me to death, it was my choice."

Kiran's fists clenched behind him. A sour taste rose in his throat. He said, "And you chose what?"

She took a sharp breath, reached awkwardly past Dara to slap him and burst into tears. The slap cut across the bruise already rising from Gulik's blow. The sharpness of it jolted him so that he heard the echo of his own words and felt ashamed.

Between sobs she said, "We worked, didn't we, Dara?"

Dara twisted around in Myra's arms and nodded gravely at Kiran.

Myra said, "Sometimes Ranga came and told Gulik not to work us so hard. At least I think that's what she said. And today we just took care of some babies and a sick woman and it wasn't bad at all, was it, Dara?" She rocked Dara against her.

"Sorry," Kiran said. "I'm sorry, Myra, forgive me. I wish I could kill him for you." His voice sounded hoarse and weak in his own ears. He wondered sickly how Gulik would take out his resentment against his new slave.

Dara slipped out of Myra's embrace and came to kneel in front of him, stroking his bruised cheek with her cool fingers. "They have fat babies here and Ranga is nice but when are we going home?"

★ ★ ★

Once Dara had fallen asleep and Myra had laid her gently on the ground and bunched the pine branches and cut bracken on the floor around her to keep her warm, Kiran told Myra everything. He wanted to make up for his own clumsy questions and in the darkness he found himself telling her even the parts that in daylight would make him duck his head in shame: his hesitation on the railing, Ser Vetel's betrayal, Bulo's fall, his father's oozing leg wound and bitter words. "In a year you'll be free," he told her. "You only have to hold out for a year."

As he finished, he became aware again of the ache in his shoulders and the sound of a few voices still talking out by the fire. Above them, the Shelonwes' fowl fluttered in their sleep and the stench from their manure hung thick in the air.

"A year," Myra said. There was a giddiness in her voice, a lightness of relief. She stood up and twirled around. "I can stand a year, because I know it will end. And because I'm away from Gulik. If he couldn't make me his wife, he wanted to make us his beasts." She dropped onto her knees in front of Kiran and leaned to look into his eyes. "He wanted us to beg for food. Me, beg!"

The indignation in her voice would have made him smile, except for the worry swirling in his head. What would Gulik do to try and make Kiran beg? He felt as if the three of them were sliding into a whirlpool. Myra would be spit out on shore and Dara would follow but he would spin deeper and deeper into darkness.

"And as soon as I'm out," Myra continued in her decided way, "I'll figure out how to get you and Dara free, too."

Oh, she thought it was so easy, did she? The negotiations just needed her clever touch? With a snort of anger Kiran turned away while she said, "What? What is it?"

When he didn't answer, she pulled the flute from his belt. He had forgotten it was even there but as he turned in protest, she lifted it to her lips and tried to blow into it. He started forward to stop her but his arms were still bound behind him. Of course she didn't know how to do it and she could get no sound beyond a puff of air.

He glared at her and she let the flute fall into her lap. "Why shouldn't a girl try?" she demanded. "Why should making music be only for priests?"

He shook his head at her. "Why not do something useful and untie my arms?"

She stuck out her chin and pushed the flute through the woven branches of the wall. He turned and tried to shift his shoulders to give her some slack to work with as she tugged at the cord behind him. How could she be taking so long? The camp sounds were quiet now and the chinks of firelight had disappeared.

"I can't get it," she said at last. "The knot's too tight. I wish I had a knife."

Kiran thought of his pack, stowed behind a bush at the edge of the clearing where he had waited for Calef. Inside it was a knife, food, fishing line. If they got out now, they could find it and Myra could cut him free. Then they could light out through the woods to freedom.

With a grunt he shook Myra off, got to his feet and stepped over to the door. He set his good shoulder against it. Something was holding it from outside but surely he could break down a door built to hold turkeys in.

"What are you doing? Kiran, don't!" Myra said, but he backed up and hurtled himself at the door. His shoulder crashed into the woven branches and the door bowed outward.

Immediately there broke out a cacophony of growls and barks just outside the pen, and paws scrabbled at the door from outside.

With a whimper, Myra threw her arms around the sleeping Dara. "It's Gulik's dogs. They sleep just outside and if they wake him up, he'll set them on us again."

"Again?"

"Last time that black one had me by the leg, trying to drag me off Dara so he could get at her. If Gulik's brother hadn't come—" She broke off.

"You were trying to escape?"

Even before she nodded, he knew that of course she would have tried to escape, being Myra and brave. He pictured one of those huge ragged dogs with Myra's leg clamped in its jaws as its companions lurked, slavering for their chance at Dara.

The hope that had momentarily leaped up in him slunk back to its hole and he came away from the door to hunch once more against the wall. He turned his head away and refused to answer Myra when she tried to talk to him again. Eventually, he heard her settle among the bracken and pine branches on the floor. From the scuffling sound she made, he imagined that she was shifting over to put her arms around the sleeping Dara. So she was taking on that duty, too, which should have been his—the duty of comforting his sister. The two girls lay enfolded together while he sat apart, slumped, with his arms tied behind him in the stinking pen.

Chapter 19

Weeding and carrying water were tasks Kiran could do with one hand; but more and more, as he dug new fields and lugged branches for Gulik's fire from deeper in the forest, he found himself using the hand of his splinted arm. Finally one morning Gulik took him to see Ranga, Setolo's wife. Plump and calm, short for a Shelonwe, she measured Kiran with her gaze before she took hold of his arm.

She cut the twine holding the halves of the wooden sleeve of his cast and bent the top half back. Watching Kiran's face, she prodded and tugged at the arm, and when he didn't flinch, she tossed the two halves of the sleeve aside. She unwrapped the cloth beneath it and for the first time in almost two moons he looked at his forearm, now shrunken and pale, with a new growth of faint wispy hairs. It looked like the arm of an old woman but it was straight enough. He turned it over, clenching and unclenching his hand.

Instead of letting him go, Ranga reached higher to probe his shoulder, which ached constantly from the way Gulik levered it back to tie him up at night. When he winced, she made a disapproving sound, a whistle between her tongue and the roof of her mouth. She spoke in a firm voice to Gulik, who seemed to argue with her before shrugging and jerking his chin at Kiran to summon him away.

That night, instead of tying Kiran's arms behind him, Gulik bound his wrists in front. But he tied his ankles, too, and when he shoved him into the pen, Kiran had to twist quickly to keep from falling on the injured arm.

"Can't you just untie me for the night?" he asked Myra for the hundredth time.

She shook her head. "He told Ranga he'd kill us both, you know that."

"He'll never know," Kiran said but he didn't press it. With his arms in front, he was able to lie on his back for the first good sleep of his captivity.

★ ★ ★

Other than sleep, his life without the cast was no easier. Now that he had the use of his arm, Gulik watched him more closely. He tied a loop of twine around Kiran's neck with a long trailing end that he yanked whenever he thought Kiran was loitering. If he had to leave him untended outside the turkey pen, he bound Kiran's hands and tied his neck rope to the branch of a tree.

As his arm grew stronger, Gulik gave him heavier work. Kiran chopped wood, moved rocks and wove houses for Gulik's neighbors. He dug new latrines for the village and filled in old ones. He lugged hundreds of buckets of water from the stream. Children who before had willingly carried water for their parents now tossed their buckets to him, pointing and grunting as if he were a beast who could understand no language. At mealtimes, nobody ever handed him food: they flung it in the dirt at his feet.

We never treated our seffidges so, he thought, each time he fished up a bit of food from the dirt. Though in truth, he had seldom seen seffidges eat. At midday in the forest or field, when the Lanath men stopped for lunch, the seffidges just dropped to the ground and slept. Kiran had assumed that seffidges, like snufflers and oxen, fed only twice a day. Seffidges weren't—in Lanath they didn't seem—fully human, no matter how they looked here in the high forest.

When he passed through the village during the day he sometimes caught a glimpse of Myra and Dara working outside the house that belonged to Setolo and Ranga. They cooked, made clothes, twined long fibrous plants into rope and knitted fishing nets. Even from the other end of the village Kiran sometimes heard the bubble of Dara's laughter or the sound of Myra's voice shaping itself to the Shelonwe language.

"They're not really savages," Myra said one night when Dara was already asleep. "You know, in their language 'onwe' means 'person.'"

Kiran lay on his back in the straw with his hands tied before him, keeping his eyes open by trying to get a glimpse of the stars through the woven branches of the roof. In his exhaustion it was hard for him to stay awake longer than Dara did but arguing with Myra was the only piece of his day that reminded him of who he was. He mocked her. "Their language! When they talk, it sounds like frogs choking on pebbles."

"You should learn their language, just the same. You should try and focus on something more than work."

He grunted. "Why are you always telling me what to do?"

Myra picked at the straw and didn't answer directly. "They think we're the savage ones, you know. They talk about how a hundred years ago the soldiers came and drove them out of the place we call Lanath. Our soldiers burned the houses and killed everyone they could reach, even children."

"That's not true!" Anger burst into Kiran's voice. "You believe everything they tell you just because Setolo's wife is nice to you. When our people first came to Lanath the Savages were dying from some sickness. Our priests helped them but then they stole into our houses and stuck knives in our people as they were sleeping. That's why we had to drive them out. They left the sick ones behind and we nursed them and healed them and gave them work. That's where the seffidges came from, as you would know if you'd listened to Ser Vetel's lessons."

"Because Ser Vetel is always truthful," Myra said.

Kiran ground his teeth in frustration.

"Setolo's mother was a chief," Myra said. "When he was a child there was a drought and the children didn't have any fruit. So his mother took her children with her to go trade with one of the barges on the river. They brought along plants they use for medicine and a lot of fish, and she and Setolo, who was five years old, paddled out to the upstream barge where it was moored by the Serpent. Do you know they call it the Serpent, too? Setolo says, 'We paddled out along the Serpent's back.'"

"So he even tells you little fables," Kiran said bitterly. "All I get is kicks and curses."

"Shut up and listen," Myra said. "When they got out to the barge, the soldiers helped Setolo and his mother come on board. She laid out the dried plants and tried to explain what they wanted but the priest took the plants and threw them overboard. Setolo's mother grew very angry and because she was used to being a chief, she stepped up to the priest and slapped him across the face. So the closest soldier stuck his sword in her stomach and killed her. Setolo screamed for help while the soldiers knocked him down and tied him up. The Shelonwe waiting on shore came out in their canoes to fight but the soldiers killed most of them or drove them away. And that's how Setolo came to be Set, the seffidge."

Kiran didn't say anything at first. He felt sick to his stomach. The story sounded true. Finally he said, "But they stole Calef."

"Yes. Years later. And now Gulik has stolen us, to show what a man he is. Gulik is Setolo's big brother, you know. He was seven years old and standing on shore the day we killed his mother. He tried to jump in a canoe with the warriors but the women held him back with the other children. When he knew his mother and brother were gone, he took up a knife and slashed his own cheek twice, for mourning. Ranga says he grew up twisted and angry and now nobody wants to be his wife. So he does brave deeds like stealing us to try and attract women. A lot of the village people are angry about that. Some of them think it pollutes the village to have us here because we're not really human."

Kiran's head whirled. "Is that what your Setolo thinks?"

"Setolo remembers my mother. She took care of him once when he had fever as a boy."

Kiran fell silent. Nora's soothing touch, the sympathy in her eyes—yes, they would make an impression on a frightened child.

"That's why he and Ranga try to be kind to me and Dara. We work but not like slaves. We work the way they do, like family members."

"People don't lock their family members in the turkey pen at night."

Myra stirred, started to say something and stopped.

"What?" Kiran demanded. "They don't make you sleep here?"

Myra turned her palms up. "They offered us a place in their house. But we said we wanted to stay with you, Kiran, to keep you from getting discouraged. They understood because they think you're my special person, my—"

"Twin."

"Yes, my *filoni*."

Kiran's face burned in the darkness. To think how often he resented her, bossy Myra with her easier life. And every night she made this choice. He said, in a low voice, "I can't believe you want to sleep in this stink."

She laughed. "They make us wash before we touch anything in the morning."

He sat up. "I mean, I know you don't have to do it. And I know I argue a lot and have a bad temper"—Myra gave an emphatic nod—"but you're right, I—I don't know what I'd do if I didn't see Dara every day, if I didn't have you to talk to."

She patted his shoulder and nodded again, looking satisfied. "So now you know why I tell you what to do. Shelonwe girls are supposed to make sure their twins grow up to be good men. I'm trying to make sure you turn out like Setolo, not like Gulik."

She wants me to turn out like a Savage, Kiran thought; but the old name sounded wrong in his head. *Like a Shelonwe*, he amended. Still, her words angered him. What was wrong with being like a man from Lanath? "What does that mean, to be like Setolo?"

"It's hard to explain. Brave enough for the long haul. Honorable. Not hating. Ranga taught me a Shelonwe saying: 'A good man makes things whole.'"

"Makes things whole? What's that supposed to mean?"

Myra yawned. "Sometimes I think it means one thing, sometimes another. Work it out yourself. And now, hush, Kiran, I want to get some sleep."

She turned over and her breathing grew quiet almost at once. But Kiran lay awake, thoughts chasing each other through his head. He tried to keep his mind on the history Ser Vetel had taught him and on how Myra couldn't possibly be right. But instead, the thought kept returning that in another nine and a half months Myra would be gone and he didn't know how he would carry on without her.

Chapter 20

As summer folded into fall, Gulik grew more violent and unpredictable. He had broken with tradition by approaching a Shelonwe girl about marriage, Myra told Kiran, and she had turned him down. At night Gulik sat by the fire and drank juniper wine from a deerskin pouch, singing loud songs and chanting poetry about a one-eyed wolf. Ranga came out from the house she shared with Setolo to try and hush him, bringing him something hot to drink, but he pushed her away. Sometimes he waved other, younger men over to his fire, where he shared his wineskin with them. Then he ordered Kiran to play for them while they danced and the dogs howled.

Once Gulik stumbled in the dance and fell into the fire. Immediately he rolled free, yowling, his long hair sizzling. When he jumped up he caught sight of Kiran, who had let the flute fall from his lips in surprise.

Gulik made for him with a snarl. Kiran dropped the flute and crouched, waiting. He managed to dodge Gulik's first swing. "Bewitching me into the fire!" screeched Gulik. "Give me that flute, I'll smash it! But first—" He launched himself at Kiran again and this time his blow glanced off Kiran's jaw.

Kiran staggered back and Gulik's dogs leaped around him, barking in a fury of excitement. He knew if he fought back they'd be on him in a moment, ready to tear his throat out. The circling dogs kept him in place while Gulik advanced. Weave and dodge as he would, Gulik's fists pounded his arms and chest until Gulik's friends, laughing and clapping him on the back, pulled him off. Singing, the drunken men left for one of the houses and Kiran lay rolling in pain in the dirt.

It occurred to Kiran, lying there, that he was outside and untied. He could make a run for it. But he was almost too stiff to move and one of Gulik's dogs was watching from across the clearing. In the end he squirmed over to pick up his fallen flute, then crawled over to lie against the side of the turkey pen where he could exchange a few words with Myra.

In the morning he couldn't remember what he'd said, just his shame that, like a beaten animal, he'd crawled back to sleep beside his cage.

★ ★ ★

Gulik seemed to be getting bored with his slave. He acted like a child grown careless of an old toy, who would be secretly delighted if it broke. He amused himself by devising dangerous or uncomfortable things for Kiran to do—gathering nettles for soup or honey from an active hive, or climbing trees to check nests he'd already emptied of their eggs. When a pine branch creaked under Kiran's weight, Gulik laughed. "You eat too much," he said in Shelonwe. "Tomorrow that branch will break under you."

Sometimes Gulik paraded Kiran through the camp, leading him by the leash around his neck, offering him out to other families for chores. Occasionally some woman, her eyes flickering over him in pity, would take him to grind corn or stack wood for her but mostly people shook their heads and turned their eyes away when Gulik offered him. When that happened, Gulik cursed and yanked on the leash and had to find something for him to do. If he couldn't think of anything, he locked Kiran in the turkey pen until someone asked for him.

One morning Ranga offered to take him so Gulik could go hunting. That day Kiran worked side by side with Myra and Dara, hauling water, stacking wood and cutting fresh pine boughs for bedding. The girls laughed and chattered as they worked but Kiran had a hard time shedding his silence. Their chatter fell around him like spring rains through the trees. Kiran was struck by how strong and healthy the girls looked.

Later, while Setolo's little daughter and her *filoni* toddled around their feet, with Dara herding them, scolding, Myra taught him how to stew a rabbit with herbs and mushrooms. Ranga, watching, nodded. "Your twin will choose you, I think," she said to Kiran.

Kiran glanced across at Myra. To his surprise, he saw a flush rise to her cheeks. She stood crushing an onion, tears forming in her eyes—Myra, strong and steady, his partner, his friend. Long ago, back in Lanath, he had thought her chin was too long. He raised his glance to Ranga, who smiled at him, a dimple appearing on her round brown cheek.

"Nobody chooses a slave," he said.

As the rabbit stewed, Ranga wanted the children to nap, so she asked Kiran to play for them. He brought out the flute and leaned against the doorpost. At first he played a dance tune, making the children laugh and clap, but when Myra scolded him, he tried the moonrise song, closing his eyes and coaxing out the tones that showed the long clear rays of light pouring down from the sky. But the notes wavered and broke. How could he play about the great expanse of sky when he was locked in every night?

At last he played a song his mother used to sing to him. Dara came and sat at his feet, leaning her head against his leg.

The little children lay down on their pine beds, sucking on their fingers until they fell asleep. Kiran started an old song of the nuath harvest and as he played, the door flap opened and Setolo came in on silent feet. Kiran hesitated but Setolo gestured for him to continue. Setolo's gaze felt to Kiran like a bass note playing under the music.

When he stopped, Setolo said, "From the place where we seffidges slept or the places where we worked we heard music in the distance. Our people don't have this tradition, Kiran. We sing for war or courting or sorrow or when we drink. But we play only drums."

"Do you miss the music?" Myra asked him. She spoke as if she asked him questions all the time, as if they were members of the same family.

Setolo just said, "I hear the flute sometimes at night."

At that, Ranga came up to her husband and touched his arm. Myra said, "Kiran, play something happy."

"If you'll sing," he said. Ranga laughed, as if she guessed the words' meaning. Myra's cheeks turned bright pink but she tossed her hair back and came to stand behind him with her hand on his shoulder and her mouth close to his ear. He played the King's Song with all its flourishes but she sang so softly that he decided to try something quieter. He had started the Morning Song when all at once Gulik kicked the door flap aside. Kiran let the flute fall from his lips.

Gulik's glance swept across them all and then returned to linger on Kiran's shoulder, which Myra was still gripping. His voice dripped with scorn. "Brother, since you have no work for my slave, I will take him back now. Slave, dress this deer."

★ ★ ★

That evening as Kiran squatted in the dust near Gulik's fire, eating the entrails that Gulik had thrown to him, Myra walked over to him with her hair hanging down over her eyes. "Kiran," she said. "Setolo and Ranga won't let us stay in the pen any longer. They say Dara and I must sleep in the house with them."

Kiran looked up sharply. A few paces behind Myra, Ranga stood waiting, standing gravely, her hands folded before her. "But why?"

Myra averted her eyes. "There's a woman, Norua-onwe, who's expecting a child. She says if it's a boy she wants Dara to be his *filoni*. People tell her the age difference is too great, but she says no, she wants that yellow-hair girl to be part of her family and a true Shelonwe. Setolo and Ranga say in honor of that, we must come inside and be clean."

For a moment, Kiran couldn't make sense of it and he shook his head. Dara adopted into the Shelonwe would no longer be a slave. Already she seemed just as happy here as she had been at home. Which meant that his sacrifice was worthless. He said, "You, too? Is someone adopting you?" As soon as he spoke, he was ashamed. He should be happy, thinking of Myra on her clean bed of pine boughs.

To his surprise, Myra shuddered. "No—they just—want me inside."

He thought he heard a hiccup in her voice as she said it. When he looked past her shoulder, he saw with a jolt that Gulik was watching from beside the fire, whose flickering lights and shadows gave his face an oddly hungry look.

Then Ranga stepped forward, blocking the view. She put an arm around Myra's shoulder and, almost motherly, drew her away toward the house.

★ ★ ★

The next day Gulik set Kiran a series of difficult and useless tasks. Late in the day he led him to the river and pointed to a tree on the far side. "Swim over and climb that one," he said. "Bring me some eggs or I'll beat you."

The shore fell away rapidly from the sun-rippled shallows to glinting dark water where the river trout lurked. Kiran took a step toward the water and felt his stomach lurch. This was nothing, he told himself, the current was nothing. But he hadn't tried to swim since he'd almost drowned at the Serpent and his fear had grown stronger. His limbs stiffened.

He shook his head. "I can't swim," he said in Shelonwe.

Gulik's teeth glinted with delight. He gave Kiran a shove. "Go!"

Kiran's toes gripped the pebbles. His legs refused to move forward. The sight of the swirling water roiled his stomach. He swiveled around toward Gulik in appeal.

Gulik slapped him, then stepped forward and punched him in the stomach. He wasn't drunk now and his blows landed, driving Kiran backward through the shallows. Kiran lost his footing and went down, flailing.

"Swim!" shouted Gulik, and kicked him.

Kiran slid into deeper water. Gulik waded after him, aiming kicks at his head and shoulders. "No," begged Kiran, scrabbling for a foothold. A kick caught his throat and he choked, gasped, toppled backward and took in water. Through the water closing over him, the sky wavered. His arms and legs churned. One hand caught his master's ankle, and he pulled himself closer, his body scraping the pebbles beneath him. "No, Gulik, please, I can't, please."

To his surprise, Gulik drew back. Kiran hauled himself out of the water, shivering so hard he could hardly place his hands on the sand to crawl. He lifted his head and saw Gulik grinning, his eyes lit with triumph. *He's done it*, thought Kiran. *He's beaten me. He's made me whine and beg like a beaten dog.*

He rested his forehead in the sand and wept with frustration and shame.

Chapter 21

From that moment, Kiran knew he had to escape. He realized that without knowing it he had been waging a battle of wills with the Shelonwe outcast. Gulik had been trying to break him, to make him a beast, and he had resisted, fighting for his self-respect. All that was gone now. Gulik knew his weakness. At any moment he could shove Kiran into the river and force him to beg. The knowledge made Kiran keep his head down, his shoulders bent when Gulik was around. To his disgust, Kiran saw himself scuttling to obey like one of the seffidges at home.

One morning, sent to carry a pot for cleaning in the river, Kiran found a knife that one of the village children had dropped near the fire. With a furtive glance both ways, he snatched it up and thrust it inside the ragged remnants of his tunic. That night he stowed it between the branches of the turkey pen.

A couple of days later, going to the river for water, Kiran saw a squirrel disappear into a tree twenty paces from the path. He remembered the spot and, later, when he was alone, he slipped through the woods to explore it. When he pulled aside a leafy branch he found a hole, hidden just at shoulder level and large enough to reach into. The next day he found a moment to slip the knife into it.

Myra started bringing him stolen supplies, too. She brought nuts and dried berries until he pointed out how much the squirrel was going to enjoy them. She brought lengths of twine, fish hooks, even one day a flint and iron for starting a fire. All of these things Kiran stowed in the hollow tree when no one was watching. Doing it, taking some action, allowed him to hold onto the hope that they would escape. Hoeing, chopping wood, carrying stones, he let his mind return to the vision of himself leading the girls through the woods. He imagined himself carrying Dara long distances on his back. The thought made him straighten his shoulders and stand more upright.

But although Gulik often sent Kiran on errands, he could never find Dara and Myra alone. Ranga and Setolo kept the girls close beside them. And even if they wandered off for a moment, how far would they get before they were missed? The Shelonwe were expert trackers.

★ ★ ★

Now he had no one to talk to at the end of the day. Each night he fell exhausted on the filthy heap of straw, but often he woke in the darkness with his heart beating heavily. Finally he sat up, felt around him in the darkness and found the flute. He played softly, songs of lament. He used a new scale, one he hadn't heard before. If the people of the village heard him through their sleep, he imagined they would think it was the voice of the forest itself singing to them.

Gulik was drinking even more of the juniper wine now, during the day as well as at night. Once Kiran saw Setolo try to take the wineskin away from him but Gulik swung around to shield it with his body. "This, too," Gulik hissed at his younger brother. "You take my slaves that I won with my own courage. You talk the chief into confining me to camp. You keep the woman I chose for myself. Hands off my wine, brother!"

The woman he chose? wondered Kiran. *Did Gulik choose Ranga once? I thought among the Shelonwe only the woman herself could choose.* Then he remembered Gulik's face, hungry in the firelight. With a sensation that he had been socked in the stomach, he understood. There was one woman Setolo could give away.

That afternoon he went to the hollow tree and took out the knife. After dark, with his bound hands, he began to dig at the corner of the turkey pen, carving away at the base of the branches planted in the ground. The scraping of his knife sounded loud in the night. He paused and thought he heard something scuff the ground outside. One of the dogs, come to investigate? But then he heard footsteps drawing away, rounding the side of the building. Hastily he shoved the knife under the straw and lay down.

The door burst open and there stood the shadow of Gulik. He strode over to Kiran and kicked him hard, cursing. "Thief! Do you think I am too stupid to find that tree, to watch it? I can track your feet anywhere. You steal from the Shelonwe. Do you think to steal yourself, you fool?" He grabbed him by the neck leash and dragged him out of the building while the turkeys squawked and fluttered. Kiran tore at the tight cord around his neck, choking, his vision going dim. His bound feet stabbed at the ground to help push him along.

Gulik picked up a branch still smoking from the fire and started to beat him with it, heavy fast blows on his face and upper body. Kiran grunted, rolling from side to side to avoid the punishment. The night sky swam and narrowed before his eyes.

Then something pushed him onto one side and fingers loosened the cord around his neck. When his vision came back he saw Setolo pinning Gulik's arms from behind, holding him close, talking in his ear. Ranga's chubby fingers were rubbing a salve into his neck. He lay on the ground, gasping.

When Ranga had finished with him, she went to stoop beside Gulik and Setolo cut Kiran's ankles free. He helped him rise and led him tottering back to the turkey pen. "Give me the knife," he said.

Kiran crept to the corner where he had hidden it, handed it over and collapsed in the straw. Setolo said, "I fear Gulik will beat you to death if I don't give him what he asks."

When the words sank in, Kiran's eyes flew open and he struggled to sit up. "No!" he said. "You can't do that! She's my twin."

"You forget," Setolo said. "A slave has nobody."

"Then just let me go," Kiran said. "You don't want slaves here. Let us all go."

Setolo looked down at him. He lifted one foot, as if the filth of the turkey pen bothered him, then placed it down again deliberately. "That time has passed. I offered to trade freedom for freedom and you refused. Now I obey the ruling of my chief."

★ ★ ★

In the morning, it was Ranga who opened the door. When she did, Dara ran across the straw to throw herself down beside Kiran. She had a pot of Ranga's salve, which she dabbed on the cuts and bruises that covered his face. Kiran winced at her touch. She was crying. "Kiran, I heard the dogs and I heard you, too, like this—" She made a choking noise. "I was so scared. Kiran, when are you taking us home?"

"I thought you liked it here. You get to fish and climb trees."

"I miss our mother."

Ranga called to Dara and sent her back to the house. Then she came and squatted before Kiran. "Can you walk, pink man?"

Kiran rolled over onto hands and knees, then slowly labored to his feet.

Ranga nodded. "Good. In two days we go upstream to fish and find herbs. Setolo and I want to take Gulik far from his wine and this village. Gulik says we all must come, except my daughter, who will stay with her *filoni*."

Kiran's head still felt groggy. "And not Myra," he suggested hopefully, "Myra shouldn't come."

Ranga sighed. "Gulik will never be tame without a woman." She shook her head. "If he steals a Shelonwe woman, the people will make him a slave or drive him away. Setolo can't bear that."

"No," Kiran said. He heard the blood pounding in his ears. "Ranga, you can't, she belongs to herself. She's not yours to give away."

Ranga looked at him sorrowfully. "If he earns her, if he is calm and kind, we will give Myra to Gulik. But only if he is kind to her and only if she agrees. Don't be afraid, when they are wed she will be Shelonwe. Gulik won't treat her as a slave. And, pink man, when that happens, as a marriage present we will ask Gulik to set you free."

* * *

They hiked along a path upriver all morning. Between them, Kiran and Myra carried a canoe overhead, though Kiran could hardly hold his hands above him. Mid-morning, Setolo took over from both of them. Gulik mocked him for doing a slave's work but Setolo said quietly, "This was a man's work, sometimes a woman's too, before we had slaves. Why should we stop doing our own work?" After that, Gulik took his turn carrying too.

Myra kept her distance from Kiran. Wherever they found themselves on the path, either Setolo or Ranga walked between them. She kept her head down, her face forward. He thought he saw the stubborn set of her chin. He was sure she would never consent to Ranga's plan. But she never looked at him and they never exchanged a word.

As the sun started its downhill journey, they came to a lake where they set the canoe on the bank. Across the water stood an island. Ranga took the girls into the birch woods to search for herbs while Setolo and Gulik went to fish on a rocky thrust of land. "Prepare the men's camp," Gulik told him. So Kiran dragged himself to gather fallen branches. He even made a lean-to among the trees and lined its floor with pine branches. *Like a good and thoughtful servant,* he thought. *If I had that flint Myra stole, I could even start the fire.*

In late afternoon, they ate fish wrapped in leaves. The air was clear, with the first cold of fall settling around them. Three and a half months, thought Kiran. He picked the bones out from between his teeth. His face still throbbed but the day felt like a holiday, a picnic. He liked being with Setolo and Ranga. Surely they wouldn't force Myra to marry Gulik. *I might like living with the Shelonwe,* he thought, *if I could live as a man and not a slave.*

As evening fell, Ranga loaded Myra and Dara into the canoe. "No men come to this sacred island," she said. "You may fish and hunt or sit by the fire, but don't come after us!"

Gulik let out a sharp laugh. "You don't have to worry about my slave," he said. "He can't swim. If he even has to wash his feet he begs for mercy!" But Gulik watched with hunger in his eyes as the canoe pulled away.

After the women left, Gulik and Setolo sat by the fire talking. It was a long time since Kiran had seen his master so calm. He told jokes and laughed quietly. He threw his arm over Setolo's shoulder. Kiran sat in the shadows, watching. His face still throbbed from his last beating and he could still feel the panic of his windpipe closing under the cord around his neck.

"I see you brought your flute, Kiran," Setolo called to him at one point. "Maybe you could play for us."

Gulik's head swung around to look at his slave and an ugly shadow crossed his face. Kiran wished Setolo had forgotten him. "My lips are swollen," he said. "I can't play tonight."

"You heard him," Gulik said, his voice hard. "My brother says play."

Kiran drew out the flute. It was rough and stained and sometimes it seemed to know only mournful music. But it connected him to home, to a place where he was a human being and not a slave. And tonight he was out under the sky. He brought the flute to his lips, blew a few notes to remind himself and played for the Moon Lady. He saw Setolo nodding.

When the song was over, Setolo said to Gulik, "Your slave could teach our children to play. He could make these flutes for them and show them how to do it."

"No," Gulik said. "This kind of music won't make them strong."

Setolo shrugged and they talked of other things. Kiran leaned back against a tree trunk in the flickering edge of the firelight. He wondered what it would be like to teach music to the village children. Gulik would never allow it; he'd sooner fill Kiran's days with meaningless labor. But no, he wouldn't focus on that; he would enjoy being in sight of the sky. He thought of the barge trip down the river, the sandbar where they had stayed that first night, the songs he had played for Dara. Idly, without thinking, he began to play again.

Gulik jumped up at once. "Who told you to start again?" he demanded. "Sending messages over the water, are you? Playing courtship songs!" He took three steps over to Kiran, who pressed himself back against the tree. Gulik tore the flute out of his hands and tossed it into the fire.

"No!" Kiran cried and started forward. Surely Setolo wouldn't let the flute burn. But Setolo sat by the fire, studying Gulik, keeping his silence.

Gulik caught Kiran around the neck and threw him on the ground. He brought his heel down hard on Kiran's hand. "You're a slave. Your hands do what I tell them. Touch that music stick, make one ever again, and I'll smash your hands with a rock, do you understand?"

Setolo rose and laid a hand on Gulik's elbow but Gulik shook him off. "You act like they're humans, Setolo!" he said. "Do you forget our mother, the sword in her belly? I'm tying this one up." He took hold of Kiran's neck leash and pulled him up. Then he threw the cord leash over a branch and tied it far enough out along the branch that Kiran would have to sit upright all night with no trunk to lean on. He looped a second cord tight around Kiran's wrists and tied his arms in front of him.

Gulik walked back to the fire. "Still want your music stick, do you?" he sneered. "Take it! Let's hear you play it now!" He pulled the flaming flute from the fire and spun around to throw it at Kiran.

Instinctively Kiran raised his hands to catch it. He caught hold of flames and cried out as he let go. The flute fell into his lap. His tunic smoldered and the smell of burning wool filled his nostrils. He tried to shift aside but the neck leash held him.

"Pick it up," Gulik commanded. "Play for us now, slave. Let me see your lips burn."

"Stop," Setolo said. But with sudden inspiration, Kiran dropped his hands to his lap and pressed his wrists against the embers of his flute before they died. In the heat and pain he felt the twine that bound him sizzle and the fibers part. When they did, he kept his wrists together and he pretended to try and lift the flute but fumbled it aside. "It's ruined," he whined. "I can't obey."

Gulik took another stick from the fire and threw it at him but he ducked and then Setolo started tossing logs from the fire into the lake. "Enough, brother," he said, his voice shaking with anger. "Enough. You will be a wolf howling alone forever unless you change your ways."

"Yes." Gulik dropped suddenly to the ground and put his head in his hands. "Just give me the girl, so I don't have to be alone. I'm your brother. I'll be good to her. I'll treat her like a Shelonwe woman. Just give me the girl and I'll be cured."

Setolo knelt beside him, laid a hand on his shoulder, and peered into his eyes for a long time. At last he sighed. "Ranga agrees and the girl has resigned herself. We will do it. But remember, brother, when you are wed, the Shelonwe women will protect her. Now come away." Without looking at Kiran, Setolo put both arms around his brother and led him to the lean-to Kiran had prepared.

Chapter 22

Kiran sat upright with the cord tight around his neck and his back aching. He waited while the fire died and the night sounds of the forest gathered close. The Sky Serpent rippled behind scudding clouds. When the moon mounted the sky, only half full, he began to work at the knot behind his neck. As soon as he did so, he knew it was no use. The knot had been there for three months or more. His probing fingers and tearing fingernails had no effect on it. Kiran put both hands around the cord above him and tried to yank it free but the cord just cut into his hands.

Despair engulfed him. Even with free hands he couldn't loose himself. He felt himself bowing once more to the knowledge of defeat and bracing himself for the beating Gulik would give him in the morning when he found Kiran's hands unbound.

His leg brushed against the charred flute at his feet. It was still warm. He picked it up and broke it on his knee. At its core, an active ember still glowed. Kiran pulled to the end of his leash and pressed the glowing flute against the cord where it stretched from his neck. He heard again the sizzle, the soft pop of parting fibers—and suddenly he jerked free.

And now what? Setolo's bow lay against a tree. How he would like to take it and shoot an arrow through Gulik's twisted, cruel heart! But then there would be Setolo to deal with. Setolo, who had also been a slave. Even if he could move quickly enough, Kiran knew he couldn't bring himself to kill Setolo.

Which meant that what he had to do now was retrieve Myra and Dara somehow. The thought brought a wave of nausea with it. He crept down to the water's edge. If only there were another canoe, if he could make a raft somehow, silently, if—

But there was no time. Moonlight rollicked on the choppy water. The wind blew in toward shore. At the best of times, in flat water on a sunny day, Kiran didn't know if he could ever swim as far as that island. And now, in darkness and wind, with winter on its way . . . How far was it, anyway? How long had it taken the women to canoe there?

He could flee on foot now, alone, but then he would have failed.

Kiran placed a foot in the water. He took several paces forward and the water still only came to his knee. At least it wasn't a river, churning and sliding. If he concentrated with all his might on the sparkling path of the moon on the water, maybe he could hold off the panic that was waiting to grab him. He waded farther. The water was chilly but not as cold as he had feared. Now it was waist deep, now chest deep, rocking and splashing at his face. His breath came faster. This was the time. He had to choose now. If he started thinking, he'd turn back. Now!

He pushed off, and sank.

What kept him from panic, oddly, was the knowledge that he had to stay silent. He kicked and pulled under the water; he moved forward, then bobbed to the top, took a breath, went under again. He felt himself undulating through the water like a snake. Even underwater he could see the path the moonlight made across its surface.

Up, gasp, down, kick, writhe, up, gasp, down. The water was cold now. He had to strike out at an angle away from the moon

The Beechwood Flute

path. This time, if he followed her unthinkingly, the Moon Lady would lead him into unending water, into death.

He swam. Sometimes when he came up for his gasping breath, a wave slapped him in the face. Down so low in the water, he couldn't tell if he was making progress. The low hump of the island seemed as far away as ever and when he looked behind him, the shore stretched as long and close as it ever had. When he paused, he felt the wind and waves push him back.

Courage for the long haul, he thought. *This is my only task. This is the path before me now. I swim, and either I make it or I don't.*

This far from shore, no one would hear him splash and flail, so he tried swimming the old way but it only made him tire more quickly. He rolled onto his back and the lake water cradled him much better. He kicked and wriggled his way through the water, staring at the sky. *Every month the Sky Serpent crosses the dark pit of the sky to rescue the Moon Lady, to restore her. A good man makes things whole.* He had to remember to veer off from the straight lit path.

The cold seeped into him. It was getting harder to kick, harder to move his arms. Cold seized his ribs. He turned on his stomach and swam as fast and loudly as he could, to warm himself up, and then turned on his back again, gasping.

The island rose higher before him. He was making progress. He turned on his stomach. Another hundred strokes, dipping underwater. Less splashing, make it steady. The long haul. A moment on his back, then another hundred. Maybe a man could keep swimming, a hundred strokes at a time.

Now the island was a patch of darkness blotting out a section of the western sky. But surely it was too late. The cold was dragging him down; he could no longer tell what his arms and legs were doing. And now the water was no longer cold but welcoming, offering to take him in its arms, to cover him, to keep him. But Dara, Myra! He thrashed free of the water's embrace and his feet fumbled at the stony bottom and caught hold. Dripping, numb, he climbed out of the water, pulling on the trunks of bushes, breaking through the underbrush like a moose. On an empty patch of ground he flung himself down to gasp in the darkness.

Shivering racked his body, waking him enough to understand that if he stayed down he might not get back up. So he stood, stupid, unable to think, pounding his arms against his sides, then stamping his feet in an attempt to get some warmth. He turned in circles. How big was the island? How would he find the girls?

Finally he decided to creep around the shore. Surely he would find some sign of the canoe and the girls would be camped nearby. If only he had watched from the far shore to know which direction they had gone. He had to find them before light.

He turned left along the shore. It was difficult to walk without lumbering noisily through the underbrush, snapping branches. Reluctantly he decided to go back to the water. Wading was quieter, except for lapping water and the sound of his teeth chattering.

Then he saw it, a bulge in the darkness, the canoe, pulled onto the bank. He ducked low under branches and crept up beside it.

When he had caught his breath, he moved like a shadow into the clearing. In the ghostly moonlight he made out the form of a lean-to and the humps of three sleepers within. How could he wake only two of them?

Kiran hovered shivering over the sleeping forms until he discerned Myra's pale face and bushy hair, and the small mound that was Dara.

Biting his lip, he reached to shake Myra's shoulder.

Her eyes flew open but she kept silent. She sat up at once. It was almost as if she had been expecting him. Without a word she slipped out from under the blanket and stood beside him.

He caught hold of her hand and drew her to the bank. "We'll take the canoe," he said. "Do you have any supplies?"

She touched his arm. "You're shivering."

He brushed her hand away. "Show me where the stuff is. You get Dara. No noise."

She indicated a bundle beside the remnants of the fire. He carried it to the canoe and stowed it without stopping to check the contents. His hands were too clumsy with cold to untie the canoe. But here was Myra again, with Dara beside her. Dara had a hand over her own mouth as if she couldn't trust herself not to speak.

Myra carried a blanket, which she threw over Kiran's shoulders. Then she untied the canoe and Kiran helped her lift and slide it into the water. It bobbed there and Myra nodded to Dara to get in.

Abruptly she jerked erect. She mimed the act of paddling. Kiran looked around. There were no paddles. Myra said into Kiran's ear, "Ranga's sleeping on them. Help me."

It seemed very dark back at the lean-to. Myra knelt and prodded under Ranga's sleeping form. She seemed to grasp something and slowly drew it forth. Ranga stirred and muttered. Myra handed the paddle to Kiran, then hesitated. He jerked his chin at her to come away but she gave her head a shake and reached again under the sleeping woman. She tugged and Ranga opened her eyes.

Kiran raised his paddle, meaning to strike her before she could cry out. But he couldn't make himself bring it down to crash into her skull. Ranga stared at him. She turned her head ever so slightly to look at Myra. Then she shifted her weight off the second paddle and closed her eyes.

They fled. Kiran's feet slapped against the dirt of the campground. He lifted Dara into the canoe and pushed it off, running a few steps beside it in the water, then heaving himself aboard, making it tip wildly. Myra was already in the bow. They dipped their paddles and drove the canoe into the choppy water of the lake.

He couldn't believe it. They were safe. They were away. Their three captors had no way to come after them. He wanted to throw back his head and roar with joy. Instead he laughed. "She closed her eyes," he said. "Myra, she closed her eyes!"

"What else could she do? You standing there like the arm of vengeance ready to strike her down." Myra shivered. "Besides, I think deep down she always wanted us to go."

★ ★ ★

Before dawn they found the outlet that led downriver. Kiran feared the tracking skill of the Shelonwe. He figured that in two or three hours, when Setolo and Gulik found them missing, they would split up, one running back to the village to raise the alarm, one scouting along the shore for signs of where they had disembarked. Better for them to get as far downriver as they could.

They paddled in darkness, with the moonlight reflecting off sliding patches of water between the shadows of the trees. Kiran felt the current shudder up the paddle, through his arm, as if the river were a living thing, talking to him. He was riding it, feeling it. If the canoe caught on a snag, they might all be flung overboard, but now he knew that if that happened he could swim well enough to save Dara. Myra, he suspected, could take care of herself.

They did bump against rocks sometimes, scrape against underwater obstacles, brush under low overhanging branches. But they swept on downstream. When the gray, misty light of dawn hovered on the horizon, they approached the cleared bank that marked the village. Steering close to the far bank, Kiran made the girls lie down in the canoe. He himself crouched low to keep his silhouette from standing out against the sky. He saw a child stand up at the water's edge, her mouth an O, silver water dripping from the pot she had come to fill. Then, as they drew away, a dog began to bark in wild frenzy. Myra sat up and the two of them paddled as hard and fast as they could until the barking faded in the distance.

Late in the day a rock tore a great gash in the bottom of the canoe. Kiran, who was dozing, took the blow on his back and sat up as the water poured in around him. He seized a paddle from Dara, who began to cry, and helped Myra steer toward shore. They reached the bank just as the canoe foundered beneath them.

Kiran shoved Dara up on the bank and threw their bundle of supplies after her. Myra scrambled up the bank on her own. Kiran stood in the sunken canoe, thigh deep, and when the girls turned to offer him a hand, he began to laugh.

They stared at him with worry on their faces. At last Myra ventured, "What's so funny?"

He shook his head. "Nothing. We're free. Before this, I was trying to decide whether we should float all the way down to Catora. Can you imagine us, paddling among the barges, looking like beggars, making it to Catora after all, only six months late."

"They'd probably call us Savages and shoot us."

Dara said, "I want to go home."

"That," Kiran said, "is what we're going to do."

When he stepped out of the canoe, he wrestled it off the bottom and shoved it back out into the current, where it spun in a lazy circle and bobbled away downstream.

Part Three:
The Beechwood Flute

Chapter 23

Scrubbed clean, with a new white tunic draping his shoulders and his hair clipped short, Kiran sat at his mother's side in the temple cavern. He was tall enough now that it was easy to look over her and over Dara nestled on her lap, to see Lir, with his beard neatly combed, tapping his foot as he waited for the ceremony to begin. But though Kiran looked down the line, leaned forward to peer farther and even turned around to search along the back benches for Myra, he couldn't see her. He hadn't seen her in the four days they'd been home, not since she squeezed his hand at the village gate, in front of Lir and everybody, and bid him good-bye.

While the three of them had been serving the Shelonwe, a new king had come to the throne, young Arluin the Fourth, twenty years old. Today, the six-month celebration of his ascension, was also the day the three slaves of the Shelonwe would officially be welcomed back into the village. The image came to Kiran's mind of runaway snufflers who had to be dipped and scrubbed free of parasites before they were allowed to rejoin their fellows in the pen. But he struggled to put his cynicism aside. Ser Vetel might be a liar but that didn't mean the temple had nothing to offer.

Broad-shouldered Ser Tolan lit the incense and the faint sweet smell of nuath filtered through the cavern. After his months away, Kiran was surprised by how cloying it smelled and how it seemed to constrict his chest. Breathing that all the time! No wonder Ser Vetel had grown so gaunt over the years.

Now was the time when there should be flute music drawing the people's thoughts to the sky but because he had no flute boy, Ser Tolan launched directly into his sermon, relating the old story of the country's founding. He told the villagers how their ancestors followed a young prince across the sea to establish an outpost in the wilderness, where they fought against winter and treacherous Savages to build a great white city that held even when their home kingdom fell to ancient enemies. They hollowed out temples and roofed them with domes to honor the stars and the Serpent who had guided them across the ocean. They spread into the fertile valleys of the south but quarrels among the people and friction among the priests weakened them.

Kiran shifted in his seat. The story was familiar but the details were wrong. The old kingdom hadn't fallen: they had broken free of it. Ser Vetel used to tell the story of the old sea battles, ships ramming one another and men swarming onto enemy decks. He couldn't understand why this new priest would leave out the most exciting parts. Kiran glanced over at Lir, expecting to see him slapping his knee and rolling his eyes the way he used to do at what he used to call Ser Vetel's "spew of whitewash." But Lir just sat stroking his beard, his eyes fixed on the priest.

Ser Tolan continued his story, telling the villagers how one day a band of explorers pushing north threw fallen beech logs on the fire and in its embers, smoking nuath raised visions that reminded them of their destiny and their connection. Lanath saved the kingdom and sustained it, so Arluin the First established an outpost here and dedicated its inhabitants to the sacred task of harvesting the nuath that upheld the kingdom.

And now, said Ser Tolan, the founder's great-great grandson had come to the throne. As a young and energetic king, he was pursuing the war to the south with new vigor. And yet there was good news for Lanath as well. For the new king recognized the vital importance of his northern capital.

Ser Tolan paused. Kiran looked side to side. The people stared at the priest, eyes wide, some of them with mouths hanging open.

The priest raised a hand. "Yes, you heard me right. Our king seeks to make our village a great city. First will come soldiers—you have seen them already—to clear the land of bandits and Savages. We will construct a great road along which messages and supplies can reach us summer or winter. We will bypass the falls, and carts full of white stone and skilled masons will pour into our village, our town."

As Ser Tolan spoke, Kiran's heart thumped harder. Wipe out bandits and Savages! His father had made the decision to leave off banditry just in time. As for the Shelonwe, Kiran wondered if they would try to fight or disappear into the forest. Imagining the fleeing Shelonwe, Kiran felt something uncomfortable swell and grow heavy within him, a sense of something unfinished, something he still had to do.

The priest fell silent and in the coughing and shuffling of feet that followed, Kiran thought again that what was missing was flute music rising in the smoke to fill the dome with a sound of peace and longing. But then Ser Tolan turned to the girls' chorus, setting them to sing in unison. While the singers carried the song, the priest beckoned and Myra descended from the back ranks of the chorus. At the sight of her, Kiran began to stand but the priest signaled him backward and summoned only Dara to approach.

Kiran kept his eyes fixed on Myra. Like Dara, she wore a white dress and her hair was braided as tightly as Dara's, the neatest he had ever seen it. She kept her eyes lowered when Dara took her hand.

With a taper, Ser Vetel lit a coil of nuath in the bottom of a censer, which he lifted and waved as the girls turned and half curtsied before him. The smoke wove around them. The girls glowed in the candlelight as they spread their skirts and dipped in their dance. Kiran's neck prickled. Dara he recognized but Myra, submissive and sedate, eyes lowered to the priest, had become a stranger.

And then Ser Tolan waved the girls to go and take their place in the chorus and beckoned for Kiran to come forward. He felt the unevenness of the stone floor through the soles of his new sandals. The priest raised the censer and Kiran bowed his head and turned. The nuath incense wreathed him and in its sweet smell he felt himself flying over a forest and swooping down to the warm hollow of home. The feeling was sweet and lulling but all at once his father's voice sounded in his mind and he stepped aside. Ser Tolan drew his head back and frowned but he set the censer down as if he had finished and Kiran returned to his seat.

Away from the smoke, Kiran shook his head to clear it. In the chorus, Dara rested her head against Myra's arm, a dreamy look on her face. Kiran still felt drawn to the sense of flying but he pushed it away and tried to concentrate on the music of the girls' song. Without the harmonies and embellishments Ser Vetel loved, the music sounded thin. The unison of voices made them bland and flat. And then he heard a rich alto hitting a wrong note and he smiled. Myra, not fitting in. He let himself remember Myra at the end of their journey. Their last day on the trail had been unseasonably warm and they had turned east toward the river so as not to miss Lanath. By midday, Kiran recognized the flattened area along the bank where he and Bulo had dragged Lir's rowboat into the river. He was stunned to have brought them so close to the village. He reached back for Dara's hand and pointed through the bushes, to the hidden trail that led to the beech grove.

"Run ahead!" he told her. "Run calling for your father. If you see him, be careful he doesn't fall out of a tree with happiness!"

Dara ran and Kiran turned back to catch Myra around the waist. He swung her around and around, splashing at the edge of the shallows. "We did it! We did it! We're home!" Without stopping to think, he pulled her close and kissed her. Her lips were sweet and cool and then the kiss was over.

He stood back, suddenly awkward. If only he had planned that, he might have had a chance to do it better. To savor it.

Her face pink, Myra danced away from him up the trail.

"Where are you going?" he called after her. "Come back!"

She twirled and laughed. "I'm going to make sure Dara is all right. Stop worrying. Don't you know already? I choose you. You're my *filoni* and I choose you. Now hurry up, we're home."

★ ★ ★

After the ceremony, Kiran paid a visit to his old teacher.

Ser Vetel lived now in disgrace in a hut by the seffidge quarters. Walking down the narrow street, Kiran pictured the events Lir had described. In the fall the new barge had brought news of Ser Vetel's lies—how Orda and the others had died and how Ser Wellim had seen the canoe pull away with the girls bundled aboard.

Irate, the people of Lanath stormed the guard tower and demanded Lir's release. The soldiers stood aside as Lir led mothers and fathers to break down the temple door and drag Ser Vetel into the square. They stripped him of his robes and drove him half naked through the streets. With a rope around his waist he confessed his lies in front of the witness tree and then they dragged him through the river to wash him clean of deceit. Only then had they given him old clothes and this tumbledown hut, where he helped prepare meals for the seffidges.

Kiran found the door hanging half off its hinges and the old priest squatting by the fire. Ser Vetel turned his head on his scrawny neck as Kiran threw back the door.

So many questions and accusations fought for exit from Kiran's mouth that he stopped at the threshold without saying anything. Vegetables lay drying on a high wooden table under the single window. Cobwebs looped down from the thatch overhead. Kiran's shoulders almost filled the doorway, while the old priest shrank into himself and twisted back to poke at a pot on the fire.

Without turning around, Ser Vetel waved the wooden spoon and spoke in his dusty voice. "The girls sound flat. This new priest, this Ser Tolan—he has no ear for subtlety."

Kiran stepped into the center of the room. Light bathed his feet and he thought the smell of nuath still lingered around his old master. "Why did you lie?"

The priest shook his head impatiently, as if the question were not worth answering. "For the greater good. To keep men from charging off to their deaths like your father."

"Like my father! My father's not dead."

Ser Vetel turned to look at him. Kiran saw him absorb the news; oddly, it seemed to fill out his withered outline, to make him look more alert, more shrewd.

"Is that so? Where did you find him?"

Kiran caught his breath and cursed himself silently. This was just the information he didn't want to give. He pictured his father hacked by swords and dragged down from the granite castle to hang on some riverside tree branch, his eyes bulging and his body twitching until it fell still.

He ran a hand over his eyes. "It's a rumor. The Savages have a story about a wild pink man who lives—who lives in some desert way beyond the mountains."

Ser Vetel's glittering eyes flitted, searching his face.

Kiran clenched a fist. "You would have left the girls to slavery or death."

The priest spoke in his smoothest voice. "I saw what I saw, Kiran. I thought they were dead already. I told you what I saw. But your stepfather, Lir, had to challenge me. That one is a blasphemer who denies all wisdom not to his liking. Yes, and neglects his duty, too. What is the purpose of Lanath, Kiran?"

When Kiran didn't answer, Ser Vetel stepped closer and closed a hand like a bird's claw on his sleeve. "How does our village serve the kingdom, Kiran? Have you forgotten your lessons so quickly?"

Kiran jerked his arm away. "We live in villages for mutual protection, so we will not be alone in the wilderness."

"Yes, yes, but that's secondary. Lanath exists, Kiran, and you know it, you learned it at my knee, Lanath exists for the harvest."

The old priest crept to the table, where he lifted a bunch of dried fungus and sniffed at it. "Look at this, Kiran, the miracle gift of the beech tree. Too many of you think of it as just some product like apples or corn. But no. Here we harvest visions for all the temples of the kingdom, wisdom for the king's counselors."

He shook the handful of fungus in Kiran's face. "This at a time when our people live under threat from Savages, bandits, foreign armies on our southern borders, deceitful diplomats from overseas! With a new king, a young king. And you, Kiran, selfish and blind, you doubted me, you disobeyed. You tried to distract the people from their duty. And yet you have the gall to come here and question me!"

"You're a liar," Kiran said. "You lead the people with lies."

"People need stories to guide them, boy. Men are weak and guided by passion. Very few have the subtlety and wisdom to see how to act. If your father had listened to reason, he would be here today."

"And my brother would be dead!"

Ser Vetel raised his eyebrows and leaned close. "Do you have something to tell me?"

Kiran clamped his mouth shut and shook his head. *I am going to have to start lying, and fast.* He exited and as he pulled the door shut, he said in as firm a voice as he could muster, "Stop imagining things. I have nothing to tell you."

★ ★ ★

The next evening, Kiran's mother spread a woven cloth of yellow and green over the table and brought out the silver candlesticks Lir had given her at their wedding. Myra and her mother arrived carrying plates of apples, onions and carrots to add to the roast mutton and the bread Enya pulled from the oven.

Ser Tolan and the captain of the guard joined them at dinner. Lir sloshed the beer into mugs, made toasts and hearty conversation, but from the sidelong looks of the guests Kiran understood that now at last he would have to tell their story. He put down his knife and spoke before the questions could begin.

"We found the track not far above the Serpent," he said.

"What became of the soldier Bulo?" the captain asked.

Kiran had already decided that he needed to provide Bulo with a heroic death. Or probable death, with just the slightest chance of survival, so that if he were ever captured, he might talk his way free.

"We made our way west and north from that spot." He spoke deliberately, making sure his words led away from the bandits' granite castle. "The track was difficult to follow. At one point Bulo fought off a bear with his sword. Then one day we heard a hunting party approaching. We climbed into a tree."

Kiran swallowed, shocked at the mistake he had just made. Would they believe he could climb a tree with his broken arm? But they were all watching him, hanging on his words. He had been gone so long they had forgotten the arm.

"The hunting party spread out to find deer. Bulo dropped down and tackled one of the, the Savages. Bulo overpowered the Savage before he could call his friends."

Kiran took a breath. This next part was the most unlikely, the part his listeners would have to swallow to make Bulo a hero and hide everything about Calef and the bandits. Kiran gave Myra a meaningful look. He saw from the way she shifted in her seat that Myra had taken Dara's hand.

"Do you remember the seffidge Set, who ran away?" Kiran peered around the table at each of them. "They told us his body was found half eaten by wolves. But the hunter Bulo captured was Set. The Savages called him Setolo and he spoke our language. And when Bulo held a sword to his throat Setolo said that if Bulo let him go, he would bring the girls and set them free in the middle of the wilderness."

The priest, the captain, Lir, all watched him silently. Myra gave him the slightest nod. It's a good story, Kiran thought, and he relaxed a little, letting himself flow into it, as if it were music.

"Bulo wasn't sure he could trust Setolo's word," he said. "So he told him to send the other Savages for the girls and we'd make the trade when the girls arrived. Then he pulled Setolo behind a tree and Setolo called out to the other men, telling them the deal. But—"

He lowered his eyes. The next part would make him sound like a clumsy fool. "From my hiding place up in the tree I thought I saw a Savage sneaking around through the woods behind Bulo.

I leaned out to see for sure and I fell out of the tree. One of the Savages threw his spear at me but Bulo jumped between us and the spear hit him instead."

He looked from once face to another. Myra raised her eyebrows. Dara's mouth hung open and Lir stared at the table, listening.

"Setolo dragged me away while the Savages jumped on Bulo and stabbed him over and over."

He took a deep breath and let it out slowly. "When we left Bulo he was still alive. I don't know for sure what happened to him but we never saw him again."

The captain looked grave and his mother had tears in her eyes. Dara ran away from the table covering her ears. Good. Let Bulo be remembered as a hero.

"Setolo brought me home a captive. He said Bulo had deceived them by hiding me, so they had no obligation to release the girls. But they would treat them kindly, with respect. We all three lived as captives until . . ." and he told them the story of the lake escape. Here he let himself sound like a hero. Why not?

Lir poured another round of beer, even a sip for Dara, whom he coaxed back to sit on his lap. The others stood and toasted the travelers on their courage and luck. I did it, thought Kiran, and Myra nodded at him, smiling.

Then the captain leaned forward to ask questions. How was the village laid out? What weapons did the Savages have? How did they organize themselves? What did they eat?

Kiran answered carefully. He heard an eagerness in the questions he didn't like. When Enya brought out apple pie, Kiran stopped answering questions and dug into it, wondering if the apples had come preserved in winterberry from the bandit highlands.

After pie, the captain pushed his chair back and patted his belly. "Now," he said. "As soon as you are fattened up and well-recovered, young Kiran, I'll ask you to lead us back to this Savage village so we can root it out for good."

Kiran dropped his spoon and stared.

The captain chuckled. "Yes, son, times are new. As Ser Tolan told you, our young king has come to the throne with new vigor and determination. Our revered old king, may the Moon Lady lead him home, grew terribly cautious in his old age. But his grandson, this Arluin the Fourth, he has the fire of youth and he wants to expand and settle the frontier. No more huddling in the walled villages. We take the battle to the enemy in his own home place. Those that dare harass us will be hunted down and destroyed. We'll come down on them like lightning now, before the snow flies."

Myra's face went white. "But you can't!"

The captain stared at her. His face said that it was a mistake to allow females to eat at a table with serious men. He didn't deign to speak to her but Ser Tolan, in a voice smooth with kindness and condescension, asked, "And why do you say such a thing, daughter?"

Myra threw a look of appeal at Kiran. She swallowed. "Because they—go to their winter camp. They depart when the leaves fall—when the leaves reach ankle deep on the paths. We don't know their winter camp, sir. They won't return to the mountains until the ice breaks up on the rivers."

The captain turned to Kiran. "Is this true?"

Kiran felt dislocated in time. The sound of flowing water played behind him. He heard his own childish voice vow to sweep the Savages from the kingdom. Was that the unfinished thing he felt weighing on him, then? Vengeance? To lead a company of soldiers against those who had enslaved him? He remembered the day Nora had assured him he would be a warrior.

The captain jiggled his knee, peering at Kiran under lowered brows. "Is it true, boy? Do the Savages move in winter?"

Kiran looked at Myra, who gripped her spoon with white knuckles. He spoke slowly, as if reluctant to admit it. "They planned to leave in just a few days, sir." He lowered his eyes. "They talked about hiding their track, concealing their secret ways. I don't know if I could find the path."

The captain tipped back in his chair, his head tilted to one side. Then he shrugged and let the chair drop. "Well, can't be helped, I suppose. We can start the road instead. At least this way we won't bog down in snow in the mountains." He stood and bowed to Lir. "Thank you, Master."

He turned to Kiran. "And you, young man, you have proved your courage and initiative. Experience in the field is better than any examination." He nodded, smiling. "Oh, yes, I heard about your springtime exploits from a young soldier in my company. But now I invite you to join us. We're a little crowded in the barracks so I'll yield you the privilege of sleeping at home." He put up a hand. "You needn't come right away. Heal and rest. Consider this your ten days' leave."

He bowed again, this time to Kiran's mother, then buckled on his sword and went out the door.

"A soldier in his company?" asked Kiran. "Who?"

"It's Ryan, haven't you heard?" Myra blurted. The adults all swung to gaze at her, and Kiran saw Nora place a reassuring hand over her daughter's. Well brought up Lanath girls didn't speak out at meals.

So Ryan had survived. Kiran remembered Ryan leaping onto the barge in the darkness and in spite of all their old enmity, he was glad.

When the guests had departed, Lir, who seemed to be in an especially good mood, helped Kiran carry the dishes out to the yard, where a seffidge woman would wash them in the morning. "It's a shame about that girl Myra," he said to Kiran. He chuckled into his beard. "She has some spirit, though, doesn't she?"

"A shame? What do you mean?"

"No one will marry her now that she's lived with Savages. Who knows what filth she's lived in? Why, even traveling two weeks with you, no chaperone but a six-year-old child—that alone would be enough to take her out of the running. But Savages!"

Kiran's face grew warm. "I'll marry her."

Lir turned to him in surprise. "I didn't mean that. You don't have to go that far. There's no obligation. It's the Savages that ruined her, not you."

Kiran thought he had never felt so awkward. He straightened his shoulders. "I want to marry her."

Lir gazed at him, then shook his head. "You speak like a man of honor, Kiran, and it does you credit. But she has no father. Her mother, though I admit she knows her healing, spends her days wallowing among beasts and seffidges. The family is low and the girl has no manners. Whatever happened between you—and don't tell me, it's best not spoken of—you'll get over it when you start mixing with girls of quality."

A bitter taste filled Kiran's mouth. "None of that matters. She's brave and kind and smart."

Lir grinned. "Not much of a looker, though, is she?" He laid a large hand on Kiran's shoulder. "Son, Serpent knows you've grown but you're still far too young to think of marriage. When you become a soldier, you'll have plenty of women after you and no chance to think of weddings for at least three years. The kindest thing you can do for that girl is keep away from her and stifle the village gossip. So let's not argue, Kiran. Come in and sing your sister to sleep."

Chapter 24

One morning a week later, Myra came for Dara. "Please, I thought I could take her collecting plants in the woods for my mother," she said as Dara danced up and down at Enya's side, her hands clasped, begging to go.

Kiran, washing behind a curtain, ducked into a tunic and came out in time to hear his mother say in a chilly voice, "And what if I have need of her myself today?"

Myra's smile dropped away as Kiran crossed the few feet to his mother's side. "If Dara has duties today, I'll do them, Mother," he said. "I learned a lot of skills among the Shelonwe."

His mother's cheeks reddened as she turned to look at him. Dara leaned against her side in appeal, then ran to the doorway to stand by Myra, who hesitated, watching Kiran, until he made an impatient gesture urging her to go.

When the girls had gone, he said to his mother, "Why are you rude to Myra?"

Enya flushed more deeply. "It's you she's after, Kiran, hanging around here. No proper girl would visit a boy's house so."

"She asked for Dara."

"Dara can do better than run around in the woods like a Savage, getting dirty, coming home with bare feet." She shook her head. "That Myra and her mother, they practically live among beasts and seffidges. The mother's quiet and respectful, but this one . . ."

Anger rose in Kiran. "Listen, Mother. When a Savage grabbed your daughter over the side of the barge, Myra attacked him. All during the long months after, she stayed with Dara, sang her songs, washed her face, shouldered her work, tried to comb her hair. There's never been anyone more worthy of welcome into your house."

Enya subsided into a chair and put her head in her hands. "You're right, Kiran. I'm sorry. But Dara's so changed. There's wildness in her. I—I still miss her, and you, too."

His anger deafened him. He hardly heard himself ask, "And Calef? Do you miss him, too? Or was he just too wild to welcome home?"

His mother dropped her hands. "What?"

"When my father came back, with the son he slaved for, and you sent the soldiers to drive him away?"

"What?" she said again, standing now, reaching for the front of his tunic. "What are you saying to me?"

He yanked free of her. "You sent him your ring and the message to disappear because you were married and had a new child."

"No," she said. "No."

He waited, his face burning.

She pressed her hands to her cheeks and backed away a few steps, then held one hand out in appeal, like a beggar woman.

"Kiran," she said, "Is it true? Is Calef alive? Did they tell you about him, the Savages?"

"I saw him." He stepped forward and caught her hand. "He's twelve years old, Mother. His hair is golden like yours and curly like—our father's. He laughs all the time and he runs through the forest like—like a fawn, quick and clever."

"But where—but they—but where does he live? How does he live?"

He shook his head. "That I won't tell you."

"They told me he was dead." She wept now, still clutching him with one hand and with the other partially covering her eyes. "I swear to you, Kiran. They came to me one evening when you and Dara were already asleep. It was Ser Vetel and Lir, while the captain of the guard we had then, a man named Landar, stood outside the door. They sat me down and Ser Vetel said, 'Corbin is back. He's outside the gates. Your son is dead but Corbin escaped from the Savages and wants to come home.'"

She drew away now, sobbing louder, full out, in a way Kiran had never heard in all the years of his childhood. But he held himself stiff and waited.

"What should I have done, Kiran? I asked to see him but Lir said no, to see your father meant to take him back as husband. I would be married to Corbin and then my tiny baby Dara would be a bastard, or I must be Corbin's widow, married to Lir, and he would care for me and my children all our lives."

She looked at him with pleading eyes. "So I sent Corbin my ring and my blessing, and the message that he was free to go, free to find some other wife. I did it for my children, Kiran, for you."

He could hardly see her through the haze of his anger. "Not for me, Mother. Not for Calef, waiting there at the gate. You did it for Lir's riches and to get nice clothes for Dara, no matter if Lir despised me."

"He never despised you." She stroked his sleeve. "He wanted you to be happy, but you reminded him that somewhere . . ." She dropped her eyes and pulled a loose thread from his cuff. "Lir's a good man, steady, strong for his family. Your father was—moody, impulsive. He had sudden ideas, he wouldn't listen to reason—"

"Don't say those things. He's my father."

She sighed. "And he was also quick and brave and funny sometimes, and he had the finest voice. But Kiran, Lir's so proud of what you've done, so proud to call you his son."

Kiran's eyes burned. He walked to the window and glared out at the watery view.

He asked, in a choking voice, "Would you like to hear about your son Calef? About what his life has been?"

She came to join him at the window. "Please. Tell me, Kiran." She touched his arm.

He turned and looked down at her. "Our father, who is dead, took him back to live among the Shelonwe, whom you call Savages. His closest friend is a Shelonwe girl and they bathe together in the river naked. He speaks the Shelonwe language and it's the only one he knows. His skin is burned red-brown with the sun. And he loves me. Of all the people I've ever known, he's the only one who has loved me from the moment he met me, just for myself, asking nothing."

His mother backed away and sank into a chair, fumbling at her apron and staring at him with dry red eyes.

★ ★ ★

The village seemed small to him. He walked through the streets, looking into shops. He paused by the door of the carpenter shop and Jovan's father looked up. When he saw Kiran, he put a hand to his forehead and Kiran ducked away. He didn't know how to speak to the man. Ryan was safe and home as a soldier but Kiran remembered the thwack of wood on bone and didn't want to think about what had become of Jovan.

Instead he lounged in the shops, leaning on counters, watching the potter turn a bowl or watching the cooper fashion a barrel. Maybe if he chose a trade he could put off becoming a soldier until he understood what this thing was that weighed on him, this thing he hadn't done. One morning he visited the brickyard where seffidges, mostly old men, women and children, shoveled mud and straw into molds. They worked steadily, mutely. Their eyes when they lifted them were dull gray, with small pupils and yellowed whites. He didn't like to see them but when their master the mason went for lunch and no one else was watching, he addressed them in Shelonwe. "Brothers and sisters, are you hungry?"

He saw them stiffen and one child lifted his head and stared until the woman beside him reached over and pushed his head down. Kiran said slowly, still in Shelonwe, "I will help you. Somehow, I will find a way." A couple of the seffidges shook their heads without lifting them and he backed away, wondering if he had just told one more lie.

★ ★ ★

In the afternoon he descended the steps to the temple cavern. Nobody was in the sanctuary, but torches around the walls lit the dome. The dark curve of the night sky arched overhead and the star tiles glittered. Like everything else in the village, the temple was too small, enclosed, suffocating. If he were a priest, he thought, he'd smash through the roof and let the villagers look at the real sky. No, he'd take them out on the meadow and let them watch for shooting stars, the Sky Serpent shaking off his scales.

The door from the priest's quarters opened and Ser Tolan entered the round room. "You've come, how convenient. I was planning to send for you."

Kiran waited.

"What's it to be, boy? I hear you always longed to be a soldier. Now that Lanath has a proper garrison, thirty soldiers in a decent barracks, you can train right here without that side trip to Catora. Or if you choose, you can work for me this winter and next summer, still float to Catora. This time you have your pick, priest or warrior."

Two ways up and out of here and Kiran wasn't sure he wanted either. "Summer? I hoped I might go on the first barge of spring."

The priest raised his bushy eyebrows. "Restless with home so soon, or eager to start your studies? I imagine you can go as soon as our little military campaign against the Savages is over."

Kiran said slowly, "Why do we need to attack them, Your Honor? We have the girls back."

The priest waved his hands. "And what of the men killed, the trade destroyed? Show weakness and they'll overrun us. This land is ours but they have us cowering in a corner." His voice softened. "Don't worry, Kiran, this time you won't go alone."

"They have children, Your Honor. They farm and fish and take care of their old people. Wise, kind women run their village."

"If they're wise, let them move across the desert to their own land. There are riches in these mountains they don't dream of, riches to make Catora the great nation our forefathers were promised. Think of history, Kiran. Remember the great songs of our destiny."

Kiran turned away, feeling sick, but the priest pursued him and set a hand on his elbow. "Come, boy, I see you're not a warrior at heart. If I claim you as my apprentice, you won't even have to carry a weapon. Except for that one little expedition, you can forget the garrison and serve me in the temple. I could use a chorus director and I hear you have a rare talent for music."

All the long way home he hadn't missed his flute but now he let his fingers play in the air, remembering the old days with Ser Vetel. "I've lost two flutes and an arloc."

"So play the trumpet! Much more suited to the times. Call men to courage, don't lull them with romance! I have a spare trumpet right in my quarters."

Kiran shook his head. "Maybe I'll order a new flute from the carpenter. Meantime, I'd like you to teach me to read."

The priest turned his head aside and regarded Kiran from the corner of his eye. "To read?"

"Ser Wellim was surprised Ser Vetel hadn't taught me already."

"Reading is a very great mystery, boy. It requires purity and devotion."

"Purity and devotion? What are you saying?" Kiran demanded. He thought of what he had done, what no one in his village had dared.

Ser Tolan spread his hands in an expression of regret. "I don't question your time living among Savages or traveling alone with that girl Myra. But there is a strain of defiance in your family, a strain almost of rebellion. Even your stepfather challenged Ser Vetel."

"Who was lying." Kiran's words came out fast and bitter. "Who used words written on paper that only he could read to lie to all the village."

The priest raised a hand to calm him. "Who was following a mistaken policy, for which he has been replaced. You're a smart boy, a talented boy. Surely you can see that a chorus where each singer selects her own tune will be nothing but a howling tempest. If you want me to teach you to read, you'll have to pledge your utter obedience."

Kiran shook his head. "I had enough of obedience as a Shelonwe slave. You teach me to read and I'll train the girls' chorus. Not to howl like a tempest but to sing in parts that blend together like—like my mother's weaving."

The priest rubbed a finger across his upper lip, studying Kiran's face, considering. Then he straightened with a grin that made him look not much older than Bulo. "Fair enough. Anything to escape those annoying little voices. For every two hours of chorus practice you spare me, I'll spend an hour with you deciphering lines of writing. The girls will be yours at mid-morning tomorrow."

"I'll be there," Kiran said. Now at least he would have some duty, some excuse not to become a soldier right away. And no one would talk if he saw Myra in the chorus.

But when he thought about spring, when everyone expected him to guide a campaign against the Shelonwe, he felt a hollow echo in his chest. He wasn't happy; and that evening, watching his mother's hands shake as she set Lir's plate before him, he knew she wasn't happy either.

Chapter 25

The season's first snowflakes whirled down from the gray morning sky as Kiran walked to the garrison. Already a dusting of white covered the cobblestones. Tomorrow he'd have to bring the chorus rehearsal indoors. But today was free.

He nodded at the sentries outside the garrison and pushed inside. Men crowded the front room, still eating breakfast. Smoke and the smell of sausages hung in the air and Kiran's stomach grumbled. The captain, seated at the center table with a sausage skewered on his knife, was telling the men near him a story which made them throw their heads back in laughter. Kiran waited for them to finish and then stepped forward.

"Sir," he said, "I have a request."

The captain rose and stepped free of the bench. "Here to join us, I imagine? Done with your ten days' leave?"

Kiran shook his head. "With respect, sir, I work for Ser Tolan now. I've come to ask a day of leave for someone else, my old companion, Ryan."

The captain raised his eyebrows, then turned to the end table where Ryan, a wary look on his face, pushed himself up from his seat.

"For what purpose?" the captain asked.

"To hunt and maybe bring the garrison fresh meat."

The captain frowned and shrugged. "Fair enough. Ryan, back by nightfall. Take two bows."

Kiran led the way north from the village, into the forest and edging away from the river. He didn't feel like talking yet, didn't even know what he wanted to say, just knew that he wanted Ryan worried. And Ryan, lumbering along too loudly on the path behind him, kept his mouth shut. Ryan's cloak swept through the underbrush and sometimes his sword knocked snow from a bush. Why had he brought a sword, anyway? Probably just too proud of being a soldier to leave it behind.

When they reached a creek, they followed it upstream. Kiran moved lightly and he heard Ryan hurrying to keep up, his heavy boots turning over the pebbles underfoot. Ahead, there was a place where the grass was bent to the ground. Just past it a narrow track led to the creek's edge. Kiran raised a hand to stop Ryan.

He led the way around to the left, slowly, until they were downwind and upstream from the crossing place. Then he found a pine whose branches started within reach. He slung the bow over his shoulder and leaped for the first branch, caught himself and climbed. Ryan followed, with a clatter of boots and sword.

They settled themselves on two branches with clear shots to the path and waited. Snow fell silently around them, but very little sifted through the pine branches to settle on them. Kiran let the bow rest on his knees while he took turns to pull one hand, then the other, up into his sleeve to warm it. Ryan wrapped his cloak around him.

Neither of them spoke.

After a long time, Kiran began to wish he had brought something to eat. Ryan shifted restlessly in his seat, sending little puffs of snow falling from the end of his branch.

At last, Kiran pulled himself upright against the trunk and stretched. He was just about to suggest to Ryan that they try at dawn another day when something rustled in the bushes. He kept still. Across the stream, a reddish-brown patch moved through the underbrush. He stooped, touched Ryan's shoulder and pointed.

Both of them nocked arrows on their bowstrings, but Kiran indicated to Ryan that he should take the first shot. Ryan wrapped his legs tightly around his branch, waiting. Through the underbrush, the deer browsed its way down to the creek. But it was a doe, Kiran saw, with a fawn, almost a yearling, trailing after her. Kiran lowered his bow. At the edge of the water, the doe took a sip, lifted her head for a quick look around, then settled down to guzzle.

Ryan let fly. The doe crumpled, staggered up, took two steps and fell again. Ryan's arrow shaft stuck out from just inside her left shoulder. The fawn froze, then leaped away.

Ryan swung down from the tree with a whoop of victory and waited for Kiran to drop down beside him. "You could have taken the fawn."

For a moment, Kiran didn't know how to respond. *We don't shoot does.* Except, he realized, that was a Shelonwe prohibition, not a Lanath one.

Unbidden, the image rose in Kiran's mind of Setolo's mother receiving a sword in her belly while her two sons watched, one from beside her, one from shore.

He tamped down a surge of anger enough to say, "That was a yearling, big enough to survive. Next year it'll be fatter."

They crossed the creek, leaping from stone to stone. Once they had dragged the doe back out of the underbrush, they looped a rope around her hind legs and hoisted her from a branch overhanging the water. Ryan slit her throat and let the draining blood wash away downstream. Kiran drew his own knife to begin dressing her but Ryan stopped him. "What are you doing? I'll send a couple of seffidges to lug it home."

Kiran hesitated. *Why don't we do our own work?* he wanted to ask, but he decided this wasn't the time.

He ran his thumb along the edge of his knife. "All right, but there's something more I want to do first."

Ryan grew still for a moment, watching him. Beads of sweat dotted his hairline. *He's worried, all right,* thought Kiran. *He's been sweating all day.*

Kiran put away his knife and led the way once more, this time striking southeast through the forest. His sense of direction was good; they came out beside the pool above the waterfall. Kiran threw down his bow.

"What are we doing?"

"We're going swimming."

"Now? It's winter. We'll freeze!"

"A short swim," Kiran said. He stripped off his tunic and shoes.

Ryan watched with a look of horror but then he began to undress also.

Snowflakes melted on Kiran's bare skin. No point going in much before Ryan; he doubted he could stay in for long. When they were both naked, Kiran edged out along the fallen log, which was slick with a coating of ice, looked back at Ryan and dove in. The cold cut his breath away.

He surfaced, treading water violently but trying to keep his face placid. "It's not bad," he lied to Ryan.

Ryan paled. He dipped a toe into the water while all the rest of him shrank back.

Kiran opened his mouth wide to stop his teeth from chattering. "What are you waiting for?"

With a look like poison, Ryan dropped into the water and came up gasping. Kiran laughed and ducked under. The cold slashed at him like a hundred knives but he was sure now he could outlast Ryan. He turned on his back underwater and swam looking up at the surface like an otter. He wound past Ryan's flailing white legs, came up and flopped under again, kicking water into Ryan's face.

With fast, choppy strokes, Ryan made for shore. Kiran took a couple of extra circuits around the pool. His body was turning numb now, the cold searing into his bones. He swam to the sandy bank and drew himself upright. He made sure to step slowly as he walked up the bank.

Ryan, hopping about in the snow, pulling his clothes on, gave out a sound like a snarl, then suddenly laughed and tossed Kiran the green army cloak. It was already damp but Kiran used it to rub his limbs dry. He was laughing, too. His limbs burned but even so, it was good to feel the blood start to flow again.

"What was that about?" Ryan demanded. "You've already proved you're tough enough. I know it. Everybody knows it. The examinations are over."

"The examinations are never over," Kiran said, pulling on his tunic. He meant it as a joke but all of a sudden he wondered if it was true, if life would keep asking more of him than he could give.

"Is that so?" Ryan said and threw himself at Kiran. He caught him around the chest and Kiran staggered backward. Kiran caught his footing, hooked a leg around Ryan's and tried to lever the heavier boy down. But Ryan had always been stronger. They wrestled, straining, until suddenly Ryan threw him down and sat on him before he could wriggle away.

"All right," Kiran said. "One for you."

Ryan got off him and gave him a hand up. "At least we're warmer now. You lunatic."

Kiran brushed the snow from his clothes. "Look, the sun's coming out." He walked the length of the pool to where a couple of boulders loomed over the top of the waterfall. He edged out, found a seat and waited for Ryan to join him.

Ryan crept over the boulders and plopped down next to him. "Come on, Kiran, let's say we go back now. Get some hot soup and someone to bring our deer home before nightfall."

Kiran shook his head. "There's plenty of time for that. I want you to tell me about the barge."

There was a silence and then, reluctantly, Ryan began. "Look, Kiran, I'm sorry about that. You were being so stubborn, I—"

"Just tell me."

"What's to tell? I caught up with it five miles downstream, below the Pomel branch, half foundering, bobbing up against the right bank. Losar with his throat cut, dead, Jovan moaning beside me, half blind, with his face bashed in, the girls shrieking and holding onto each other, all the kids and the priest whimpering below. The little kids were trying to do something, bailing with their hands and dishes and anything they could find."

He shook his head, staring at the water boiling below them.

"There was a big gash in the hull. I got a couple of the kids pulling barrels apart, and Jovan, mashed up as he was, nailed them over the hole. I set the girls as lookouts up on deck and that priest stood by the mast moaning and praying like an idiot." He rocked in imitation. "Then as evening fell, one of the girls started screaming that she saw something and Jovan and I ran up on deck and helped them push off. We gave this great heave and just as the barge got free, Jovan collapsed. I think something broke inside his head. He flopped like a fish all over the deck and then he gave a rattle and stopped breathing. It was the most horrible thing I've ever seen."

Ryan turned his hands over as if examining them.

"After that the barge just kept floating. We were tipping, listing to starboard. We kept chucking heavy stuff overboard and bailing. And that useless priest sat on the highest part of the deck, rocking and praying. I got a couple of the girls to help me steer—man, they had no idea how to pull an oar—and we kept floating downstream."

He shrugged. "And that's it. We kept afloat, sort of, and we made it downriver. The kids mostly huddled on the deck and cried. I could have used Myra to tell them stories, that's for sure. Or you—I kept thinking what your flute could have done for them."

Ryan paused and stared at the waterfall for a while. Then he looked at Kiran. "You know, the weird thing was, I liked it. Not the bad parts. I hated Jovan dying and I hated that sniveling priest. I was frightened all the time. But I liked being the one who had to think and work and stay awake to save them. I figured I turned out to be something more than my father with all his kicks and curses ever thought I would."

Kiran waited a while and then picked up a pebble and tossed it over the waterfall, down into the pool below. "How'd you end up back here?"

Ryan kicked over a pebble of his own. "Eventually this other barge picked us up and brought us down to Catora. They were having a huge celebration—coronation for the new king. I was sent off to the barracks to train but after a month they gave me a new cloak and sent me to meet the king because I was a hero. By that time our company was getting ready to march south to put down a rebellion and I had to miss our marching date."

He passed a hand over his face. "Tell the truth, I didn't mind them going without me. Every couple of days there were wagons bringing back wounded soldiers to the field hospital at our end of the barracks. Every night with their moaning I kept seeing Losar with blood spurting from his throat and Jovan flopping on the deck.

"So I had an audience with the new king. He's our age, Kiran. He sat leaning forward with this very intense look on his face and asked me what we should do to secure the northern frontier villages. I couldn't believe the king was asking me. 'Build a road,' I said. 'Let people travel whenever they want and not have to wait for a barge.'

"And then his old counselor leaned in and whispered in his ear that a road would lead to people going back and forth willy-nilly, too much freedom, we needed discipline on the frontier, what if everyone decided to come south for an easy life? So I interrupted and said there were plenty who would choose adventure on the frontier if they could have their own place and some freedom to move about.

"They ushered me out of there quick, and I knew I'd talked too much. I started getting ready to march out with the next company but before I knew it, I was transferred to a new captain and a month after that we were coming upriver with a company of men carrying axes and shovels along with our spears.

"When we got here, Lir had been in prison two months already and the village people still believed Ser Vetel that the attack had been nothing. So there was a lot of uproar when we brought our news." He grinned. "That old phony should be grateful the water was still warm when we dragged him through the river. I've never seen anyone look more like a drowned chicken."

He shook his head. "The one really bad part was when I had to go visit Jovan's family and tell them how he died. That part was terrible."

Kiran said, "And what did you tell them about me?"

Ryan froze, like that fawn before it fled. "I didn't say anything. No one seemed to know we'd . . ."

"I didn't tell anyone about you," Kiran said. *I didn't tell them how you abandoned your post or how you tricked me and ran out on me.* He bit his lip to keep from saying it. Ryan and he were not that different. They'd been away and now they were trying to make their way back. At least Ryan had found a purpose in being home. He said, "I haven't seen any road-building."

"First we enlarged the barracks for the bigger garrison. Thirty soldiers, Kiran, did you think Lanath would ever be so important? Other than that it's just been scouting so far. They planned to clear out the Savages first but now that's put off until spring so we'll be hacking away at the forest in the next day or two. You should join up."

Kiran stood. "I don't know. I think a road's a good idea. But since I came home, I can't stand anyone telling me what to do."

Ryan gave a hoot of laughter and stood also. "Can't be a soldier, then. But maybe you can still train with us sometimes, like you used to. And you should come play your flute by the fire."

"I thought it was all trumpet music now."

"That's fine for marching but even soldiers like to go dreamy sometimes. They're not animals, Kiran. They have homes, sweethearts. Speaking of that, what's this I hear about you and Myra?"

"What do you hear?" Kiran was surprised at the edge in his own voice. He had followed Lir's advice and stayed away from Myra. To his disappointment, he'd found she no longer even sang with the chorus. What talk could there be?

Ryan looked at him sideways. "You're a hero now. You don't have to settle, Kiran. You saved her. You don't owe her anything."

Kiran clenched his fist and rested it under Ryan's nose. "Listen. Myra is brave and beautiful and if you say another word there's a good chance I can knock us both over this waterfall before you beat me to a pulp."

Ryan raised his hands, leaning back. "Hey, anything you say, man. She's tough, she's good-looking, she's got a great voice. I agree. Not another word."

Kiran dropped his fist and Ryan threw an arm across his shoulders. "You still have to tell me your adventures but how about we do it on the way back? 'Cause if I freeze to death you'll get stuck lugging home my corpse."

Chapter 26

Winter coughed and drew back. The snow melted and Lanath enjoyed a couple weeks of almost warm weather. But the air inside Lir Coman's house had a chill the fire didn't seem to drive away. Enya's eyelids were red and puffy; at mealtimes she set Lir's plate down in front of him with a bang. At table Lir watched Kiran from under his brows. Kiran got out of the house as much as he could and even Dara slipped away when she was supposed to be indoors mending.

One time Kiran came in to dinner to find Dara kneeling in her shift, crying as she leaned over a washtub in front of the fire. Lir stood by the window, arms crossed over his chest, staring out. "What's going on?" Kiran demanded, starting forward.

His mother turned on him. "She's washing her dress. Your father found your sister on her belly in the mud, writhing around next to a filthy seffidge child!"

"We were catching fish, Kiran," Dara wailed. "I was showing him. I almost caught one!"

Enya shuddered and Lir turned from the window. "Don't talk back to your mother, child. Your brother didn't risk his life to save you so you could act like a Savage in front of the whole village."

Kiran felt as if Dara's fish were flopping over inside him. "Go easy on her, mother. She was fishing. You should be proud of her. She helped feed us on the way home, catching fish. Dara, come on, I'll help you." He started forward.

His mother stepped into his path. "You stop right there. No son of mine is going to wash clothes. That's for seffidges and disobedient girls. Kiran, your sister turned wild out there. But she's home now and she has to learn."

Kiran looked over his mother's shoulder at his sister. She caught his eye, then stuck out her lip and pulled off her shoes. With a squeal, she jumped into the tub to tromp on the soapy dress. Water splashed onto the floor.

Lir took two strides to the tub, grabbed her arm and hauled her out. Her heels dragged over the edge of the tub and he dropped her onto the hearth.

Kiran dodged around his mother to gather the sobbing Dara into his arms. "Respect!" Lir shouted overhead. "Both of you, we're glad you're back, but where's your respect for your mother?"

Kiran stood, holding Dara's head against him. "Leave her alone! You expect her to forget everything in a week or two?" He took a couple deep breaths. Enya was crying into her shawl and Lir bit the edge of his beard, puffing like a bull deciding whether to charge. "You don't understand. She's used to more—"*Freedom*, he wanted to say but that was ridiculous. Freedom, as a slave?

Still patting Dara's hair, he leveled his gaze on Lir and made his voice as flat and calm as he could. "With the Shelonwe, girls and boys are raised together and do all the same things until they're about my age. The girls are strong and healthy—"

"Your mother doesn't need child-rearing advice from you. I thought it was your girlfriend planting these ideas in Dara's head. Now I see it's you, too." Lir shifted his weight and sighed.

"Kiran, you mean well, but Dara has to learn what's right for a civilized girl now, or—"

"Or else what? You'll throw her back into the forest like my brother?" Kiran stepped away from Dara, shouting now.

Lir lunged toward Kiran with his fist raised. Kiran twisted out of his way and his mother, with a loud sob, launched herself to catch hold of Lir's arm.

"Out!" Lir's voice shook. "Out. Go stay with that girlfriend of yours. Live with her like a Savage and see how people treat you. Don't come back until you can speak with respect to your elders."

Kiran stood in the middle of the room with his hands hanging by his sides. The fire danced, he smelled dinner, the roof thatch hushed the outside world. How far had he traveled to bring Dara safely home?

His mother's form was a gray blur. He blinked hard to clear his eyes, grabbed a cloak from its peg and pushed out the door.

Darkness came early now and a damp chill hung in the air. He could go to the barracks, join up, live like Ryan, a man among boisterous men. Wasn't that what he had always wanted, to be a soldier? It must be what he still wanted because he hadn't even tried to get a flute to replace the charred memory of the one Gulik had burned. The one that had set him free.

But his steps turned away from the barracks and led instead to the rear of the village. Myra lived back here, in the low cottage flanked by the barn and paddocks where people deposited their sick animals for Nora to tend. Should he follow Lir's bitter order and ask Myra and her mother to take him in?

He faltered at the thought. He and Myra had hardly exchanged a word since their return. She didn't come to chorus practice and he hadn't visited her house. Was it really concern for her reputation that kept him away or something else, some doubt of his own? He saw her sometimes when she picked up

Dara for a walk. He felt his mother's distaste as she passed Dara out the door, as if she were being generous to let her sweet golden girl help Myra of the bushy hair and uneven dress.

But surely none of that mattered. Myra was Myra, his partner, his twin. How could he defend her from talk on the one hand and avoid actually talking to her on the other? Yet his feet seemed stuck to the ground in front of the cottage. In the darkness the steamy odor from the barn and paddocks rose and mixed with that of the herbs and flowers planted around the base of the cottage.

Myra and her mother would take him in. But in Lanath that would be like announcing their marriage. He told himself it wasn't fair to impose that on Myra. Her words in the forest—they were probably just the drunken excitement of homecoming. Like his kiss. There, he'd said it to himself. Yes, at the time, the kiss in the sparkling water had passed too quickly, too sweetly, but now he wasn't sure.

He wasn't sure of anything. To have walked so far, fought so hard and still to be sure of nothing, not even who he was or what he should be!

He turned aside from Myra's cottage. He might as well go sleep with the seffidges. At the thought, his heart thumped painfully in his chest. What was this? Curiosity to know how they really lived, there in their shed, but more—a sense that in a pen, enslaved, reviled, was the place he, too, really belonged.

He turned right, toward the long, low seffidge shed. A sentry standing at the front door gave him a nod. The sentry had a spear in his hand, a sword at his belt and at his other side a horn to call for help in case of trouble from the seffidges. A torch thrust into the ground near his feet threw his writhing shadow against the wooden wall.

Kiran hesitated.

"Looking for something?" the sentry asked.

"Checking," Kiran said. He stepped to the door, tugged on its heavy iron lock and sidled rightward to peer in through a chink between the logs. In the shadows and faint flickering light he saw bodies sprawled practically on top of one another. Shocked, he drew back. He had never stopped to figure it out—the number of seffidges, the amount of space in the shed.

Misinterpreting, the sentry laughed. "Yeah, quite a stink, isn't it? Practically knocks you over."

"Don't you give them clean straw?"

The sentry shrugged. "Don't want it, do they? Filthier than animals! You should see how they eat."

Kiran thought of scrabbling for entrails in the dirt and a wave of disgust rolled through his empty stomach.

He shouldn't have looked. And Myra lived right next to this.

Beyond the seffidge shed squatted the once-abandoned cottage where the disgraced priest lived. Kiran paused in front of it with distaste but in truth, he needed a place to sleep. He could go to the temple, beg a spot from Ser Tolan, but what price in labor would he have to pay, what lectures would he have to endure? This was better; he knew Ser Vetel and nothing the old priest could say would touch him. He knocked.

A scuffling sound, a chair pushed back, soft footsteps. An old man's tremulous voice came from behind the door. "Who is it?"

"It's Kiran. I need a place to sleep."

A pause while Kiran decided that he'd refuse to say "Your Serenity" even if it meant huddling all night in the cold. But then the door creaked open and Ser Vetel's face, greenish in the shadow, peered out.

"Have you come back to serve me, then?" the old voice creaked.

Kiran pushed the door farther open and stepped inside. "I'll chop wood and bring water in return for a bed but I'm not your servant."

"They bring me hardly enough food for one."

"I won't take your food," Kiran said as his stomach gave an exceptionally loud growl. He shot a glance at the huge pot resting on the hearth.

"Don't look at that, that's seffidge food. I suppose I could let you have some nuts and a chunk of old cheese." Ser Vetel picked up a plate and dumped the crumbs off it onto the floor. "How are the girls behaving for you? Oh, yes, don't look so surprised, of course I noticed. The chorus sounds better already. But surely you haven't apprenticed yourself to that warmonger. No ear for music, can't even hold a flute!"

"He's teaching me to read," said Kiran.

Ser Vetel's eyes narrowed. "Oh, really. And how do you find your lessons?"

"Sparse. He begrudges me every one."

"Well, I'll make a deal with you, Kiran." The priest's voice turned breathy, conspiratorial. "You bring me paper and pens, lots of paper, mind you, and I'll supplement those lessons. I'll teach you writing, too. And don't you ask what I need the paper for." He leaned closer, his stale breath blowing in Kiran's face. "They have the nerve to post me in this wilderness for thirty-five years and then sweep me aside. The unsavory secrets I know shan't die with me, my boy. I'm writing my memoirs!"

Kiran took a turn around the small room with its blotched and yellowing mortar and its close, old man smell. He felt a sudden curiosity about Ser Vetel's memoirs. Maybe the old man would write some of the true history of Lanath, the history of Kiran's own family. How bittersweet, to learn the way to see through lies from a man who had told so many of them.

"I'll bring you paper," he said.

★ ★ ★

Kiran slept wrapped in a blanket on the brick floor, dreaming he was back in the turkey pen. He woke with cold seeping into him and Ser Vetel prodding him with a foot. It was still dark but the priest said, "You promised me water and firewood, so kick yourself awake."

Kiran rolled to his feet and saw that the priest had poked the fire to life. "You should sleep longer."

"The seffidges aren't worth much till we feed them. I need to add water to this mush and heat it up. Move along!"

A new sentry stood at the door of the seffidge shed and he looked surprised to see Kiran emerge from the priest's cottage, carrying a bucket and rubbing his eyes. By the time Kiran returned from the well the first time, the sentry had unlocked the door. In the time it took him to haul four more buckets of water, bunches of seffidges plodded out of their quarters, scratched, squinted at the sky, visited the outhouse, then squatted in front of their pen, picking bugs off each other's skin.

As Kiran carried the fifth bucket into the cottage, Ser Vetel turned away from the pot, wiping some kind of brown powder from his hands. "That's water enough. Leave that one over there for me."

"You add spices?" Kiran asked, looking at the priest's hands. "I never even knew you could cook."

The priest gave a wheezy laugh. "Cook? I just make the seffidge mush, morning and night. Anything else they need, the soldiers bring them. But me—yes, I've stooped to this. 'You're to work for your living,' the council members said, as if all the music and preaching, record-keeping and visiting the sick meant nothing, all those years."

"But why mush? Why the seffidges?"

Ser Vetel regarded him through narrowed eyes. "Too many questions. Fetch me more wood."

Kiran stacked wood beside the fireplace. The pot was now simmering and a sweet, sickly smell rose from it. "It smells like nuath."

"Nonsense. Nuath smells sharper. This is just the fortifying power I add. We need our seffidges strong." The priest snickered. "But not too strong. Now fetch the sentry and tell him it's ready."

The sentry wrapped a cloth around his hands and helped Kiran lug the pot out to the seffidge yard. Holding wooden bowls, the seffidges filed by as Ser Vetel spooned shapeless globs of mush out of the pot. The seffidges put the bowls close to their faces and used dirty fingers to scoop the food into their mouths. The sentry, standing next to Kiran, wrinkled his nose in distaste.

"So give them spoons, then," Kiran said.

The sentry gave him a puzzled look and sidestepped away.

Ser Vetel plopped the last dollop of mush into the bowl of a returning seffidge. "That's it, now. More tonight." He jerked his chin at the sentry and the seffidges gazed after the pot with dull longing as the sentry rolled it back toward the cottage.

The sun was up now; three more soldiers arrived to herd the seffidges out for their day's work. Kiran moved away from the priest's cottage so he wouldn't get saddled with any more chores.

He found himself standing once more in front of Myra's house. Firelight showed through the window and he stepped onto the threshold, then hesitated, his hand lifted to knock. What must she think of him now? His fingers felt clumsy. Home almost a month already and he hadn't visited her once. He had defended her, spoken up for her and avoided her. How she must despise him!

The door flew open, making him step rapidly off the threshold. She stood there with a bucket in her hand. A sense that she was foreign sizzled through him. Her hair was a bushy brown mess.

"There you are, you foot dragger," she said. "I thought you'd never come. I'm just getting water. Go on in."

He let out his breath in a long sigh. She was just Myra, bossing. His twin, not his girlfriend. Relief washed over him as he ducked inside.

Chapter 27

"Lir should have given you a new flute at least," Myra said after Nora had fed them both on oatmeal bread slathered with jam. "Before he got around to throwing you out, I mean."

Indignation made her cheeks pink.

Kiran shook his head. "I don't want to be the village flute-boy any more."

"Don't, then. Be Kiran the musician."

Nora smiled and moved her chair to the edge of the room. She climbed onto it to reach for a bundle of purple flowers dangling from the thatch. Herbs and flowers hung all over the room and bowls of crumbled petals lined the shelf.

Kiran tumbled over himself in his hurry to reach Nora's chair. "Let me help you get that."

"No, no. You and Myra go check on the animals."

The paddock behind the house, crowded up against the village wall, held two sheep whose eyes were weeping mucus. Myra threw them some hay and wiped their eyes with a damp rag. In the next paddock, a thin, tottering cow came and laid her heavy chin in Myra's outstretched hand. Myra scratched her cheeks, then lifted a bucket into the paddock and climbed over the fence. She righted a stump and sat on it at the cow's side. When she tugged, she got only a thin trickle of milk.

She passed the bucket through to Kiran. "Toss it out. We're not sure the milk is any good."

While he poured the milk away, she turned the cow around. Looking back, Kiran caught a whiff of something so rotten it made his head whirl. The cow had a deep hole in her right flank and it was dripping pus.

"Oh, good," Myra said. "It's draining." She tugged a tangle of sodden wool that hung from the opening. With a sound like a foot pulling free of mud, the matted wool came out of the wound, yellowed, stinking, covered in pus and pale watery serum.

"Here!" Myra tossed the wool to Kiran. He recoiled, letting it fall at his feet, and she laughed. "Never mind, don't pick it up. We'll bury that one."

She climbed out of the paddock and led him back to the cottage.

"Mother, the cow's ready to be packed again."

Nora came to the cottage door carrying a bowl of what looked like a clear green soup. "Kiran, will you carry this? Just a minute, let me get the packing." She returned a moment later with an armful of clean, dry wool.

They filed back out to the paddock, where Nora gave her daughter a keen look. "Ready to try it yourself this time?"

Myra said, "Kiran, will you set the pot right here? And then if you can just hold her head."

Too surprised to beg out of it, Kiran took hold of the cow's halter and gazed into her dull brown eyes. Myra rolled up her sleeve, dipped a hank of wool into the pot of liquid Kiran had carried and reached into the wound. Kiran gagged and the cow jerked her head.

"Hold still," Myra said. Kiran caught sight of her scornful face, steadied himself and murmured soothing noises to the cow. Myra scrubbed inside the wound, then tossed aside the soiled hank of wool.

Kiran swallowed and looked at Nora. "What's in the soup?"

"Hensbane, feverfew. Dara knows them." Nora smiled at him. "Boiled together overnight. We boil the wool, too, then hang it up to dry."

"Boil it?" Kiran asked at random, trying not to breathe through his nose. "Why?"

"Boiling makes bubbles and we think bubbles help cut the pus. But this cow . . ." Nora paused. "Look at her ribs. She's suffering and if she weren't Grandma Sola's only wealth, I'd let her go. Are you any good at catching snakes?"

"Snakes?" Kiran looked back in time to see Myra stuff wool into the cow's wound, more and more of it, until she left a twist trailing from the opening.

"Goldenrod snakes. Those little green ones with the yellow markings that make your foot swell up black and blue if you step on them. A little of their venom mixed in with the soup, scrubbed around the edges of the wound, would make it bleed clear."

Myra stepped back from her work, then passed the leftover wool to her mother and picked up the pot. "You can let her go now, Kiran. Yes, let's fetch Dara and ask her to catch snakes with us!"

"Dara's got herself in trouble. They won't be letting her out today. And I have to rehearse the chorus. Why don't you come sing anymore, Myra?"

Nora twitched an eyebrow, smiled and left them.

Myra lifted her chin. "I don't need any examiners to choose me. I'm not so keen on Catora any more."

"Why not?"

"I don't want to be a servant." She looked at him and he felt an answering lurch in his own heart. "I've had enough of it. I want to choose what I do, the way my mother does."

"So do I," Kiran said. "I can't stand anybody saying, *Do this*, or *You can't do that*."

"Girls can't learn that. Out of our way. That's not proper for women."

"What do you want to do instead?"

Myra flushed. "Healing. I want to take what my mother knows and what I learned from Ranga. The only reason I would go to Catora would be to study with the healers there, so I could put it all together and teach people so they don't lose their babies to fever and their husbands to injuries that go bad and—"

She broke off. "I don't even know if there's a school for healing in Catora but there must be, to teach the priests and take care of the army, don't you think so?"

A strand of hair hung over her face. Kiran reached to push it behind her ear. "I could ask Ser Tolan, or Ryan might know. His company was camped next to a hospital. Come to chorus practice."

She shook her head. "Not if you won't even get a new flute."

"I'll go see the carpenter this morning. Jovan's father."

"What about the goldenrod snake?"

"Just before sunset, meet me by the rock wall behind the meadow. Maybe we can find one sleeping in its winter home."

★ ★ ★

Not that day, but another, at midday when the sun warmed the field a little, they found a sluggish snake on the stone wall. When Kiran poked at it with a stick, it withdrew into a crack where it shared a nest with five others. With his forked stick, Kiran lifted them into a basket and they carried it back to the village.

Nora showed them how to get venom from the snakes. She spread a thin membrane like the skin of a sausage over the top of a jar, then pinched one of the snakes behind the neck. When its mouth yawned open, she jammed its fangs into the membrane. It discharged its venom and when she lifted the membrane, two gleaming drops clung to its underside. She let them take turns to milk the other snakes and then she set the basket in a dark corner of the room and covered it with a lid. "We'll keep them inside this winter," she said. "Every ten days we can milk them and what we don't use we'll dry for future need."

Nora dipped a twig into the snake venom and then swirled the drop of venom into the green healing soup. "Just what comes on the stick, no more," she instructed them. "We only want the cow to bleed where the tissue is scarred and scabbed over. There, shall we try it right now? Be sure you don't have any cuts on your hands."

Kiran held the cow while Myra soaked a handful of wool in the soup and used it to scrub out the wound.

"Rub hard," Nora urged. "Get out all the dead flesh."

Myra scrubbed so hard the cow staggered, rolled her eyes at Kiran and lowed in protest. When Myra pulled the wool out, a trickle of red blood followed.

The next morning, the sick cow finished her hay and mooed for more.

★ ★ ★

Kiran moved along the shelves of the carpenter shop, hefting short lengths of hardwood perfect for flute-making: cherry, birch, walnut. Jovan's father reached past him and picked up a block of cherry. "See how straight and tight the grain is. This one will dull you a chisel or two, but she'll make a fine flute."

Kiran took it, turned it in his hand and heard no music. He put it back. None of the pieces of wood inspired him. It was like a sickness of the soul, he thought, not to care enough even to choose.

He wandered out into the yard behind the shop. Leaning against the wall was the aged limb of a beech tree. Someone had dragged it into the yard after the branch broke under a seffidge's weight. Kiran could see where Lir's workers had tunneled into the meat of the limb to draw out the fungus after it had fallen. The smaller branches looked intact.

What would a beechwood flute sound like?

Kiran ducked back into the shop with its clean sawdust smell and waited until Jovan's father had finished taking an order for six new bowls. "Can I make a flute from the branch of that beech outside?"

The carpenter shrugged. "I've no other use for it. I know your stepfather meant well having his seffidges drag it here, but I never trust a beech tree. Make someone a marriage bed and even though you think it's clean, there's fungus eating away at the heartwood. All of a sudden on his wedding night the buyer gets too vigorous and the wood breaks. Ill omen for the marriage and ill business for me. But take a look if you want to." He handed Kiran a saw.

★ ★ ★

Kiran's days fell into a jagged rhythm. Up before dawn to haul water and wood for Ser Vetel. Breakfast with Myra and Nora, after which he helped Myra with her chores, or watched and listened as she and her mother worked with sick animals the villagers had brought them. Then he went to the carpenter's shop, where he swept and sawed and did odd jobs for Jovan's father in return for instruction in flute-making. The carpenter's wife brought them bread and cheese at midday and sat watching Kiran with such a look of longing for her own dead son that the food fell heavily on his stomach.

In the afternoon, if there was no chorus practice, Kiran followed the sound of spades and axes out of the village to Ryan's road, which was cutting south of the village along the river. Soldiers scouted ahead while Ryan supervised the team of seffidges felling trees, uprooting stumps and clearing rocks. In his excitement, Ryan often stooped to pull at a stump right alongside a seffidge. Kiran chopped branches off felled trees and loaded wood onto the ox cart to haul back to Lanath to strengthen the village wall. He watched the seffidges, trying to see if he could glimpse another Setolo among them—a man somewhere with rebellion flashing in his eye—but he saw none.

The soldiers took turns leaving the road and walking back to the open space just outside the walls for training. They let Kiran join them, though they gave him no real weapons, just a wooden sword and a staff in place of a spear. He felt stupid thrusting and parrying against imaginary enemies in time to the sergeant's grunted orders. Sometimes it seemed to him that the life of a soldier must be tedious indeed.

Toward evening Kiran returned to the village and descended the temple stair for his reading lesson with Ser Tolan. Kiran tended the fire and swept the floor as he used to do for Ser Vetel, making sure he was nearby when a village woman—they took turns—appeared with Ser Tolan's meal. The women always brought too much for even a hearty young priest to eat, so Kiran got his share, sitting cross-legged on the floor. After dinner he went to Ser Tolan's study for a sheet of paper and quill, which he laid before the priest. Each time, he tucked another couple of sheets of paper inside his tunic to bring to Ser Vetel.

They had worked through all 43 letters now and Ser Tolan was beginning to show him how the letters fit together into words. "Of course, this is just the surface meaning," the young priest said, sitting back with his hands folded over his belly. "For the symbolic meaning you'll need to wait several years yet."

Ser Tolan warned him not to share what he learned about reading with anyone. "Such knowledge can only mislead the ignorant," he said, in a voice so condescending that Kiran resolved to disobey him. When Nora asked, he showed her how to make the letters of her name. He even carved the symbol for the start of Myra's name into the edge of her table so she could learn the shape of it with her finger.

When Ser Tolan grew tired of teaching him and shooed him away, Kiran made his way back to Ser Vetel's to sleep.

With variations—a fishing excursion with Ryan, extra chorus practices, a day when Jovan's father asked him to help set up a new doorframe—these were Kiran's days and he should have been happy. He had shaped the strands of his life together the way he was shaping the girls' chorus and all of it was his choice, from eating breakfast under the dried flowers in Nora's house to taking his supper in the starry underground temple room that had once meant so much to him. He should have been happy; he couldn't understand why he still felt a hollow at the pit of his stomach.

Of course he missed Dara and his mother. Truth be told, he even missed Lir, with his bulk and bluster. A good son, wrong or right, would go home, apologize, ask to be taken back. *A good man makes things whole.*

But for that Kiran decided to wait until he finished his new beechwood flute. Once he had shaped the outside, he braced it and drilled into it with an auger. After he had drilled an inch, he blew the wood dust out of it and discovered that Jovan's father had been right: a wisp of fungus hung from the hole. He thought about throwing the piece of wood away, but there was something about its grain and color he still liked. So he decided to burn the fungus out. With an ember from the shop fire, he set the wisp of fungus alight. It smoldered, filling the shop with the smell of incense and making Kiran feel both calm and mysterious. When the ember extinguished itself, the rotten heartwood had burned away. Kiran worked to scrape the inside of the flute smooth. Because of the track the fungus had taken in its growth, there were serpentine grooves along the bore of the instrument but when he started to drill the finger holes, the sound was still good.

Once the flute was ready, Kiran sat at night in the corner of Ser Vetel's hut, learning its tones. Ser Vetel made a sour face when he played but didn't interrupt. This flute was fashioned for playing laments instead of the merry village songs people requested. Kiran improvised a song of his broken family, a song of his father's unhealing wound, a song of captivity and the taste of dirt in his mouth as Gulik ground his face into the earth.

But even music wasn't enough.

Chapter 28

A month after the midwinter feast, infection spread through Lanath. Its symptoms were cough, fever and shortness of breath, and it hit the young, the old and seffidges most heavily. When the sentry opened their shed door one morning, the seffidges staggered out, some of them crawling, hacking and coughing, gasping. Even when the soldier went inside to prod at them with the butt end of his spear, some of the seffidges just rolled over on the filthy straw, groaning. Those who emerged turned their heads away when their fellows offered them their bowls of mush.

"Fetch that woman Nora," Ser Vetel told Kiran.

Nora came, with Myra trailing after. The herb woman walked from one seffidge to another, peering into mouths, tapping her knuckles against their chests, shaking her head.

The sick seffidges sat with their hands braced against the ground, laboring to breathe.

Impatient with waiting, the sentry started herding the healthier ones together to send out to work. Nora stopped him. "Tell the captain no work today and not till they're better."

The sentry stared at her, then turned on his heel.

"Now Kiran, Myra, help me," Nora said. She asked some of the healthy seffidges, the ones still on their feet and breathing easily, to help, too. They hauled the filthy straw out of the shed to the courtyard, where Kiran brought smoldering logs from Ser Vetel's fire to set the sodden bedding alight. Then Nora made Kiran and the seffidges haul bucket after bucket of water into the shed to splash on the walls while she and Myra scrubbed with brooms.

Ser Vetel disappeared into his hut. As they finished cleaning, he appeared again, trailed by a soldier lugging a pot of some hot drink. "If they can't eat, at least make them drink this," he said to Kiran.

Nora looked over at him. "Is that what Ser Tolan's been giving the children in the village?"

Ser Vetel's face turned an unseemly color. "My concoctions are none of your business."

Nora pressed her lips together and nodded at Kiran. With Myra, he carried bowls of steaming liquid to one seffidge after another. Most of them took the bowl dully and sipped at it with chapped lips but some turned away or even batted at the bowl in refusal, spilling the liquid over the ground.

One mother held a baby to her breast. The baby refused to suckle but the mother pressed the limp body against her again and again until Nora took the child and peeled the mother's hands away. As the baby drooped lifeless in Nora's arms, the mother looked at the small body, then at Nora's face, then back again. When she understood, she slid and lay with her face on the ground, her body rippling with sobs.

★ ★ ★

That day and the next, Kiran didn't go to the road or the temple. There was no chorus practice. Village people came to pick up seffidges to do their chores but with a firm quiet word Myra sent them away. Ser Vetel limped off to help Ser Tolan minister to houses that had been struck with the illness but none were as hard hit as the seffidges. Soon enough the villagers who came to see backed away, shaking their heads. Ser Tolan sent Tad for Kiran but Kiran pretended not to hear. Before long the priest himself arrived and called him over behind the file of houses that backed onto the seffidge camp.

"Kiran, you brainless fool, come away, you'll catch the sickness."

"I'm all right so far."

Ser Tolan's eyes flicked over him. "Yes, you're a tough one. But listen, it's not so much that I need you for chorus practice right now, it's that..."

"Yes?"

"Too many people have seen you down here. I have mothers telling me they won't send their daughters any more if you wallow up to your elbows in filth with these seffidges."

"The filth comes from the way we make them live."

"The chorus, Kiran, the chorus."

"People are dying here."

The priest startled and looked swiftly around. Then his face relaxed as he appeared to realize that Kiran was talking about not village people, but seffidges. *Not people at all*, Kiran thought bitterly.

Kiran said, "Are the women frantic, with no seffidges to haul water and grind grain and wash clothes for them?"

Ser Tolan nodded, watching him.

"Well, here's an idea. Let them teach their children to do those things: firewood, water, cleaning."

Ser Tolan reddened, sputtered and turned away.

★ ★ ★

By the third day, some of the seffidges began to shake and rave. "Delirium," Nora said. "It comes with the fever."

But Myra came back from bathing them and said to Kiran, "They're not all hot. I think the ones raving are the ones who haven't been eating."

Kiran wouldn't have expected hunger to make people thrash and rave so. But then, he reflected, seffidges were different. There was no use denying it. He had found among them no trace of the fierce Shelonwe pride; sometimes it was still hard for him to believe they were the same people. They submitted, heavily, stupidly, to whatever they were ordered to do.

The delirious seffidges thrashed on the ground, rolled to their feet. Their eyes grew wild, with the whites showing all around the green iris. They shook their heads and ground their teeth. When Myra tried to bring them water they turned violently away and one of them shoved her. The sentry stepped forward and brought a club down on the offender's shoulder, and he collapsed to his knees, saliva bubbling from his mouth.

The commotion brought Ser Vetel to the door of his hut. When he saw the writhing seffidges, he called to Kiran, "Come here, you numbskull. Make them drink, make them drink the brew!" His words ended in a string of coughs that ran down and diminished until he was left leaning against the doorframe, gripping it to hold him up.

Kiran ran to support the old man. He helped him back into the hut and half lifted him to sit on his bed against the wall with the blankets drawn up over his knees. The priest leaned forward, gasping. Kiran felt a kind of panic grab him. Angry he had been at this old man, but the priest had been his teacher for many years—had taught him music, after all.

"I'll get you some of the brew," he said.

The priest's long fingers wrapped in Kiran's sleeve. "No. That's not for us . . . our kind. Get me some of that glop, that soup, the stuff the woman makes."

Puzzled, Kiran obeyed. Ser Vetel dozed off and on, and at the end of the day, he tried to rise but Kiran pushed him back.

Ser Vetel slapped weakly at his hand. "Help me up, boy. I have to make the seffidge broth."

"Tell me how to do it. Do you use that brown powder?"

Ser Vetel narrowed his eyes, peered at Kiran and then suddenly nodded. "You'll have to grind some fresh. Open that box over there." His long finger pointed.

Kiran lifted down the box and opened it. Inside coiled fibrous, dry stems of old nuath. "You use nuath?"

"Stems, boy. Not fit for regular humans but yes, stems. No part of the fungus wasted, that's what makes it so valuable."

"But why?"

"Keeps them docile, boy, what do you think? They're beasts otherwise. Maybe they'd be tame enough if we fed them scraps from our tables and let them sleep on our hearths like snufflers but people aren't going to allow that, are they? Who knows when they might rise up and throttle the children in their beds?" Ser Vetel barked out a laugh, which broke into coughing. When he had wiped his mouth and managed to catch his breath again, he added, "So we give them a little something to damp down their vicious ways."

"You drug them," Kiran said. All at once he understood the dull eyes, the slouched posture, the seffidges' mute stupidity. "You put it in their mush every day. You drug them to keep them slaves."

"Don't be an idiot, Kiran! You see them out there, the ones who haven't drunk any, babbling and thrashing like madmen. Do you want to see them start tearing their hair, scratching their clothes off, attacking each other, attacking the soldiers? Then it will be swords, not clubs coming down on them, you soft-bellied wriggling excuse for a Lanath man!"

Kiran trembled with anger. But out the door he could see a wild seffidge swaying his head back and forth, starting, indeed, to tug at his hair and cry out in a language neither of Lanath nor of the Shelonwe. His cries were desperate. Hastily Kiran threw a root down on the table and ground it with a granite pestle. When he had finished he followed Ser Vetel's instructions, measuring the powder out into the water, boiling them together and then letting the broth cool.

But Setolo had survived, he thought stubbornly. Setolo was too sick to eat and instead of dying, he woke up. When he recovered from his sickness, he knew who he was again and from that moment he burned to escape. And the seffidges that Setolo and Gulik stole from the barge—the Shelonwe hadn't given them nuath any more and when Kiran saw them a month later they looked like men, not shuffling beasts.

When the broth had cooled far enough, Kiran called to the soldiers. They lugged the pot out to the yard. Kiran dipped up bowls full of broth and with three soldiers helping him now, took them around to the seffidges, starting first with the wildest. It helped that they were thirsty and though often as not they knocked the first bowl away, Kiran found that if the soldiers held a seffidge's arms long enough for him to spill a little of the broth on the thrashing man's lips, soon he would be licking his lips and looking about wildly for more. He went back to the cottage to make more broth and gradually the floundering and raucous shouting in the yard grew quieter.

Chapter 29

When the sickness was over, Kiran didn't return to the temple. He remembered the stories of his childhood, how the Sky Serpent's scales fell from the sky as starry seeds that sprang up as men and women, and how the men and women formed seffidges out of mud to be their servants. *Well, now I'm tainted with mud,* he thought. *I've been that way ever since the Shelonwe made me their slave. I know what it is to think like a slave. I can't see the great distance between us. I can't rise back up to the sky level and grind the mud people beneath my heel.*

He thought in despair, *I don't belong in my village anymore.*

Now he spent his days with the soldiers, working on the road or practicing in the field outside the village walls. He learned the sword thrusts, the maneuvers of men with spears, the sudden shouts and turns. When the soldiers marched through the snow, sweat sprang to his face and his breath mixed with theirs in hot steam. He was part of something elemental and unthinking like water rushing in its channel. In the evening he drank beer and ate meat in the barracks and banged his mug against the table until a seffidge came scuttling to refill it.

He still breakfasted with Myra and Nora and slept at Ser Vetel's place. Once, passing Nora's house on his way to the old priest's, he spied Ryan leaning on the gate deep in conversation with Myra. "What were you talking about?" he demanded the next morning.

Myra tucked her hair behind her ears. "He's not such an oaf anymore. He has dreams. He tells me about his road." She looked at Kiran sideways. "He's been asking about the hospital in Catora for me."

A pebble rolled in Kiran's stomach. He had promised to ask for her. He had hung back from doing it—why?—and she'd turned to Ryan instead. He didn't like the way their heads had bent close over the fence. Though why shouldn't she listen to Ryan? Ryan had dreams; what dreams did Kiran have? Since the seffidge sickness he just wanted to fell trees, jab with his wooden spear, march, his mind empty.

One day Lir met the company as they marched through the gate at dusk. He stepped into the flow to touch Kiran's shoulder and beckon him aside. Hesitating, Kiran lost a step, took a shove and a curse from behind, then broke out of the company and faced Lir.

His stepfather gazed past him at the gate. "Your mother invites you to dinner," Lir said. He took a breath and looked Kiran in the eye. "We were worried when we heard about the seffidge fever. We want you to come home."

Kiran ducked his head. A surge of emotion rushed into him and he feared his eyes might brim over with tears. He gave a nod and followed his stepfather home. He smelled the wood smoke rising from the cottages, sweet in the sharp night air.

Dara ran to throw her arms around him and bury her head against his stomach, and his mother embraced him, weeping. The food was a stew of vegetables and mutton, with herbs that the barracks didn't know. The family spoke carefully of progress on the road, the weather—hadn't there been a lot of snow this winter?—and Lir's experiments with saplings in the nuath grove.

After dinner Kiran rose and thanked his mother. She fretted and pulled him to see the bed she had made for him by the fire but he shook his head and told her politely that Ser Vetel, old and feeble now, still needed someone to care for him at night.

"What about the potter's boy, that Tad?" she asked, fussing to smooth out the front of his tunic.

"Tad's with Ser Tolan now. Everyone's abandoned him, Mother."

Behind her, Lir shook his head. "Kiran, this fascination you have for the disgraced and degraded, the lowest of the low ..."

Enya whirled to hush him and he stopped mid-sentence.

Kiran said slowly, "If my actions are disgracing this family, I will keep my distance from you."

Dara burst into tears and Enya cried, "No, no!"

Even Lir shook his head. As he walked Kiran to the door, he said quietly, "It's just that we miss you, son." He let his hand rest on Kiran's shoulders for a moment, then released him.

"Come back tomorrow!" his mother called after him as he trod away through the gently swirling snow.

★ ★ ★

One day as the men gathered to march out to the road head—an hour's quick march now—the captain called Kiran out of line. He jerked his head and Kiran followed him back to the barracks, up to the walk along the rampart of the wall. The sky was a clear, surprised blue and bits of vegetation poked through the snow cover where they looked across the fields and toward the forested hills.

"You seem ready to join up," the captain said.

Kiran's stomach jolted. He should have foreseen this. In spite of all the time he was spending with the soldiers, in spite of the beer and the camaraderie, he knew he didn't want to bind himself. But the captain could draft him in an instant.

He spoke carefully. "I'm doing a lot of different work in the village. But I'm happy to volunteer my time."

The captain raised his eyebrows. "A lot of different work? Nursemaid to seffidges and old men? I hear you abandoned the chorus. But never mind. The point is we're planning our spring campaign and it's time for you to help with the maps and the guiding."

"The spring campaign?" Winter had passed too fast.

"We expect reinforcements on the first spring barge. You will guide us to the Savage village from which the cowardly attack on our river traffic was launched and we will wipe it out. It's already been too long. Punishment should come swiftly, like lightning out of the sky."

"What if . . . if the Shelonwe aren't back yet?" For a moment Kiran pictured it as if Myra's lie had been true, as if the village lay empty, waiting for its people to return.

The captain's eyes narrowed. "They return when the ice breaks up, that's what the girl said. If not, we ambush them when they come."

Kiran closed his eyes. In his mind the Shelonwe village became furnished with mottled bodies, sprawled face down among the houses. *And what do I care?* he thought with fierce anger. *They enslaved me. They are my enemy.*

The captain's voice carried an edge of impatience. "You will assist us, as a volunteer guide or under compulsion. I must say, I expected a prompter willingness to serve."

Kiran met his eye. "Sir, I volunteer. I'm just thinking. There is an instinct that guides us home, sir, and still we didn't come the most direct way. Getting back . . . I don't know. I'm trying to make a picture in my mind."

The captain grinned. "Ha! That's more like it. Come along to the barracks and talk to the mapmaker. We'll see if your memories and his colors can draw out the way."

★ ★ ★

At dinner that night Kiran asked his stepfather, "What do you think of this spring campaign against the Savages?"

Lir tipped back his chair and clasped his hands. "I hope it works. We can't have them attacking barges."

"There's another way," Kiran said carefully.

Lir watched him from under his black eyebrows, waiting.

"They stole the girls to make them slaves like we do with the seffidges. It was a kind of revenge. I know they'd make peace with us if Lanath would free the seffidges."

Lir let his chair drop. "Not a chance."

Kiran's face grew hot. "That's what I told them when they offered to trade the three of us for all the seffidges. But listen. Suppose we opened the door—just let the seffidges go, a few at a time, as a gesture of peace."

"Don't be childish, Kiran. I can think of at least seven reasons that's the stupidest idea I ever heard."

Enya jumped up and began clearing the table. Dara stared from her father to her brother. Kiran fought to keep his voice polite. "Tell me the reasons. Please."

"One: they're seffidges, they know nothing better than working for us. Two: they're stupid and won't survive on their own. Three: Savages don't care for anyone and won't want to be burdened with useless half men. Four: Who's going to do the work they leave behind? Five: The purpose of this village is to harvest nuath. We can't do that without their labor."

Lir shot up from his chair and paced, his boot heels striking the stone floor. He threw a look at Kiran, who was still waiting, and with a growl he added, "Six and seven! What, you'd take the word of these Savages? Show any sign of weakness, they'll swarm over us like a pack of wolves."

Kiran set down his spoon. "It's the nuath, isn't it? Where would we be without nuath? Let's see, we'd have priests that don't see visions. But you don't believe their visions anyway, do you, Lir? What else? We'd have seffidges that we can't control, because we drug them, don't we, to keep them stupid? And you, well, you wouldn't be the richest man in the village, would you? So is that what we have to march out and die for?"

"Kiran!" shouted his mother, running back to the table. She leaned across it with a clanking of plates and caught his wrist. "You may not speak to your father that way."

"My father?"

She stuffed her fist in her mouth, but Lir stared at Kiran, his big head bobbing slightly, his mouth open.

"I do my part," Lir said at last. "I do my part for the kingdom and I don't ask questions. Neither should you."

"Then you're a slave, too. Slave to the nuath, just like all of us. Else why can't we move to Catora if we want? Why'd you send Dara off to the city and not go along to watch over her? Because of the nuath."

"I do my part," Lir said again. "You're young. What do you know of empires and how they're built? If you can't treat your family with respect, at least show loyalty to your king."

Kiran gripped the edge of the table, struggling to hold his tongue. He didn't want to fight. He waited; Lir waited, too, breathing heavily through his nostrils.

Finally, in a voice as calm as he could make it, Kiran asked, "Is it disloyal to try and find a way without bloodshed?"

His mother was crying silently now, her face crinkled up, leaning into the table as though shielding him and Lir from one another.

Dara came around behind her, slipped her hand in Kiran's.

Kiran squeezed Dara's hand and let it drop. He said, "Thank you for dinner, mother. I'll go now." To Lir he said, "Can you tell me when the first barge is expected?"

Lir grunted. "No more than ten days." He passed a hand over his face. "I wish it could be as you say, boy. No warfare, no slaves. But that's not the way the world works."

He cast a look of appeal at his wife. She turned to Kiran, one hand held out, the other gripping the chair back.

"Kiran, don't you see?" his mother pleaded. "If you don't like things—if things about Lanath seem wrong to you—Catora, too, if you think the way they tell us to live is wrong—well, that's why you should become a priest, to change things. You can't do it by yelling and insulting people and striding around, Kiran, you can't. You'll just end up in jail or banished, and we'll have lost you for no reason. Just do this one last thing they ask you, Kiran, and then you can go to Catora and change the world."

Then, as if exhausted by her long speech, she pulled the chair out and sank into it.

Lir walked his stepson to the door and when Kiran passed, he gave him his hand. "You'll be back tomorrow, then?"

★ ★ ★

"It's not just the seffidges," he told Myra later.

"What's not?" They were talking in low voices at a corner of the table. Myra ran her finger around the letter of her name that he had carved into the table edge. Nora was out attending a birth.

"Trudging around like they're drugged, not fighting back. It's not just the seffidges, it's all of us." He put his face in his hands. "Ryan would kill for the chance at glory I have. I get to map the camp layout, advise the captain on the terrain, lead the company in for the kill. The Savages are our enemies. They broke my family and I swore to sweep them away. There should be trumpet music playing in my head but all I hear is a broken flute."

"So why don't you refuse?"

"The captain will just throw me in jail and then they'll march out anyway. You know what the campaign plan was before we showed up, you and me and Dara? They were going to throw a couple of seffidges out in the woods. They thought their homing instinct would take them to the Savages, like animals finding their own kind."

"Maybe you could lead them wrong, get them lost in the woods."

"And look like a hopeless idiot. They'd go back to plan one." He shook his head. "I keep thinking about what he offered me. Setolo."

"What do you mean?"

"When I first walked into the village, he offered a trade, our freedom for the seffidges'. But I knew Lanath wouldn't go for it, because we rely on the seffidges too much. So then . . . do you ever wonder if he wanted us to escape?"

"Setolo?"

"What if that's why he took us to that island?"

She stood up, shaking her head, and cleared his cup away. "They took us to that island to gather herbs and prepare for my wedding to that wolf Gulik. Setolo and Ranga, for all their scruples, would have fed me to him. Anything for Setolo's brother, to heal his damaged soul, that's the way they talked about it."

"But at the end Ranga let us slip away."

"Yes." She sank back into her seat beside him, biting her lip.

"And now she'll see her husband slaughtered and the village children enslaved and the village burning and she'll know what we're really like."

Myra reached for his hand but he jerked it away and stood up. "I never made a promise to Setolo. Do you hear me? I never said I could make it happen because I knew I never could."

"What are you talking about?"

He strode back and forth the length of the room. "I feel it pounding inside me, Myra, as if I made the promise. Our freedom for theirs. Ever since the sickness, when I found out about what Ser Vetel gives them, I hear it roaring in my ears at night. Our freedom for theirs."

She stood and touched his arm again. "Kiran, I hate the way we treat the seffidges. I always have, even when you thought it was the natural way of things. But the way you're talking is crazy. Say you did let them out somehow. First of all, the seffidges would get lost and die in the woods. Second, the soldiers would string you up and hang you as a traitor."

Kiran reached a hand to his throat, where the scar of Gulik's cord still traced a thin raised line like a collar. Myra was right.

She watched his fingers run along the mark of his servitude and spoke as if to seal the argument once and for all. "You'd be better off back with the Shelonwe yourself."

He stared at her. At that moment, the door swung open and Nora stepped over the threshold, unwrapping her shawl.

"A fat pink little girl," she announced. "The father looks so proud!"

Chapter 30

He had ten days. If he was going to do anything to quiet the roaring in his head, he had only ten days. As soon as the barge arrived, he would belong to the army. Already the captain was pressing him to sleep in the barracks.

It would have to be at night. During the day the seffidges were divided, the men out on the road or in the nuath grove, the women and children working in the village. And if at night they could somehow slip past the guards and away from the village, they would have a head start of several hours.

But the seffidge shed was at the very back of the village, farthest from the gate. How could he lead a hundred-twenty seffidges through the winding streets of the whole village without being seen? How could he make the dull, lethargic seffidges follow him to begin with? He lay awake all that night, staring through the darkness at Ser Vetel's roof, trying to think it through.

Toward morning he worked out that in eight days it would be the new moon, a night of full darkness. If he was going to do it, that should be the night. He felt sick at the thought. He would be choosing exile and the condemnation of everyone who had ever loved him. If he led the seffidges away, he could never return home. But the plan kept forming, playing itself out in his head.

By dawn the plan was swelling inside him so that it seemed he must tell somebody or burst. He slipped out of Ser Vetel's hut, brought the water and started the fire. The bubbling pot mirrored his insides, as if anyone looking at him could see his plan boiling over. He had to tell Myra; she would call him crazy again and once he had spilled all his thoughts, this terrible pressure inside him would be released. Myra would talk him out of it.

All through breakfast at Nora's he fidgeted, while Nora shot him puzzled looks and tried to get him to eat more. Once he and Myra were outside, he tried to form his lips around what he needed to say but the words were so outlandish, so treasonous, that he found it difficult to speak. Only on the way back from the paddock, where the cow was fattening up nicely, did he pull Myra aside.

"Listen, I have to talk to you. You made me think. The only way to free the seffidges is for me to go with them. First we have to stop drugging them, then I have to hide supplies in the forest." Arms waving, he let the plan pour out of him.

As he knew she would, Myra shook her head. "You're crazy. You'll never get away with it. How will you deal with the guards? Unless . . ." She broke off, looking thoughtful, then shook her head again. "Even if they don't catch you, imagine the disgrace for your family! They'll throw Lir in prison again."

Kiran pictured Lir in the guardhouse. He wasn't sure the picture bothered him that much. But another thought struck him.

"Myra, you're the one they'll throw in prison!" The certainty clanged in his head; he let his shoulders drop and felt the tension leave them. Of course the village would suspect Myra. Of course he couldn't put her in that danger. Relief flooded him: it couldn't be done.

Myra set her jaw. "So I'll come with you."

She stood there, the milk bucket swaying against her leg, her shoulders thrown back and her eyes smoldering in that stubborn way they had. A shiver went through him. From her look, he knew she would really do it—leave everything behind to help him finish this task.

He took a deep breath, let it go and shook his head. "They'd just go after your mother."

"My mother's tough. She can handle them."

He studied her face. "But you're going to Catora to study healing."

She hesitated, dropping her gaze; then she threw her hair back and said, "That can wait. I still have plenty to learn from the Shelonwe." But then her face turned white. "Oh, Lady, I didn't think. Gulik will claim me back."

Kiran pictured a wolf, crouched and snarling, and in spite of himself he felt all the old fear and self-loathing he'd experienced as a slave. "That can't happen, Myra. We can't ever let that happen. I knew I was crazy. I couldn't stop thinking about it, about freeing them, but you're right, it's crazy. I'd never get away with it anyway."

Myra fell silent, biting her lip. He waited anxiously, searching her face. Her gaze shied away from him, as if he'd disappointed her.

"There still might be a way," she said. "We could turn aside just before we got there and send the seffidges on."

"And if we got caught?"

Myra flushed. "Gulik couldn't touch me if we were married."

His jaw dropped. "Married?" he repeated stupidly.

"Yes, married. You and I. I know all about the ceremony. We could do it on the way there. The seffidges would speak for us."

Kiran shook his head. "I couldn't let you. It's too dangerous. It's not that I don't want to marry you, but . . ."

She set the bucket down and glared at him. "Are you sure? It's not because of all those girls in the chorus blinking their lashes at you?"

"No," he said. "No! You're the only one I'd—"

"Then you wouldn't let Gulik take me. You're not talking me out of this. I can see it, Kiran. You're going to make things whole. Besides . . ." She picked up the milk bucket, climbed the steps to the cottage door, and spoke over her shoulder. "Besides, you're my *filoni*, and I'm claiming you."

Before he could answer, she slipped through the cottage door.

★ ★ ★

Kiran had never felt so alert and full of purpose. His skin tingled with it. Whenever he thought of Myra coming with him on the journey, his breath caught in his chest. To have her beside him, believing he was right, made him feel as if his feet hardly touched the ground when he walked. The only problem was that sometimes the image of holding her in the night struck him so powerfully that he stopped in a task and smiled like an idiot until someone—Jovan's father or Ser Vetel or Lir—called him to attention.

Time was so short. Myra offered to take over the first part of the plan, feeding the seffidges. She visited Ser Vetel, charmed him and told him he should be sleeping later in the morning; she would have Kiran teach her how to prepare the seffidges' porridge. The old man hesitated but she winked at him and told him she already knew about the special ingredient, so he agreed, chuckling. The next morning the priest snored as Kiran and Myra measured out a little less of the nuath powder than his instructions directed. A little less each day and they would wean the seffidges off the drug.

That day on the road, Kiran planted in Ryan's head the idea that the barracks should have a night of carousing before they headed out to war. "Not the night just before, I don't mean that," he said. "We'll need to be in top form when we march out after the Savages. But a good night of drinking, a farewell to winter. We don't want to leave a lot of beer behind. The night of the new moon, that's when I'd do it. Light up the darkness."

Ryan clapped him on the back. "Now you're talking like a soldier!" Ryan brought up the idea to anyone who would listen. Even the officers, who usually tried to keep a close eye on the beer supply, scratched their heads and nodded.

After dark that evening, Kiran crept back into the woods to retrieve an axe that he had hidden during the day. He concealed it under his heavy winter cloak, walked stiffly past the sentry at the gate and stowed it far back under Ser Vetel's bed. Over the next couple of days, Kiran managed to abscond with two spades before the sergeant in charge of the supply wagon became more vigilant, frowning and counting the tools returned at the end of the day.

The mapmaker, who had threatened to complain to the captain that Kiran was either a fool or hiding something, listened eagerly when Kiran told him that the images and memories were coming back to him more clearly now. Kiran sketched the camp layout, the two streams, the bean fields and the placement of the houses. He told the mapmaker that when they escaped he had led Dara and Myra always downhill and toward the rising sun, so the village must lie in the hills almost due west of them.

The mapmaker wrinkled his forehead. "Doesn't make sense," he said. "If they're up west of us, why'd they go so far south to attack the barges?"

"Because of the Serpent," Kiran said quickly.

The Beechwood Flute

The mapmaker peered at him, his face skeptical.

"Look," Kiran improvised. "They call that place the Serpent, too. And their war god is also a snake. They figure with the Serpent beside them they'll always win. In fact, they want to take back that whole part of the river. They figure it's rightly theirs because—"

The mapmaker put up a hand to hush him. "Wait up, I got it. So you mean they live just up there in those hills? So close to us, hanging right over us? We should have moved against them years ago. Wait till the captain hears!"

* * *

Food was going to be a problem. They would have a hundred-twenty hungry seffidges, most of them not that well fed to begin with, at least ten days of walking through the woods to find the Shelonwe village, and almost nothing to forage in the woods so early in the season. Myra showed Kiran some shoots in the woods that had an oniony bulb at their base but each one yielded only half a mouthful. There might be some hunting but none of the seffidges knew how to hunt. Kiran skulked about the village, ducking into cellars to stuff potatoes into the front of his tunic. He hid a sack of potatoes and a sack of porridge grain under the woodpile behind Ser Vetel's cottage. Surveying it, he calculated that it was enough for only a couple of meals.

What they needed was money. How well Lir had provisioned the boat when Kiran fled with Bulo! If only they had some coins, they could buy bacon and dried apples. At the carpenter's shop Kiran had handled money and he knew the box where it was kept. He could take it, smash it and quick, before anyone noticed, buy all the supplies he needed.

But that was crazy. He couldn't steal money. *You're stealing the seffidges*, a voice in his head pointed out. *You're stealing Myra.*

★ ★ ★

The last few days of the waning moon, Kiran felt so full of his plans that he wondered people couldn't see them swelling within him. At dinner, accepting a plate from his mother, he looked into her eyes until she exclaimed, "What, Kiran?" and laughed. Afterward, when he played his flute for Dara in the corner, fingering a mournful farewell song, she skipped away telling him she wouldn't listen unless he played something happier.

Lir caught up with him as he crossed the village to Ser Vetel's after dinner and said, "You have that far off look in your eye, son. It won't be long until you're setting sail for Catora again."

Kiran kept walking. "Not before the Savage expedition."

"If weather and luck cooperate, that won't be long. And then? Still interested in being a priest? Or is it a soldier now?" When Kiran didn't answer, Lir stopped and stood in the middle of the road. "You know it would make your mother happy, Kiran, if you stayed in Lanath. I'd be glad to have you in the nuath grove."

Kiran turned and measured his stepfather with his gaze. Had he forgotten all their arguments, then, and did he expect Kiran to do the same? To forget his banished father, his grieving mother, to join in harvesting the nuath that twisted like a cord of slavery around all their necks?

Lir stood waiting and Kiran realized he no longer had to tip his head up to look Lir in the eye. Lir had lost his swagger and with it some of that sureness that had made men follow him. What must it be like for him, Kiran wondered, to have his stepson come home a hero, expose his lies and challenge the worth of his life's work?

He made his voice courteous. "I can't promise I'll go the nuath grove but I can tell you I don't have plans to go to Catora just yet." He gave Lir a nod and stepped around him.

Ser Vetel greeted Kiran that night with a snarl. "I've had three separate visitors today complaining that the seffidges are acting troublesome."

"Troublesome?" Kiran's heart did a dance step as he cast about for something to say. "Aren't seffidges always troublesome?"

"Talking back, refusing work. That seffidge woman Loa got a beating for tossing the wash water at her mistress's head. I'll tell you what it is, Kiran. Your lovely Myra doesn't know how to measure out a dose. Incompetent interfering women! Tomorrow I go back to preparing the mush myself."

That would undermine the whole plan. Kiran found himself stuttering like Bulo. "M-maybe it's an aftermath of the sickness."

Ser Vetel shook his head, looking grim.

Kiran added quickly, "I'll go talk to Myra about it."

He ran across the courtyard, past the seffidge shed and knocked on Myra's door. She came right out, pulling a shawl around her shoulders. As he explained the problem, she tilted her head back, sticking out her chin.

"Tell him you and I are going right now to check on the seffidges," she said. "Kiran, it's time we explained to the seffidges and got them on our side. They need to know what's coming."

★ ★ ★

An hour later he walked her back to the door of her cottage and, oblivious to the sentry lurking nearby, took both her hands in his. "I never saw seffidges act like that," he said. "The way they were listening! You—There's something about you, Myra: just with your voice you can steady them. Here I have this big plan to free them, but you're the one who speaks to them as if they're already free, already . . ."

"Human?" She pulled her hands away. She sounded angry.

"It's not just them, Myra, it's the way you talk to me, too, like an . . ." *Equal*, he thought, but he didn't want to make her angrier. "Like my twin."

She turned aside but he clasped her shoulders and pulled her back around to face him. "Listen, Myra, you're strong like a Shelonwe woman and you give some of that strength to me. Without you, I—"

In the faint glow of the sentry's torch, he saw the tears glimmering in her eyes. He stopped trying to talk. Instead, he pulled her close and she pressed her wet face against his shoulder. He kissed her hair, then lifted her face and kissed her long and deeply.

Then, with a sudden sob, she shoved him away and bolted through the door.

Chapter 31

Kiran tossed most of the night, full of doubt once more. How could he tear Myra away from her mother, her plans for becoming a healer? What did it mean that he was putting the good of a band of seffidges ahead of what was good for her?

He awoke to the murmur of voices and thought for a moment that he was home, with his mother bending over the fire, toasting bread. But when he sat up he saw Myra standing in front of Ser Vetel, nodding as he watched her measure out the dose of nuath. She said, "Yes, I see. Yes, Ser Vetel, I'll do it just that way."

That day there were no complaints about the seffidges' behavior. They slouched around with their shoulders rounded and their heads low. But when Kiran stooped to look, he saw the glint of awareness in their eyes.

"How did you work it?" he asked Myra, when he managed to pull her aside the next day. "I mean right under Ser Vetel's eagle eyes."

She gave him a sidelong glance. "Ser Vetel's eyesight's not that good. I sat up half the night burning sticks. That pot of nuath powder is mostly pine charcoal now."

★ ★ ★

By now Kiran's hoped-for night of carousing had swollen into plans for an end-of-winter feast for the whole village. Ser Tolan had taken it up, telling the villagers it was time to shake the gloom of winter from their souls. "Of course it really should be at the full moon," Ser Tolan said. "But who knows where our brave soldiers will be in fourteen days? We'll make a new festival, when the Sky Serpent starts to feed the starving Moon Lady, to mark the end of winter."

Because nights were still too cold for a feast outside and because there was no building large enough for the whole village to assemble, Ser Tolan asked householders to arrange a moveable feast that would proceed from one house to another. Lir, of course, volunteered his house and so did nine other heads of household. Wives from across the village, along with their seffidge women, cooked and baked and scrubbed for two days in preparation.

The feast began at sundown, as soon as the seffidges were locked away in their shed. Revelers carrying torches rolled from street to street, crowding into houses, snatching delicacies from each table and moving on with songs and laughter. Beer and elderberry wine sloshed over the side as drinkers raised their cups in celebration. Kiran watched quietly from the corner of his mother's house until he decided it was time to move on. He went to kiss his mother, leaning down to do so, but flushed and laughing, she batted him away with her serving spoon. He wrapped his arms around Dara and twirled her in the tight space between two loud visitors.

His mother pressed food on him as he left and with sudden inspiration he took a sack from a hook and filled it with rolls, jellies, sweetmeats, as many as she could give him. "Take them to that skinny old Ser Vetel," she said. "Stock up his house. He always loved his sweet things."

Kiran wandered the streets, ducking into other houses, filling his sack, politely declining drink as the singing of the soldiers grew louder and more boisterous. The night was very dark now. The streets were beginning to empty—mothers calling their children, cuffing them, scolding them into bed—by the time he made his way with laden sack back through melting patches of snow to the poor end of the village.

Ser Vetel snored in his corner as the sounds of revelry in the village faded at last. Kiran lay on his stomach and reached under the old priest's bed to drag out the axe and two shovels he had stowed there. He ducked outside and made his way to the back of the seffidge shed. No sentry was pacing this section of the wall right now. Kiran reversed the axe and rammed its handle heavily three times against the back wall of the shed. Then he dropped the axe and ran toward the front of the building.

The axe blows were the signal, and as Kiran circled the building a long anguished howl rose from the seffidge shed. By the time Kiran arrived at the front door, the two sentries were beating against the door with their spear butts, yelling at the seffidges to quiet down. "What are they up to?" asked Kiran, panting. "What was that banging?"

One of the sentries meandered over and peered into his face. "That you, Kiran? Home so early?" It was Ryan, drunk. Kiran grimaced. Ryan would not come out of this well.

Ryan laughed and swayed. "Ironic, you think? I come up with this plan for a great revel and they stick me and Jor here on sentry duty. Lucky I have friends looking out for me." He aimed a kick at a barrel rolling empty on the ground beside him.

The wailing inside the shed rose higher. "Shouldn't we find out what's wrong with them?" Kiran asked.

"Yeah, sure," said Ryan. He fumbled at the lock while his companion, a tall shy quiet youth, hung over him, watching.

"Sick, we're sick!" shouted a couple of the seffidges, just as Myra had coached them. "We want Myra, we're sick!"

Ryan pushed the door shut and leaned against it. "Wouldn't send your girl in there, would you, Kiran? Stinking seffidges!"

"I don't mind going in with her," Kiran said. "I'll fetch her." Before Ryan could object, he ran to Nora's door, where Myra stood waiting.

Myra carried a basket of cheese and another bundle.

"More food?" he asked, nodding at the bundle.

She shook her head. "Medicine. Herbs. Even a packet of that dried snake venom."

Kiran shook his head. "We won't have time for doctoring sick seffidges."

She set her jaw. "You never know what we might need."

He thought he heard her voice tremble, so he took the bundle, threw an arm around her and gave her a quick hug. "You're right. Thanks, Myra. Now, are you ready? Are you sure?"

"I'm sure. If those seffidges keep yowling they'll wake my mother. Let's go."

Kiran carried the bundle of medicines and Myra brought the basket. They crossed the mud to the shed, where Ryan, shaking his head, pulled back the door and let the two of them enter.

The wailing ceased the moment they stepped inside. Kiran heard the seffidges' breathing and then he began to make out their forms in the darkness—men, women and children standing ready, their eyes flashing white. He pulled two of the largest men to stand on either side of the door. Then he looked at Myra and nodded.

Myra hid herself behind the first rank of seffidges and then let out a long, despairing scream. Before it trailed off, he yelled out, "Not Myra! No!"

The door burst open and Ryan stood in the entry with his sword drawn and a torch in his free hand. All signs of drunkenness were gone. He stared at Kiran with that same alert intentness that Kiran remembered from the barge. Kiran froze, unable to lure him deeper. But the other sentry, behind Ryan, lurched against him, crying, "What's going on? Lemme see, Ryan!"

Ryan stumbled and the two seffidges by the door seized his arms, flinging him to the ground, knocking his sword free. He scrabbled after it, still holding the torch high, but the seffidges reached out and grabbed Jor as well. They wrenched Jor's sword away and used the hilt of it to knock him on the head. As Jor's knees buckled, the seffidges flung him down on top of Ryan. Ryan's torch rolled on the ground, setting the straw bedding alight. Flames leaped up around the fallen soldiers.

"Watch the fire!" shouted Kiran. "Stamp it out!"

But Ryan struggled to his feet and instead of obeying, the seffidge men swarmed around him, shoving and kicking him into the flames. Screaming, Ryan fell, stood, fell and struggled up again, his tunic alight and face twisted in pain. A seffidge swung a club and with a sickening thump, Ryan crumpled.

"Stop, stop it!" Kiran shouted, trying to push through the mass of seffidges. "Put out the fire!"

The seffidges fell back from the rising wall of flame. Kiran managed to push past them in time to see Myra fling herself through and onto Ryan's burning body.

Seffidge women and children cowered against the wall. Kiran grabbed a blanket from a child and leaped after Myra.

Inside the circle of flame, smoke choked him with the smell of burning hair and wool. Kiran flung the blanket down over the heap of Myra and Ryan and rolled on it until he was sure Ryan's burning clothes were extinguished.

"Ouch, get off," Myra said.

Kiran stood. Three of the seffidges, having come to their senses, beat at the spreading flames with blankets, while others pulled the unburned straw out of the way. Smoke filled the shed, but the flames dwindled and died.

Kiran held his hand for silence. Seffidges stifled their coughs and women comforted children who were moaning with fear. Kiran pushed the door open a crack and peered outside. Nobody was coming.

Under Myra's direction, the seffidges carried the unconscious Ryan and Jor into a corner. Jor's clothes were charred but Ryan's tunic was burned right through. Blisters covered his face and his chest and legs were raw and weeping. His eyes had rolled back in his head. Looking at him, Kiran felt himself about to vomit. Myra knelt beside Ryan, picking bits of charred straw from his wounds.

"I'll need water," she said.

Kiran sent two seffidges skulking to the well, then called them back and went himself just in case there was anyone still awake in the houses. But in the moonless night, the village was silent, as if fear and death had no place here. He passed two buckets into the shed. He had no time to check on Ryan. Some of the seffidges crowded at the door, stamping from foot to foot, murmuring. He felt a current rising in them, the way wind rises before torrential rain.

He drew three men out, brought them around behind the shed and handed them the axe and shovels. Then he led them along the drainage ditch. Sticking close to the wall, they followed the ditch to the place marked by two scraggly bushes where drainage water scooped under the wall. Kiran handed the men the axe and shovels, getting them started prying away rocks and dirt. "Stay hidden," he told them.

In a series of runs, he led seffidges ferrying bags of food to the spot. Now there was room to enter the pen and he found Myra bathing Ryan's body, her bundle of medicines open beside her. The ends of her hair had sizzled in the fire. It stood out in tight, acrid-smelling coils.

Rather than hurry her, Kiran went back to the wall. The seffidges at the ditch worked fast, grunting. Already the hole under the wall was large enough for a child to tunnel through.

Time to gather up the rest of the people. He returned to the shed. Some of the seffidges held bundles and stood ready; others crouched around the edges of the room, their eyes wide with confusion or fear. Kiran approached and touched Myra's shoulder.

She looked up at him. "I can't go." She gestured at Ryan's bruised face and burned body and the blood matting the back of Jor's head. "They could die tonight if we leave them."

"No," he said. "Someone will come."

"Not soon enough. And think of the pain. If Ryan wakes up I have to give him some nuath broth."

"Your mother—"

"I can't pull my mother into this," Myra said. "Look, Kiran, it's better this way. I can tell the story, how the seffidges tricked us and burned the shed, and dragged you away with them as prisoner."

Kiran fell to his knees. His voice shook. "No. You can't be choosing Ryan over me."

"I'm a healer, Kiran." Her voice pleaded. "This is my burden, as freeing the seffidges is yours." She took a few items from the medicine bundle, wrapped it up again and stood to hand it to him.

"I don't want that," he said.

"Take it." She put it in his hand and left hers there, waiting. Her eyes held an appeal that he had no way to answer. Turning his back on her, he waved at the seffidges watching the drama with their mouths hanging open.

Myra said in Shelonwe, "Go with him now. Go with Kiran."

The seffidges lined up and Kiran walked to the head of them. At the last minute, as he pushed the door open, he looked back over his shoulder and saw Myra leaning over Ryan, tears streaming down her ash-streaked face, a hank of scorched hair stuffed into her mouth to stifle her sobs.

He almost turned back. Then, from the far end of the seffidge yard, he heard a shout and the sound of running boots striking against cobbles.

Chapter 32

It was a soldier. In the darkness, Kiran saw only a shadow and the glint of a drawn sword. He lifted his arm to halt the seffidges but as he did so, they separated and spread out, moving like shadows along the wall. In the darkness, they circled around the soldier like a river parting and closing around an island. Then they flowed over him.

"Don't kill him!" Kiran called out sharply in Shelonwe. He heard the soldier's choked cry and saw the dark arms of the seffidges rise and fall rapidly. Fists thudded into flesh and then he saw a flash of metal.

He waded into the mass of men, pushing one after another aside. They fell back, breathing heavily. Kiran stooped and reached for the soldier. The soldier's own sword through his abdomen planted him to the ground. Kiran felt his stomach heave.

He recoiled and croaked, "Hide his body."

The seffidges shuffled and jostled their shoulders together. Rage at their laziness and violence flared up in Kiran and with it, a sickening guilt. He had released these men and they had turned out Savages after all, the murderous brutes. Ignoring him, they could flow this way over the village, knifing people in their beds.

Then he remembered himself telling Ryan how he couldn't stand anyone telling him what to do any more. These were slaves awakened, fighting for their freedom. He had no reason to expect meek obedience.

"Listen," he said, speaking again into that dark murmuring seffidge mass. "We have to hide him or people will know something's happened. They'll chase after us and catch us all. Help me carry him to the shed."

Grudgingly, one broad-shouldered man stepped forward and pulled the sword from the soldier's belly. Two others took the body by the arms and legs, but instead of bearing him to the door of the shed, they lugged him to the back and swung his body into the shadow. At least Myra wouldn't be staring at a dead body all night, Kiran thought with sudden gratitude.

He locked the door of the shed and stuffed the key in his pocket. Maybe there would be an extra few minutes' delay in the morning while the soldiers searched for a duplicate key.

A crowd of seffidges huddled by the drainage ditch. The men who had been digging stood back and Kiran jumped down into the freezing water. The tunnel was wide enough now. He took the arm of the closest man and waited in silence until a crossing sentry passed overhead, then gave the man a shove toward the tunnel. "Go through. Be silent and fast. Wait just inside the edge of the forest." The man stooped, then lowered himself onto his belly and slithered through the mud and water.

Kiran cursed himself. They should have stopped up the flow of water first. All of them would be wet and freezing by the time they got through. And not all of them had brought their blankets. But with so many soldiers about, they had to hurry. He stood in the ditch urging the prisoners on, silently pushing them toward the opening. Children clung to their mothers, whimpering. As he handed the seffidges along, Kiran's mind filled with the memory of Ryan's burnt body and the blood springing from the dead soldier's belly. But at last the knot of people inside the wall grew smaller. He hoped they were fleeing quickly on the other side, gliding across the snow and out of sight.

Only a few more now. Kiran pushed them, his heart beating faster. The last seffidge ducked forward and now it was his turn. He splashed onto his belly and slithered through the narrow passage, then pulled himself up in the muddy opening beyond the wall.

The last seffidges, almost invisible in the darkness, scurried across the open snow-covered field between here and the forest. One leaned down to scoop up a child. Kiran wondered whether any of them really expected him to come along. Maybe they could make it alone after all. For a long, yearning moment, he considered turning back.

But these people were not Setolo, with a memory of their mountain home. They were nothing more than escaped slaves, who had never found their own way or slain their own food. Half of them were still sick with the need for nuath, jumpy or lethargic. If he was going to fulfill his promise—*but I never made a promise!*—he would have to lead them home.

Kiran cut across the field with its patchwork of snow. This close, he could see the faint shadows of footprints everywhere. Soon after dawn, the villagers would realize that the seffidges had flown and immediately they would find these footsteps. How many hours before their pursuers caught them? The thought was so frightening that Kiran broke into a run.

He found the seffidges huddled just inside the woods where he had told them to wait. He gestured to them to follow and ran deeper among the trees, up toward the hilly ridgetop southwest behind the village. They followed, crashing and grunting, until he stopped in a clearing, realizing that he could lose them rapidly in the darkness unless somehow he managed to stifle his fear. Already the band had fractured and clots of seffidges came straggling in to hide at the edge of the trees, their breath coming in grunts, their glances wild.

How could he continue without losing any people? In the circle of hulking bodies, he saw here and there a head lifted, an eye glinting with shrewdness. Yes, some of them, men and women both, looked alert and ready. He reached out and pulled them, his new team leaders, into the clearing. "Now, each of you take ten—no, twelve—people on your team," he said. "You're responsible for them. You understand?" He was speaking Catoran, but now he switched to Shelonwe. "These are your family. You are the father and mother of your family. You have to bring them home."

Some of them nodded; others just stared. He gave the one nearest him a push. "Now! Choose twelve people." Eventually they seemed to catch on. Although the crowd milled around far too long with argument and hushed instructions, finally they stood ranked in groups.

He led them west and upward through the trees, walking fast in the darkness, across patches of snow and patches where the grasses and snowdrops were pushing their tips up through the soil. Their tracks would lead in the direction he had given the mapmaker. Now if only they could find a stream or some other place to hide their footsteps, he would veer south and try to conceal their direction. Why hadn't he planned this better ahead of time?

Mothers and fathers carried the littlest seffidges, who rode bobbing, silent and wide-eyed, in their parents' arms. Kiran remembered carrying Dara on his back. He wouldn't see her again. He wondered what Myra was thinking right now as she tended her injured soldiers. She had abandoned him; she had never meant to come along. But he remembered her tears when he looked back and he knew that wasn't true. Why hadn't he thanked her, kissed her, even said good-bye? How bitter it would be for her if after her sacrifice, Ryan and Jor died anyway. The handsome, virile Ryan, scarred now for life. If he lived. Kiran prayed to the absent Moon Lady to keep the soldiers safe through the night.

A light touch brushed his hair. Looking up, he saw the stars blotted out and scattered flakes of snow drifting down. Kiran breathed the cold fresh scent and felt his heart lift just a little. Now they had a chance. As they pressed on, the flakes grew large and fluffy. Snow would smudge their tracks and in a few hours, if they were lucky, erase them. Kiran called back to the seffidges, "Hurry! The snow will hide us!"

Gurgling through the valley past the first ridge ran just the kind of stream he had been seeking. It burbled and frolicked toward the south. Kiran stopped the seffidges and beckoned to the team leaders. Standing beside the stream, he tried to get them to understand.

"No tracks. We walk in the stream here and make sure to leave no tracks. If the soldiers follow us we want them to be confused."

One of the team leaders, Thol, who had massive shoulders and almost no neck, nodded and began explaining to the others. Then, before Kiran could stop him, he called to his group and led them, splashing, across the stream to the slope beyond.

"No! What are you doing?" Kiran called after him, but one of the other seffidges placed a hand on his arm. Kiran yanked his arm away. On the far side of the stream Thol led his team at a run up the slope, then made them walk backward, sidle over a few steps, and run up again. It looked as if a hundred people had fled up the slope until their footprints lost themselves on the bare granite of the hillside.

Not bad. Kiran wished he'd thought of that.

Afterward, the teams of seffidges splashed downstream in the freezing water. Some of them stumbled with fatigue and cold, losing their footing on the loose stones and falling onto their knees. Team leaders gave directions and their followers took an arm or supported an elbow of those who were faltering.

As the black night slowly faded into a dull gray, Kiran saw that they were walking toward the lightest part of the sky. They had veered east, which would bring them back too close to the river and Ryan's road. He called a halt. The snow had stopped; he didn't know if it had been enough to cover their tracks.

Looking back at the seffidges in the first light, Kiran was alarmed by what he saw: too many were shivering, clutching onto each other to keep standing. Behind him a slab of granite sloped up from the stream into the shadow of pines. He signaled to the team leader behind him to take his team up it and duck under the trees, leaving no tracks until he was far under their shadow.

"Stop when you get away from the stream," he said. "We'll rest and get warm."

The people struggled with cold-numbed feet to find footholds in the sloping rock. Team leaders and stronger men stationed themselves at intervals up the rock, so they could hand the weaker seffidges up the slope. Kiran stood in the water, urging the last ones, the women and children, the elderly, the stumbling, up the rock; then he came scrambling after them.

As soon as they had moved far enough from the stream for the trees to conceal them, the seffidges flung themselves down. They drew off each other's soaking footgear and rubbed one another's feet. Team leaders walked around directing who should huddle under which blankets.

Kiran kicked away some snow to make an empty patch and dropped onto the ground, exhausted. But Thol, the broad-shouldered giant, came and stood over him. "I'll make a fire."

"No! They'll see the smoke."

"The people are too cold."

Kiran dragged himself up to look. Under their blankets the people still shivered convulsively. Their lips were blue, and some of them had a dazed, blank look. He had a sinking conviction that he had kept them in the stream too long. And maybe the nuath addiction made some of them less resistant to cold.

He said to Thol, "Let's get them over the top of this hill. In the next hollow we'll build a fire. We'll make a proper camp where we can rest and eat."

Thol stood with his legs splayed, thinking, then nodded. "Give me the fire things," he said. As if, thought Kiran with sudden irritation, as if *he* were the boss. But Kiran handed over the flints and Thol strode around the circle of seffidges, urging them to their feet again, talking in fast low tones to the other team leaders. Two of them ran ahead, while the people labored up, clutching one another and groaning. Wrapped in their blankets, the people trudged up the slope. But as they came down the other side, a thin smell of smoke encouraged them, and then they saw the flickering tongues of flame.

★ ★ ★

In the afternoon they pushed on until twilight touched the treetops. The next day, which was sunny with a sky of high, cold blue, they walked through most of the hours of daylight, heading always southwest. Two days' journey away from Lanath, Kiran was much less afraid of being followed. They took time to make a proper camp in a grove that sloped gradually beside a stream, with multiple campfires and bedding of pine boughs.

More and more, the seffidges seemed to be thinking for themselves, coming up with ideas, like people stretching after a long sleep. Maybe they didn't even need him any more, Kiran thought. He could just point the direction and tell them to keep walking until they found the Shelonwe encampment. But he wasn't sure of the exact direction; he was counting on recognizing the contours of the land as they drew closer to find the camp. Besides, he had nowhere else to go. And he wanted to deliver the seffidges to Setolo in person, to be able to say, "See, I kept the promise I never made."

They were running short of food. The seffidges did not plan ahead, even though he told them the journey might be ten days. They had cooked all the apples in the fire that first morning and gulped them down to warm their frozen bodies. The first evening they boiled up as much of the grain as they could fit in their stolen pots and before Kiran could stop them, they had thrust half their potatoes to roast in the ashes.

Maybe nuath had dulled their hunger and now their appetites were too large for their ordinary rations. At this rate the food would be gone in another day. Kiran thought they would have to linger by this stream in the morning long enough to fish and dig for roots.

But they would manage. They had made it this far. Kiran lay wrapped in a blanket and gazed up through the pine branches above him to the faraway sky. He saw only a thin swath of the Sky Serpent laboring through the darkness. In the night air he wanted to play what was in his heart—the beginning of hope, the sense that he had set down a rotten burden and picked up another that was heavy but clean. He sat up, set his back against a tree trunk and brought his long low-voiced flute to his lips.

He played a wavering song of weariness and sorrow and then made it change. The sudden fear of the escape, the long slog through the woods, then the quiet snow falling and firelight, the people bedded down. Around him as he played, some of the people stirred, while others remained still in their sleep of exhaustion. But Kiran felt that he had said what he needed to and he crawled back into the blanket with the flute clutched by his side.

He woke with cold dew on his face. The sky above was a deep violet and he had the sense that the woods were alive with people around them. No, they couldn't have been followed. He raised himself on his elbows and peered around him at the sleeping forms and the scattered glow of the campfires. He refused to let these people be captured, not after they had come so far. Among them all they had no weapons but one axe and two stolen swords. Instinctively Kiran closed his fingers around the flute beside him.

A shout broke the darkness and feet slapped the earth as shadows jumped among the sleeping forms. Kiran threw back his blanket with a cry, but someone stepped in front of him. A foot on his chest shoved him back and a spear point pressed against his throat.

Chapter 33

The man holding the spear shifted and a patch of his skin glowed red and brown.

Around him other voices exclaimed in Shelonwe, "But these are all our people! Look at them! These people are ours!"

"Not this one," said the man holding the spear at Kiran's chest. "Mine is a pink skin. Do I take him or kill him?"

Kiran choked out in Shelonwe, "Brother!"

The man leaned closer to look at him.

"I brought these people, your people, to freedom. Ask them."

The spearman let the point of his weapon fall as he reached down to grab Kiran and pull him up. Kiran scrambled to his feet, clutching his flute as he rose. In the stronger light he saw the Shelonwe warriors gathering close, their faces curious.

"Look at this!" his captor exclaimed. "It's Gulik's slave who ran away." He gave Kiran a shake.

"I didn't run," Kiran said. "I went back to my village and freed the seffidges." The words sounded weak to him, as if he were a boy pleading to his mother that he hadn't done wrong.

"Let me see," came a bitter voice. The warriors in front of Kiran parted and to his horror he saw the angular form of Gulik thrusting through the crowd. "The thief," he said, leering at

Kiran. "It's all right, I don't want him back. Kill him."

The warrior holding Kiran didn't move.

"Did you hear me?" Gulik snarled. "I am the chief of this raid. I said kill him! Are you a woman? Do I have to do it myself?" He started forward, his spear lifted high.

The Shelonwe put Kiran behind him. "I want to hear the story." He raised his voice. "Children of the Forest and Mountains, free brothers. Did this pink man free you?"

From his place behind the Shelonwe's broad back, Kiran heard shuffling and murmurs as former seffidges made their way into the circle surrounding him.

"It's true, he helped us escape." That was Thol's voice.

"He brought us food and an axe."

"He helped us fight the soldiers."

"He showed us the path."

Their Shelonwe was accented and awkward, and they sounded frightened.

Kiran's captor stepped back beside Kiran and rested a hand on his shoulder. "This one is under my protection, Gulik."

Gulik stepped forward and leaned his face close to Kiran's. He smelled of sweat and stale alcohol. "Where is the girl?" he demanded. "The one you called Myra?"

Kiran caught his breath. Is that what these warriors were after? Were they a raiding party bent on recapturing Myra so she could be Gulik's wife?

"Myra has gone to Catora," he said. "She lives in the great city now." As soon as the words had left his mouth he looked about in alarm. The former seffidges knew Myra's name, knew he was lying. He caught Thol's eye, and tried to plead with him, then glanced around to give the same silent message to all the runaways he could see. They gazed back at him gravely and kept their silence.

Gulik growled, then abruptly shrugged. "All the better. Build up the fires and we'll hold council."

Kiran's captor let go of his shoulder and Gulik's men hastened to pull dead branches from the trees and throw them onto the fire. It was full light now. The seffidges came forward gladly to boil water and the Shelonwe passed around slices of dried meat cut from the bundles they carried.

Kiran kept his silence. He thought of trying to slip away into the forest, but three silent Shelonwe stood close around him. Altogether there were about twenty-five warriors, almost the same number as there were soldiers garrisoned at Lanath.

The runaways and Shelonwe ate together, and one of the former seffidges brought Kiran a turnip, bouncing it from hand to hand. The Shelonwe questioned the runaways, laughing at their accents, suddenly exclaiming when they discovered a common ancestor. And now Gulik was questioning Thol about the layout of Lanath village and the number of soldiers stationed there.

When the meal was done and the fires stamped out, Gulik stood to speak. Shelonwe and runaways crowded closer. The warriors on either side of Kiran took his arms and drew him forward to the edge of the circle where they could see Gulik.

Gulik peered around the circle, his green eyes flickering and his nostrils flaring.

"We have great good fortune, brothers. Now we know the exact strength of the pink people's village. Half the soldiers will be out searching the woods for these runaways. We can ambush them if we need to. Others will be south of the village building this great path, this road of theirs. We can cut them off, too, if we have to.

"Best of all, there are no more of our brothers in the village. Now we have no fear of hurting forest children in our attack. In the middle of the night we will shoot fire arrows onto the straw roofs of their houses. When they open the gate to flee to the river we will kill the ones who run and then swarm into their village and slaughter the ones who cower behind."

He laughed in triumph, glaring around the circle at his warriors.

Some of the Shelonwe shook their spears and stomped. But others looked down and shifted their feet uncomfortably, their grip loose on their spears.

"Do not do this thing!" Kiran said.

They turned to look in amazement that he would speak. He felt himself quail. They had known him only as a lowly, filthy slave boy. They would sweep him aside. But he had to try.

"What Gulik is saying makes no sense," he said. "You hate the pink people because they enslave your people. Now all the seffidges of Lanath are free. Lanath is full of soldiers. If you attack, many of you will die, and for what? If you burn Lanath, more soldiers will come up the river, hundreds of them, to seek you out and destroy you. They will kill your women and children in vengeance for what you have done. Return to your village. Take your free brothers and sisters with you. Help them make a new home among you."

With a howl of rage, Gulik made a lunge for Kiran but his warriors closed around him. Then the debate broke out in earnest. What would they gain from attacking Lanath? Would it be dishonor to return home having killed no pink skins? But they would be bringing the freed seffidges. Yes, and where would they put them all? The village was crowded enough as it was. Maybe it was time to start a daughter village, farther north.

The debate was turning and now it seemed to be about how to return, not how to attack.

But then Gulik shook himself free of those who had been holding him. "This man stole from me. He stole my wife. I demand the chance to destroy him."

The crowd fell silent, except for whisperings, until one of the men said, "We should take him back with us to the village to be judged."

"No!" Gulik cried. "I know what should be done. Let me fight him. One man against the other. If I kill him, it shows that as well as being sneaky thieves and cowards, these pink skins are weak. Then we'll go on to attack his village of Lanath."

"And if he kills you?"

Gulik shrugged. "Then you peaceable warriors, you warriors who are not really men but women who want to hurt no one, you can go home and say 'Gulik the Fierce died because we were women who abandoned him.'"

The men grumbled at the insult but the one who had captured Kiran stepped forward. "Though Gulik's words are ugly, his plan is a just one, if the fight is fair. I consent to putting my captive in the fight. Gulik, what weapons do you choose?"

Kiran's body stiffened with fear. How had it come to this, kill or be killed? But wasn't that the whole life of a warrior, the life he had longed for? *Let it be spear or bow and arrow*, he thought. Thank the Serpent he had trained with the soldiers, all through the months of winter.

Gulik's eyes glinted. "Knife!" he said, and he drew from his belt a blade almost the length of his forearm. He crouched low and swayed from foot to foot as the warriors around him drew back to give him room.

Right now? Kiran thought in a panic. *I'm going to die right now!* He looked down at his hand, still gripped tight around his flute. He had been a fool to think he could walk between two worlds. He pushed the flute through his belt. Crazy, because it would only hamper his movement. He had to be a warrior now, for these last few moments of his life. But he couldn't bear to throw the flute away.

A Shelonwe stepped forward and thrust a knife into his

hand. The warrior looked straight into his eyes and Kiran thought he saw encouragement there. Yes, some of them knew Gulik was crazy, that he would lead them to their death. But a knife—Kiran had no chance. When he took it, the warrior turned his hand and folded his fingers around it so that the blade pointed up, not downward.

See, it's no use, Kiran protested silently. *I don't even know how to hold it.* He scuttled backward to put more space between himself and Gulik.

The Shelonwe drew back, leaving a fighting space between them. At the edge of the trees, Kiran turned to face his attacker. He felt rather than saw the Shelonwe close ranks behind him, cutting off the possibility of flight. Gulik, low to the ground like a stalking wolf, crept toward him with long, fluid steps.

Chapter 34

Kiran crouched, waiting. As his fingers grasped the knife handle in a death grip, his heart pounded so hard he thought his chest would burst. He tried to envision swiping the knife upward into Gulik's belly. But instead he imagined Gulik's own knife slicing into his throat.

He sidled to his left. Gulik turned slightly and kept advancing.

The ground was uneven, sloping up from the stream, with little hummocks of grass and bits of root looping up from the forest floor. Kiran stumbled backward, while Gulik took each step deliberately, planting his foot and grinding it into the dirt just a bit to make a firm foothold in case he needed to leap forward. He moved up the slope toward Kiran.

I didn't agree to this, thought Kiran wildly. He shot a quick look backward but the two Shelonwe closest behind him moved silently closer together. They would never let him pass.

Gulik pulled his lips back into a smile. "Want to run away, do you, little dirt mouse? Run here, run there, with your little head spinning. Poor little dirt mouse, there's no hole for you to hide in!"

Gulik took another step forward, his glittering eyes holding Kiran's gaze. No, thought Kiran grimly. He hadn't agreed to any of this. Not to the attack on the barge, not to all the lies his

The Beechwood Flute

people told themselves, not to enslaving the seffidges. He hadn't agreed; he had acted. He had made mistakes, but he had tried to atone and he didn't deserve to die. He wouldn't just stand here and let Gulik carve him up.

He thought of fire roaring through Lanath at night, his mother's screams, Lir's beard alight, Savages pouring over the back wall to seize Myra and her mother. "No!" he screamed as he ran toward Gulik.

Surprise crossed Gulik's face but then he grinned, showing his teeth. Just as Kiran crouched to launch himself, Gulik sprang forward. Kiran threw himself sideways and kicked out his legs. Gulik's knife thrust shot past him and Kiran's legs tangled in Gulik's, bringing him down. They both scrambled to their feet but Kiran was farther down the slope now.

Gulik sidled to his right, his face dark with fury. *He wants to get past me*, Kiran realized. *He wants to get downhill from me because I'm shorter. He wants to slice up at me from below.*

Instead of circling with Gulik, he hastened backward, down to a steeper part of the slope. Cursing him, Gulik followed. He moved fast, like a wolf closing in, his face grimacing.

Gulik leaped and his knife arm sliced forward and upward. Kiran twisted aside, his own knife slicing uselessly at the air and Gulik's knife scored his belly along the side, just above his hip. He felt a tearing, burning pain as he scuttled backward.

Without hesitating, Gulik lunged again, his knife flashing upward in an arc aimed at Kiran's ribs. Jumping back, Kiran brought his own arm down to strike Gulik's hand away. He yelled out as his forearm sliced down on Gulik's blade. He felt his bone strike hard on Gulik's knife and then his hand fell open and his knife fell to the soil.

Blood poured from his arm. Gulik jumped forward and stood over Kiran's fallen knife, his lips pulled back in a snarl of delight.

"Run, little dirt mouse," Gulik said.

Kiran whipped around and ran. He fled down the slope to the stream. He wanted to thrust his arm into the water to stop the burning but he splashed across and threw himself onto the cliff on the far side. He heard shouts and hoots of derision behind him as he scrabbled up the rock face to a ledge twice the height of a man. And that was it. He could climb no farther. The cliff leaned over him.

Gulik splashed into the stream and looked up at him, laughing. "See how the little dirt mouse finds a hole to hide in? Is this your courage, is this how the people of your country fight?"

Behind Gulik, the massed Shelonwe crowded down to the edge of the stream, then spread out across it both up and downstream from the cliff where he stood. They formed a pen, with Gulik at the center and Kiran trapped up against the wall.

Kiran clutched his torn arm, blood welling between his fingers. He looked down at the red liquid running from his arm and side, soaking the flute that still hung at his belt. It was the flute he had made with his own hands and he hated to see it soiled so. He slid his finger along it, then pulled it from his belt and lifted it. *What am I doing?* he wondered. *Will I play my own death song?*

A shadow of puzzlement crossed Gulik's face. Kiran raised the flute to his lips and blew a low wavering note.

Gulik yelped as if in pain. *He hates that I can still play*, Kiran thought. *Well, Gulik, don't worry, I won't delay you long.* Already he was feeling light-headed. He played another note, then another, notes falling in sorrow.

Gulik turned to address the watching Shelonwe. "Shall I throw my knife at him?" He lifted his arms and the blade caught the sunlight, dipping and turning as Gulik breathed hard in his rage. Up the slope Kiran saw the freed seffidges lurking at the edge of the clearing. Not one of them had stepped forward to help him. In Kiran's vision the forest closed in on the seffidges. This was happening faster than he had expected. Darkness wavered at the edges of his sight.

"Or shall we just wait here while he bleeds to death?" Gulik asked, far below.

Looking down, Kiran saw darkness rising to swallow him. Far, far down, the dancing figure of rage that was Gulik seemed to founder in a dark river. In that moment Kiran remembered the leap he never made, a desperate leap into a retreating canoe. Blood thundered in his ears.

Kiran grasped the two ends of the flute and jumped.

He crashed down onto Gulik's back, his flute coming over Gulik's head. He jerked the flute toward him. Gulik fell backward on top of him in the streambed. Rocks pressed into Kiran's back and cold water swept over him. He could see nothing but shifting planes of light. He pulled the flute backward as hard as he could against Gulik's throat.

Gulik's hands tore at his fingers and wrists. His weight ground Kiran against the streambed. *So I drown in the end,* thought Kiran. *No wonder I feared water. But I won't let go.*

The fingers of Gulik's right hand dug into the knife wound and tore. Kiran jerked the flute backward in a spasm of pain and he felt something break. He had broken the flute and now he had nothing. His right hand dropped, empty.

At the same moment, Gulik's grip loosened. The warrior's weight lifted away from Kiran and Kiran's head found its way up out of the water. He gasped in great breaths of air and fought to sit up.

Darkness still hung at the edges of Kiran's vision. As if through a dark tube, he saw Gulik, far away, stagger with a hand at his throat. Gulik's breaths came in long rasping rattles. His face contorted as if he were trying to speak but nothing emerged except a strident moan.

Kiran scooted backward in the water. As he did so, he felt the flute in his left hand and looked down at it. It wasn't broken after all.

Instead, something in Gulik's throat had broken. A wall of Shelonwe closed behind Kiran, but struggling to his knees in the stream he watched Gulik gasp, stagger and claw at his own throat, leaving red scratch marks in his skin.

Then Gulik doubled over, coughing, while blood poured from his mouth into the stream. When he raised his head, his neck had swollen like a sheep bladder blown up with air. His wild eyes, ringed with white, caught sight of Kiran and he lurched forward. Now even his chin was sinking into the swollen globe of his neck.

Kiran managed to stand. Gulik tripped forward, his eyes bulging, one hand at his throat, one hand held out to Kiran in appeal. *He thinks I can help him.* In horror, Kiran shook his head.

Then Gulik stumbled, fell to his knees and sank sideways. His body flopped onto its back in the water. His green eyes stared and his mouth gaped as the stream flowed over his face.

Chapter 35

Hands grasped Kiran and pulled him from the stream, back to the place where they had camped. His vision was narrowing, closing down. The world swam around him and he could no longer stand. Now hands pushed him down; he lay in the dirt with his head toward the stream. All he could see was a round patch of sky, with faces crossing it briefly.

He was weak with blood loss but he knew he was also weak with Gulik's death. So this was what it felt like to kill a man. He wanted to vomit up the experience and never feel it again, never again hear that gasping nor even in dreams see Gulik reach out to him in that last appeal.

He was my enemy. And now Kiran felt someone pulling his injured arm straight and some sharp object pierced it.

Like you, he lost a parent when he was young.

Something pulled through the flesh of his arm.

He would have killed me. He wanted to kill all my people.

Now they were wrapping the arm. *They won't kill you now. The Shelonwe keep their promises.*

An arm behind his neck lifted his head. He opened his eyes and saw one of the seffidge women looking down at him. She tipped a bowl to his lips and he took a sip. He was more thirsty than he ever remembered being. He tried to reach for the bowl with his good hand but he was wrapped in a cocoon of blankets so he just thrust his head deeper into the bowl as the broth spilled all down his front.

Some time later—a day later?—a firm hand shook him awake. It was a Shelonwe warrior he recognized as a friend of Setolo's, a man named Woloot. "We travel today."

Kiran could see again and his arms had worked free of the blanket. His left arm was bound in strips of cloth and loosely tied with leather cords. Something at his neck bothered him. He touched it with his left hand and exclaimed bitterly—a cord of slavery.

"You are a prisoner," Woloot said. "Try to stand." He tucked his arm under Kiran's and drew him up.

The world swayed and Kiran clung to him until it stopped. "But why? Why am I a prisoner?"

"We argued. Some say you defeated Gulik fairly. But Gulik's friends say you did not kill him with the chosen weapon. Instead you used that." He nodded toward Kiran's waist and Kiran's hand fell to the flute bound there.

Woloot's hand still supported his elbow. "So we are turning back. We take Gulik home and we bring you to be judged."

"And the seffidges?" Kiran heard the tremor in his own voice.

"The freed ones come with us. You're lucky. Some of us wanted to leave you behind to find your own way to life or death but they refused."

Kiran bowed his head. So they had stood up for him in the end.

★ ★ ★

The trip back to the Shelonwe village took several days. Kiran had a hard time keeping track of the journey. He knew somehow that the bearers of Gulik's body had run ahead, to get him home and buried before his body rotted. But the rest of the war party took the slow road with him and the seffidges. He lost count of the days.

All Kiran knew to do was put his head down and step forward. Shelonwe and freed seffidges took turns supporting him as he walked. It was enough for him to put one foot in front of the other, in spite of the waves of exhaustion washing through him. Whenever they stopped, he ate whatever he was given and fell quickly asleep.

During the days he wondered if he could ever have brought his band of seffidges so far. He had been crazy to set out with so little food, to take all these fragile lives in his hands.

All one day a cold rain fell but Thol draped a blanket over his head and half carried him as he walked.

And now Setolo knows his brother is dead, he thought. His brother whom he loved so much in spite of all the darkness and cruelty inside him.

Kiran grew stronger on the march, his footsteps surer. One day the feeling of the land shifted and he knew they were approaching the Shelonwe camp. They stepped faster now, their heads high in anticipation of home. Kiran pushed away the hand of the former seffidge helping him. "I can walk alone now," he said.

They approached the village through a grove of young birches and in a moment children and dogs romped about them. The whole village turned out, singing a chant of welcome to the newcomers and praise to the returning warriors.

One warrior walked in front of Kiran and one on either side. Behind him came Woloot; Kiran knew from the light tug on his neck that the warrior was holding the cord of his imprisonment.

The four warriors led Kiran to the council building. Outside it Setolo stood waiting, with Ranga beside him. Kiran stepped forward and the four warriors drew aside.

Kiran looked Setolo in the eyes. Setolo's face was hard and blank. His eyes seemed to be lit with a hot fire.

"I brought the seffidges," Kiran said. "They are free Shelonwe now. I have done what you asked."

"You killed my brother."

In self-defense, Kiran wanted to say. But he knew that wouldn't be enough to pierce the other man's sorrow. Gulik was the brother Setolo had left behind all through his long years of slavery. *It's because I've killed his brother that I understand,* Kiran thought. *Gulik was only a man. He started off like me, like all of us, a frightened child.*

Setolo entered the council building and Woloot nudged Kiran to follow. More people came in behind him—Thol, the seffidge woman who had sewn his arm and Ranga. For a second time Kiran stood in front of the bank of women and waited for a chance to explain himself.

The old woman who sat at the center spoke first. "You are an escaped slave who did not serve out his sentence."

Kiran opened his mouth to speak, but to his surprise Setolo stepped forward first. "I offered this man a trade, freedom of our three captives for all the Shelonwe enslaved in Lanath. At first he refused but now he has fulfilled our bargain."

The old woman nodded. "Then we move to the second crime. Pink skin man, you have murdered Gulik, son of the Shelonwe."

All the Shelonwe turned to Kiran. Their eye sockets looked like shadows in the dim light.

Kiran took a breath. "I grieve for Gulik's death." That much was true. "But he challenged me to fight to the death. Do not dishonor him by twisting the agreement he made."

The judges questioned Woloot and other warriors about the terms of Gulik's challenge and the way the battle played out.

Then Labwa turned her gaze back to Kiran. "You agreed on knives but you used a different weapon."

I never agreed! Kiran lifted the flute from his belt. "Labwa-onwe, this is no weapon. When I lived here before, I had a flute that I played for the children sometimes. Gulik threw it into the fire." He felt Setolo shift impatiently behind him and knew it had been a mistake to speak ill of the dead man. He said, "The sound made Gulik angry, but at home I made this new one, with a better sound. The flute was never meant for killing."

From beside Setolo, Ranga said softly, "Play the flute, Kiran. Show that this is not a weapon."

The Shelonwe fell silent, waiting. Kiran hefted the flute. Blood had soaked it and he had used it to kill a man. Where could the music be in that?

He said, "This is a song to honor Gulik, who fell a warrior."

He closed his eyes and played the mourning song. *I thought about playing this song for myself, but now I'm playing it for the man who hated me, who tried to crush me. The man I killed, and may I never kill another.* He focused on changing the song, making it Gulik's. He added the swing of Gulik's step, the sharp ice of his gaze, his terrible hunger for revenge. Perhaps he was going too far, taking too long. What did he know of Gulik? He let the song return to its beginning and die away.

"Go outside now," Labwa said. "Setolo, you stay here."

They stood outside in a bunch, Woloot lightly holding Kiran's leash. He turned around slowly in place but none of the Shelonwe met his eye. *They think it looks bad for me.* Thol shook his large head in puzzlement. Kiran turned farther and met Ranga's eye. She nodded at him but her eyes were filled with tears.

Setolo ducked past the door and came out. His long shadow crossed Ranga's feet as he spoke to Kiran. "Once again I offer you a choice. You are freed from your first service because you brought us our people. But you killed my brother with a weapon he did not choose and did not have. That is murder. Among us, a murderer suffers enslavement unless the family forgives him."

Ranga was looking at Setolo with her hands pressed together. Setolo regarded her for a moment, then shook his head and turned back to Kiran. "I do not forgive you for killing my brother. But if you serve my household for three years, at the end of that time I will call you brother and make you part of our village."

The injustice of it was bitter in Kiran's mouth. He clamped his teeth together to keep from protesting but he lowered his head and shook it in refusal.

"You know I am not a harsh master," Setolo said.

But I cannot bear to be a slave again. "You said I had a choice."

"Your choice is to leave this place before the sun sets and never return. If ever I lay eyes on you again, I will call you my enemy."

Kiran thought, *I will be like my father, homeless, despised by all those I served.* He looked westward; the sun was not far above the horizon.

"Then I will leave," he said. "Men were not meant to be slaves. You know that, Setolo."

Thol turned and ran away. Kiran looked after him in disappointment, then back at the little group standing by the doorway. "Before I leave, Setolo, walk with me down to the river. I have something to tell you."

Setolo shot a glance at Ranga, then nodded. Woloot dropped the cord attached to Kiran's neck and the two of them walked together through the village, past the turkey pen, past Gulik's empty house, over the ditch to the squash garden and down to the bank of the river. Setolo glanced up at the sky and Kiran followed his look. The sun hovered just above the western horizon.

"Lanath is collecting soldiers to attack the Shelonwe," Kiran said quickly. "Thirty of them trained all winter, and we expected thirty more on the first spring barge. They asked me to lead them to your village" —Setolo shifted and looked about to speak— "but I drew them a map that showed you in the hills due west of Lanath and then I ran away.

"I don't know what they'll do now. They may know I betrayed them or they may think the seffidges carried me off and killed me. They don't know where your village is but they may be looking. Or Lanath may be in crisis without its seffidges.

"Setolo, it's not a good time to attack. I tried to tell your brother that. Oh, yes, you would kill lots of pink-skin people and burn their houses. But they have soldiers, and they will come after you."

Setolo bowed his head. "I never favored the expedition, but Gulik wanted his revenge."

Kiran's anger and disappointment spilled over. "Yet now you want to make an enemy of me, although I kept even promises I never made and fought to keep your people safe."

Setolo said, "I follow the laws of my people."

Kiran slapped the flute against his leg. "And for your people I have broken the laws of mine."

Setolo's head shot up. He searched Kiran's face with uncertainty in his eyes. He looked as if he were searching for something to say but just as he opened his mouth, Thol came running down the slope. His hands were full and as he pulled to a stop beside them, he glanced over his shoulder at the sun, which had now dropped halfway below the horizon.

"I brought food, Kiran. One family gave me a bow for you. Here's your blanket and that pack of remedies you carried when we left."

Kiran stood amazed and then, like a child, threw himself at Thol and hugged him.

He looped the pack of medicines onto his belt, slung the food and bow over his shoulders and tucked the rolled blanket under his arm. There was no time now; only a sliver of the sun still showed. The sky was smeared with red.

Setolo said, "Thank you for your warning, Kiran. I . . ."

Kiran turned to look him in the eye. Then he raised one arm in farewell and, turning west, jogged upriver into the last red beams of sunset.

Chapter 36

Kiran moved upriver, fishing and eating the potatoes and cornmeal Thol had packed for him. He lay close to the fire at night, wrapped in his blanket, watching the Sky Serpent swim across the sky to restore the Moon Lady.

He, too, had floated down rivers and fought his way through forests to restore families and villages, but like the Sky Serpent he had seen everything he built up wither away. His own family was shattered into three parts. No doubt in Lanath the trumpets still called for war. Gulik was dead. Ryan might be dead also. Myra was lost to him.

He was an exile, a traitor in Lanath and a murderer to the Shelonwe.

For three days he contemplated the loneliness of that fact in silence. His heart tightened with resentment at all those who had opposed or betrayed or rejected him: his father, Lir, Ser Vetel, Setolo—all those who had sought to imprison him or drive him away. On the fourth night the brightness of the waxing moon woke him and he decided to make a song of his loneliness.

He brought out the bloodstained flute, polished it with his blanket and began to play. He played Myra leaping through the flames, his mother combing Dara's hair by the fire and Lir with his legs wide and his head thrown back looking up a beech tree at the nuath harvesters. He played Ser Vetel shriveling away in his hut, scribbling down a complaint about his life and brewing up poison for slaves. He played his father Corbin raging and tossing on his stinking cot while restless bandits milled below plotting his overthrow.

Kiran dozed for a while but when he woke before dawn he played his father again, free after years of slavery, standing at the edge of the forest as Lanath closed her gates to him. He played his father's yelps of rage and pain, his desperate assault on the walls and the battle that followed, when soldiers swarmed after him with poison-encrusted spears.

Then he slept. When he woke again, the sun had climbed halfway up the sky. He cleaned up his camp and set out eastward toward the granite castle. He had no clear reason for choosing it—the bandits might not even return this year—but he wanted to see his father's cave again and to sit in the high lookout post watching over the river.

He arrived at moonrise three nights later. The bandits had done a good job sweeping the area clean but he could still see from the broken lichen and tramped-down earth that people had lived here. He dropped his pack in the eating place and climbed with only his blanket to the lookout crag.

The full moon shone over the whole expanse of the forest, which looked under its light like a quilt thrown over the sleeping land. Like a seam through the center of the quilt ran the Snake River, silver in the moonlight. Mist lingered above the treetops at the place where the Serpent roared with its low and distant sound.

Kiran played the moonrise song. He played Dara teaching her doll to dance. He played Calef lying on his belly with his hands in the sparkling water, waiting for a fish to flicker into view. He let the voice of the flute fall into its lower register as he played Myra standing at the railing of the barge, floating down to Catora to become a healer.

The songs were imperfect, all of them, but as he played his heart soared with the happiness of being alone, like the Moon Lady sailing in her boat of clouds across the sky.

★ ★ ★

In the days that followed, Kiran fished and hunted. He slept in his father's old cave, where the scent of sickness had blown away with the wind. He dug under the dirt floor of the storage cave and found a box still full of sacks of grain. All the time that he wasn't working to find or prepare food, he worked on music—exploring how the notes fit together, playing something new or shaping old songs or dances or long, free pieces.

The moon went through its phase of darkness and then started to grow again before he began to feel lonely. Even here on the mountain the snow lay only in patches and tiny yellow flowers appeared among stunted blades of grass. In all this time he had seen no barge pass on the river. Did that mean the soldiers were still massed in Lanath, preparing to raid the Shelonwe? But someday a barge would come downriver and maybe Myra would be aboard.

Kiran walked along the ridge until he found the old Shelonwe path down to the river. In the early morning mist he swam the river below the Serpent with a knife clenched between his teeth. He crept up to Serpent Camp but there was no sign of sentries there; perhaps the captains had decided that leaving just a few soldiers was an invitation to mutiny. Kiran found the tree by the riverside where he and Myra had lingered and talked a year ago as children splashed in the shallows. He remembered being drawn to her even then, feeling that the two of them stood apart from the others, both of them out of place. How he missed her! But she had been right to stay behind. She could no more have abandoned a dying Ryan than he could have left the seffidges enslaved.

He ran his hand along the smooth trunk of the tree. If Myra pursued her dream, if she sailed to Catora to become a healer, she would stay in Serpent Camp and maybe she would linger by this tree and think of him.

On the trunk, at a spot just at eye level, he carved the first letter of Myra's name. He spent a couple of hours on it, making the track of it smooth and rounded. None of the soldiers would know what to make of it. But if Myra passed someday and saw it, she would know he was alive, know he had succeeded. She would understand that he was sorry for the bitter way he had left her in the seffidge shed.

Climbing back to the granite castle, Kiran took his time, tracing the path he had followed with Bulo but turning aside to explore tracks and pathways on the mountainside. It took him a couple of days. Playing always in his mind, though he tried not to think about it, was the image of a barge that might be passing unwatched below, carrying Myra away. He wondered if in a year or two he could make his way to Catora to find her. Could he slip into the city or would everyone recognize him as a traitor? He wondered if he could give out the story that he had escaped the Shelonwe a second time.

The clamor of men's voices rose from the bandit hideout as he approached. Kiran slipped off the path into the woods, waited and then made his way to the lookout crag. He found it unmanned. That was odd but he decided to let himself be found there. He settled on the far edge of the rock, his legs dangling, and began to play the beechwood flute. The wind had risen and he played the swaying of the pine boughs below him.

Before he had finished the first song, footsteps sounded on the rock behind him and Calef's voice rang out.

"Kiran! I knew you would get away from the Shelonwe, I knew it! I wanted to stay and wait for you but they all said no. Winter was good across the mountain, we caught so many salmon and the orchards are growing and two babies were born and I think Bulo's going to get married to a girl who ran away from his very own village except she has to wait for the end of summer because he came along to sneak to the Shelonwe with me and check on you but now—"

Kiran interrupted him. "Is Father here?"

Calef's eyebrows drew together and he stopped chattering. He nodded. "He had a bad winter but he wanted to come. He walked part of the way but then he got worse, so the men had to carry him. That's why we're so late. We just got here and now . . ." He ducked his head. "Yaysal's put him in that room where Bulo stayed last summer because he says it's good enough for sick people. And Yaysal's going to stay in the top room."

Kiran laughed. "Then he can share it with me, because that's where I'm staying."

Calef looked up, surprised.

Kiran shrugged. "It's just a room. When Father's well I bet Yaysal will move out fast enough."

Calef drew in the dirt with his toe. "He doesn't really get well any more. The other men keep fighting over who should be leader and if Yaysal wins we'll go back to robbing barges and he says if it weren't for dragging invalids along we could have attacked one already."

"That's a rotten idea. Calef, will you go tell Father I want to come see him?"

"He's not in the best mood."

"Just tell him. Go ahead."

Calef chewed on his lip, then nodded and jumped away. Kiran waited, sitting with his hands clasped around his knees and the flute lying beside him. A cold wind blew up the slope from the river and Kiran thought of all the people he had parted from without a good-bye: Nora, Ser Vetel, Lir, Ranga, Dara, Myra, even his mother.

He stood and started down the path to the castle. Calef met him halfway. "I told him but I don't know if he even heard me. He seems so tired."

Kiran picked up his speed. As they walked into camp, men lifted their heads in surprise. Some of them raised a hand in greeting. Kiran said to Calef, "Do you have any loose wool?"

"No. What for?"

"I want you to boil me a big pot of water."

Calef looked at him sideways but Kiran clapped him on the shoulder and Calef walked over to the fire to talk to the cook.

Kiran climbed to the upper room. Yaysal stood at the entrance with his hands on his hips. "Are you the one who's been staying here?"

"Yes," Kiran said simply. "Do you want to share the space?"

"Of course not. You'll clear out."

Kiran gave a laugh. "We'll see. Right now I just want to get something." He ducked past Yaysal and crossed the room to rummage in the folds of his sleeping blanket. He pulled out Myra's pouch of medicines.

Yaysal came after him, bundled up Kiran's blanket and followed him to the edge of the cave. As Kiran climbed down the steps, Yaysal threw the blanket after him. When it hit Kiran's shoulder, anger flared up inside him. But he caught the blanket before it dropped onto the dirt and carried it to where Calef stood by the fire.

"This is wool," he said. "It'll do for now. Cut it up into strips for me, will you, Calef? I'd like you to boil four or five strips in the water—no, half that much water—along with these two herbs." He pulled the dried plants from Myra's pouch. Feverfew and hensbane—he hoped he remembered the right ones.

Calef stared when Kiran handed him the plants. "Crumble these into the boiling water." Kiran closed the half-empty pouch and carried it to the cave where Bulo had stayed during his recovery.

Kiran nodded at the blacksmith standing by the door as he entered the room. There it was, that stench that staggered him. His father lay in a heap of blankets against the back wall. When he heard Kiran enter, he struggled up onto his elbows. His cheekbones stood out like stone ledges in his haggard face and his eyes were dark smudges against his gray skin.

Swimming through the stench, Kiran approached his father, fighting to keep his face still. He knelt beside the jumble of heaped blankets. "Father, I finished what I had to do and I came back."

Corbin snarled. "Came back for what?"

Kiran reached and pushed a strand of hair away from his father's forehead. "What hurts you, Father?"

Corbin's eyes flickered over his face and he gave a bitter laugh. His lip lifted in a sneer. "Ingratitude. Betrayal. All the lost years."

Kiran nodded as Corbin's body twisted in a sudden spasm. "Loneliness!"

"But now you have two sons to stay with you."

The skin at the corners of Corbin's eyes crinkled and he said, "Two sons? You mean to stay?"

"Father, I mean to see you healed."

"Healed?" Corbin gasped with laughter and pulled himself straighter. "That's kindly of you, Kiran, but I think you're more likely to see me dead. What hurts? Let's see, I forgot to mention my leg."

"Then let me look at it," Kiran said. He threw back the blankets and pulled at the wrappings around his father's right leg. Soon he could peel no more away because the strips of cloth were stuck to the leg with dried yellow-green ooze.

Kiran went to the door and called up toward the kitchen area. "Is my pot boiling, Calef?"

While he waited for Calef, he began to tell his father the story of his time with the Shelonwe.

His father listened, grunting. "The turkey pen? They never threw me in there."

Two men helped Calef lug the pot on a long branch into the chamber. They peered curiously at Corbin, but he gestured for them to leave. Calef folded himself onto the floor with his arms hugging his knees. Kiran let the pot cool, while he told his father and brother about how bitterness festered in his heart until his escape with the girls. He described how he was received like a hero in the village but how he seemed to have no home there anymore and how the slavery of the seffidges became unbearable to him.

When water in the pot had cooled enough that he could stand to put his hand in it, Kiran pulled out a strip of wool blanket and squeezed the hot water onto his father's bandages. Slowly, while Corbin clutched Calef's hand, he peeled the crusted bandages away.

There lay the wound, not much longer than a spearhead, piercing the muscle of the thigh, leaking pus. The blotched skin around it looked ready to burst, while the wasted leg muscles below the knee resembled strips of old leather.

"Now, Father," Kiran said. "This is what I learned from a wise woman and an injured cow. Will you trust me?"

"Just keep talking. Finish your story, son."

As he told of their escape, Kiran washed all around the wound and then pressed the leg from both sides until more pus poured out. When he told about his banishment from the Shelonwe, Corbin said, "They banished me, too, even though I served my time. I think they don't want strangers living there."

"And we're strangers everywhere, aren't we?" Kiran asked. "Now, are you ready?"

"I'm ready."

Kiran thrust his fingers into the wound, where he felt a hollow space crossed by fibrous bands. He tugged on the edges of the wound, opening it wider, as his father gasped in pain. Then Kiran reached his hand into the wound and washed it to its depths with hunks of wool that he tossed aside when they were saturated.

At last he opened his pouch and drew out the pocket of dried snake venom. He took a pinch and sprinkled it into the wound, then poured in a bowl full of clean water, squeezed the wound opening shut and massaged his father's thigh.

His father grunted and beads of sweat stood out on his forehead. He clutched Calef's arm, his knuckles standing out like white stones.

Kiran let the wound fall open and out of it flowed water tinged with clean red blood. Leaning into it, Kiran massaged the leg until the water was gone, then leaned back on his heels. He heard a commotion behind him at the door of the cave but ignored it.

"That's it for today," he said. His arms and neck ached, and his own chest dripped with perspiration.

"But no, you still have to pack it," said Myra's voice behind him. Kiran whipped around, leaping to his feet.

Myra stood there with a grin on her face, a pack slung over one shoulder and her hair short and ragged, all the burnt ends cropped away. "I never thought you were paying attention," she said. "But now I see maybe you were."

Kiran started toward her but she knelt on the floor of the cave and indicated to a staring Calef that he should pour water over her hands. Kiran's father muttered and tried to sit up, rearranging his blanket around his waist, but Myra pushed him firmly back down, folded back the blanket to expose his wound and began to pack his leg with the boiled strips of wool. As she worked, she spoke to Kiran.

"Ryan made it. He had a couple of bad weeks and he'll have scars but he's strong. I was taking him down to Catora where they can cut away some of the scarred flesh and restore the use of his hands."

She prodded Corbin's leg and picked up yet another strip of blanket. "And then at Serpent Camp, I saw the mark you left me. So I came. I made Ryan row me across before sunup. I told him almost everything, Kiran. Does that make sense? We trust each other because I saved his life. He didn't like it but he knew he owed it to me, so he rowed me across, with those bandaged, curled-up hands pulling the oars. I guess he kept it secret until the barge was gone."

She tucked the strip of wool into the wound. "And then Bulo met me on the path and brought me here," she said. "He said he was scouting for runaway soldiers but when I told him our adventures, he was amazed."

She let the last bit of wool trail out of the leg wound like a wick and leaned over Kiran's father. "How's that, now?"

Corbin's lips were white. "By the Serpent," he croaked. "It's a miracle the two of you haven't killed me. I must be tougher than I thought." There was something new in his voice, some hint of hope. *I could put that in music for him,* Kiran thought. *A sudden upturn, a run of notes.*

He felt his own heart swelling and he took Myra's hand. "Father, Calef, this is Myra, my *filoni*." *She has chosen me.* "She's going to be a healer. No, she's a healer already. She learned from her mother and the Shelonwe."

Myra drew her hand free. Her eyes shining with pride, she nodded at him to continue.

"Father, we have to clean your wound out every day. We can trade with Pomel village for wool, and Calef and I will catch goldenrod snakes. It might take months, Father, but I know I can cure you because it worked with the cow."

"The cow?" Corbin asked. "Am I to be cured like a cow?" He wiped his hand across his forehead, clenched it and let it fall beside him. His voice fell lower. "And in the evening, son, will you play for me?"

Kiran reached for Calef and placed their two hands together on their father's chest. Corbin's heart galloped, straining against the ribcage. Kiran thought of the fungus that ran through the veins of the great beech trees of Lanath until it rotted them from within and they crumbled to the forest floor. He thought of how the leash of slavery had twisted around his neck and bitten into his skin as hatred and bitterness tightened their hold around his heart. He thought of Gulik, who had never learned to let the strands of bitterness go.

He thought of music unwinding the strands into lines of melody, one by one.

"I'll play for you," he said. "I'll make a flute for Calef, too, a higher-voiced one, sweet as a spring breeze. I'll teach him to play. And Myra will sing for you, Father."

Corbin gave a long sigh and unclenched his hands, letting the creases of pain in his face smooth out. He reached for Myra's hand and brought it to rest on top of Kiran's and Calef's. He studied her and she gazed back at him, her eyes steady.

Corbin turned his head toward Kiran once more and gave him the smallest of nods. "When I'm well, if you'll have me, I will sing, too," he said. "Bless you, children. Think of the music. How that will bring me joy."

He sank back, releasing their hands, the hint of a smile on his face.

As soon as Corbin's breathing quieted and his eyes drifted closed, the young people drew away. Kiran took Myra's hand and she let him keep hold.

Acknowledgements

I would like to thank Ian Leask for his close reading, comments, and encouragement as I completed this manuscript. And thanks to Steve McEllistrem for his careful line editing.

About the Author

Pendred Noyce is a physician, advocate for science education reform, writer, publisher, and mother of five. For twenty-five years she helped run the Noyce Foundation, which supported improvements in mathematics and science education nationwide. She continues to advocate for exciting, hands-on after-school programs in science and engineering. In 2010, Penny co-founded Tumblehome Learning to publish science adventure books and create associated science activities for children. She has written eleven books for young people and has edited and nurtured many more.

CPSIA information can be obtained
at www.ICGtesting.com
Printed in the USA
BVHW041445120223
658283BV00007B/296